malka

Also by Mirjam Pressler

THE STORY OF ANNE FRANK

SHYLOCK'S DAUGHTER

MIRJAM PRESSLER

malka

Translated by Brian Murdoch

YOUNG PICADOR

First published 2001 in Germany by Beltz Verlag, Weinheim und Basel
as *Malka Mai*
Translated from the German by Brian Murdoch

This edition published 2002 by Young Picador
An imprint of Pan Macmillan Ltd
Pan Macmillan, 20 New Wharf Road, London N1 9RR
Basingstoke and Oxford
Associated companies throughout the world
www.panmacmillan.com

ISBN 0 330 41550 6

1 3 5 7 9 8 6 4 2

A CIP catalogue record for this book is available from
the British Library

Phototypeset by Intype London Ltd
Printed and bound in Great Britain by Mackays of Chatham plc, Kent

SEPTEMBER, 1943

The day it all began wasn't the least bit different from the days before, except that it was maybe a little hotter. Malka noticed that as soon as she opened her eyes. The sun was shining brightly through the flowery curtains and and threw oddly shaped, coloured shadows on to her white bedspread. When she poked her finger at a blue flower, her fingernail took on a blue tinge, and green stripes showed up in a pattern across the back of her hand. She prodded at the coloured patches with her finger, and watched as the bright colours became matt and less vivid against her brownish skin.

Her room was gradually filling with familiar noises. The stream was gurgling outside her window, just a little way from the house. After the long, dry summer, the water was so low that you could make out the stones on the stream's bed and see the fish as they shot through the water and disappeared into the grasses at the edge. Malka often sat there by the stream, picking flowers and throwing them into the water, then watching as the current whirled them away until they disappeared behind the juniper bush. Sometimes, when it was especially hot, she even bathed in the stream, although the water came from somewhere high up in the mountains and it was cold even in the summer. In any case, she only dared go into the water if someone else was there – either her big sister, Minna, or her mother. There was no need for anyone to tell her not to go into the water alone. She would never forget that day at the beginning of last winter when she had nearly drowned.

Outside on the street, a horse-drawn cart was clattering past. The wooden wheels with their iron rims rumbled across the stones. Malka listened. She could hear from the clip-clop of the hooves that there was only one horse pulling the cart, so it wasn't Yankel, the travelling pedlar, who often had things for sale that weren't so easy to find since the war had broken out. He hadn't been here for a long time; it must have been weeks – Minna had said so herself the other day. 'We've only got a tiny bit of the violet-scented soap left,' she had said. 'It's time Yankel came round again.'

Downstairs in the kitchen someone was rattling about with the knives and forks, and then a bucket fell over with a crash on to the stone flags of the floor. That was either her mother or Minna. Zofia, their last maid, had left months before and gone back to her parents in Wyszków because the lady doctor hadn't been able to pay her any more, and because a Christian girl wasn't allowed to work for Jews anyway, even when there wasn't a man in the family. They had all been sorry when she left, especially Minna, who had made friends with her. Zofia had been friendlier and more cheerful than many of her predecessors, and Minna said she was also cleverer. Both girls had cried when she went away, and afterwards Minna had become very quiet and bad-tempered.

Zofia had been nice, but Malka still missed Olga, the nurse who had worked for so long in her mother's surgery. On the day the Germans had come, Olga had left the house in a great rush and had disappeared with the Russians as they withdrew. Malka put her finger on a splash of blue on her bedspread. Olga had had blue eyes – a proper blue, not like her mother and Minna, whose eyes were a watery blue-grey. Malka hummed softly to herself the song she had learned from Olga: *'Then comrades, come rally, and the last fight let us face, the Internationale unites the human race.'* She tried, as she always did, to imitate Olga's voice, and she still remembered very well its deep and gentle tone, but she couldn't do it, and in her voice the tune sounded wrong and silly and she soon stopped singing again.

After a while Malka got bored with her game. The sun was higher and the coloured shadows it threw on the bed were fading away. She jumped up and slipped on the dress that Henja, the seamstress, had made for her at the beginning of the summer. It was from a curtain she had unpicked, because it hadn't been possible to get hold of new material for ages. It was a very nice dress, and it would have been nicer still if it hadn't been for the stupid yellow star. Malka did her best not to notice it now, although at first she had made a fuss and cried and begged them to take it off again. But both her mother and Minna had said that that was absolutely impossible. As long as the Germans were here, she would have to wear the yellow star.

Malka squatted down on the floor and put her sandals on. They were German, too – wooden sandals with long, red laces that you crossed over one another halfway up your calf and then tied in a bow. They were still very new, these sandals, given to her not long ago as a present, together with a pot of apricot jam, by Mrs Schneider after she had come back from a trip to Germany. Malka had never had such nice shoes before. She laughed with delight. Mrs Schneider often gave her presents when she went to the villa down the street to play with Veronika. The Germans had made them wear the star when the Russians pulled out, but apart from that, things hadn't been as bad as people had said they would be.

Malka ran downstairs to the kitchen. She ate the bread and apricot jam that Minna gave her, was already half standing as she drank her milk, and then ran out of the kitchen. 'Don't forget that you've got to go to Miss Lemberger this afternoon,' Minna shouted after her.

'I won't forget,' replied Malka, as she put her feet together and jumped across the doorstep, then ran off down the street to the big house where Veronika lived.

When the kitchen door closed with a bang it startled Hannah Mai, Malka's mother, out of her train of thought. She was sitting downstairs at the desk in her surgery. Since they had taken away her licence to practise as a regional medical officer she no longer received a salary. But since there were no other doctors for miles around she was still called out when she was needed. However, that was happening less and less frequently now, and she often had more time on her hands than she liked. She looked automatically at her watch. Ten past nine. At eleven she would go to the Jewish quarter on the other side of the little town to visit the shoemaker's wife, who had had a son three days before. Until then there was nothing for it but to sit here and wait. She sighed. She felt she was the victim of a set of circumstances that forced her to be idle, and this didn't suit her at all. She missed the long trips around her area – the work, the challenges. Sometimes she felt almost like a prisoner in this house, in this godforsaken hole near the Hungarian border, and that the Germans were her jailers.

She heard Minna doing things in the kitchen, impatiently and carelessly, and she sighed again. No wonder Minna was so bad-tempered – a sixteen-year-old with no company, no real friends, and no chance of learning enough for a proper career. Minna was at a difficult age, and since Zofia had left, everything had just got worse.

Hannah clenched her fists a couple of times, then stretched out her fingers and looked closely at her carefully trimmed nails before opening a drawer in the desk and taking out the letter. For weeks now she had been doing that two or three times a day, reading over and over again the words her father had written, staring over and over again at the two photographs. On one of the photos her father looked just as she knew him – an Orthodox Jew with a beard and earlocks, a gaberdine buttoned to the neck and a round black hat on his head. A serious-looking, dignified elderly man. But the man who looked at her out of the other photograph was a stranger, with an old, scrawny, naked face, with no beard and no earlocks. The receding chin that had been concealed behind the beard made him look nondescript, frightened, helpless.

Hannah, my dear, he had written, *thank you for sending me the change-of-residence permit, which arrived a few days ago, but I can't come to you. I'm staying here with your sister and her family just as your mother – may her memory be a blessing upon us all – would have wanted. When someone is in trouble you can't abandon them.*

Hannah wondered whether these words were just a variation on the old reproach about her decision to go

5

away and study, to lead her own life without a thought for her parents and her family. Maybe. He had never forgiven her for it.

Hannah had her elbows on the desk and was still staring at the two photos when there was a knock at the door. Reddening, as if she had been caught doing something wrong, she quickly pushed the letter and the photos into the drawer, ran a hand through her hair and picked up a pencil as if she had been working, before calling out, 'Come in.'

It was Mrs Silber, a dark, heavy-set woman, who moved slowly and wore a perpetually vague expression, behind which was hidden, Hannah knew, a sharp mind. She had had six children, and Hannah had helped her with the last, which had been an unexpectedly difficult birth. Only after a particularly tricky episiotomy had little Moyshe come into the world weighing ten pounds, six months after her husband had emigrated to America. Since then she hadn't heard a word from him. She managed to feed the children by her sewing.

Mrs Silber moved more quickly than she usually did. She dropped into the chair on the other side of the desk and, without any ado, came right out with what she had to say. 'They've been to the tailors and collected all their things. And they've been to Netti the laundress as well.'

'Who has?' asked Hannah Mai, baffled.

'The Germans. The border guards. They went to Mendel Abraham and to David Scheor and collected everything, even the suits that weren't finished. It can only mean one thing, doctor. They're mounting an operation.'

The two women stared at each other. Hannah Mai didn't know how to conceal how frightened she was, because of course she had heard of these so-called operations; it was that very word which had weighed so heavily upon her for the past few weeks. One of her patients, a German officer, had told her about an 'operation' in Kraków, and had said that all Jews would be resettled somewhere else. She had written to her father right away, but hadn't had an answer yet. Even though she didn't know what the words really meant, 'operation' and 'resettlement' were the reason that she kept on looking at the photographs and reading the letter. She felt strangely weak and powerless whenever she thought about her father, or her sister and her family.

She wasn't particularly worried as far as she herself and her two daughters were concerned – or, to put it more precisely, her worry was no more than a vague disquiet which was quite easily pushed to one side by the thought that she was still working, and that she had a certain position even under the Germans, since there wasn't another doctor for thirty miles. Besides, her profession wasn't the only reason why the Germans needed her. She was, after all, one of the few educated people in a region mostly occupied by peasant-farmers who couldn't read or write.

The German officers had always been polite to her and liked to talk to her about books or the theatre, and had often visited her socially. And not only Heinz Peschl. Hannah thought of herself as being closer to the Germans in social terms than to the Polish or Ukrainian farmers, even if she had to admit that in the last few months the visits from German officers had become a lot less frequent. Even Heinz Peschl hadn't been there for weeks.

Nevertheless, she wasn't frightened. Not really. She was needed, she was protected by her profession – unlike

Jews like Mrs Silber who was clearly in a quite different position. Hannah looked at the woman who was sitting in front of her with her head bowed and her hands in her lap, and said the only thing that came into her head. 'A lot of Jews have fled to Hungary. The border is so close.'

Mrs Silber looked at her. Suddenly her vague expression had gone and she was alert and direct. Her voice was clear, too, when she said, 'Am I, Rachel Silber, supposed to take my children and go begging? Leyser and Yankel are nearly grown-up and they can decide for themselves what to do, but I'll go with the girls and little Moyshe wherever they send me.' Then she was silent.

Just for something to do, Hannah started to tidy things, as she always did when she was agitated. She pushed a notepad from one side of the desk to the other, stood up and put a book back on to the shelf, then straightened a medical journal that was lying in front of her so that its edge was exactly parallel to the side of the desk. She put her pen and a pencil into the wooden bowl, folded up the cuff of her blood-pressure monitor, placed her stethoscope next to it, turned the key to lock the desk drawer and unlocked it again. All this time Mrs Silber sat motionless on the chair, her eyes on the ground. The sun shone through the open window and everything looked completely normal, just like any other fine day in late summer. I ought to go down and sit by the stream, thought Hannah – dangle my feet in the water and watch the dragonflies skimming over the water. Suddenly nothing seemed more important to her than the dragonflies.

Mrs Silber cleared her throat. Hannah looked at her. She wanted to say something but didn't know what. Then the decision was taken out of her hands. There was the sound of someone walking along the pathway, the door to the house opened, and then the kitchen door. Minna came into the surgery, followed by Zofia's mother, Mrs Wolynski from Wyszków. The woman kissed Hannah's hand and blurted out, 'Doctor, the Germans are up to something! They've given orders for twenty carts to be taken from Wyszków to Lawoczne at five o'clock this afternoon. My husband sent me to tell you about it, ma'am, you were always so good to our Zofia, he said, and if Zofia hadn't learned such a lot when she was with you she would never have got the job in that office in Stryj, he said, and you oughtn't to be seen outdoors today, the best thing would be for you to go to someone's house who's not Jewish, you and Minna and the little one and just wait for it to pass, he said . . .'

Hannah took her hand out of the other woman's hands and thanked her for coming all that way to warn her, then she asked Minna to give Mrs Wolynski some tea and something to eat before she set off home. Mrs Wolynski kissed Hannah's hand again when she left. Hannah asked to be remembered to Zofia, and then she was alone again with Mrs Silber.

Mrs Silber stood up. 'Do you know what you're going to do?' she asked.

Hannah shrugged. 'I shall probably take the children and go and ask my neighbours – they're not Jewish – if we can stay there this afternoon. What about you?'

Mrs Silber gave a sad smile. 'I'll go where all the Jews go.' Then she suddenly put her arms round Hannah, something she had never done before, and said in Yiddish: *'Geyt in gesinderheyt'* – Go in good health.

Hannah hugged her back, and then went into the kitchen to tell her daughters to get ready.

Malka went in, as usual, through the back door of the house and straight up to Veronika's room. Veronika was sitting on the carpet with her toys laid out all round her – her dolls, a toy kitchen, a doll's pram and bed, an open case with clothes and a little box with a pink brush and comb. Before Veronika and her mother came to Lawoczne, Malka had never seen so many toys in her life, not even in Kraków. She hadn't known that toys like these existed, because up to then all she had known about were balls, skipping ropes and spinning tops. The Polish and Ukrainian children she had played with before didn't have any toys at all, and not much time to play, because instead of dolls, most of the little girls had even littler brothers and sisters to look after. In summer and autumn they were sent out into the woods to pick berries and mushrooms, and it was only in the winter that they had less to do. Winter was the time for snowmen and sledges and snowball fights.

Veronika was wearing her red dress with the shoulder straps and the white blouse with the lace collar that Malka liked so much. Maybe one day she would find the courage to ask Mrs Schneider to get her a blouse like that when she went to Germany again. Veronika's hair was done in two plaits, each one rolled up and pinned in a flat spiral by her ears. Her head was bent over as she combed the long blonde tresses of her favourite doll, Marion. Every time Malka saw the pink parting on Veronika's head with the tight, smooth blonde hair on each side of it, she couldn't help thinking it looked like someone's bare bottom, but of course she never said so. She didn't want to annoy Veronika, because she might not be allowed to play with her any more.

Malka joined the other girl on the floor and picked up Liesel, the little rag doll with the striped socks and the red woollen hair. Liesel had a pretty painted face with blue eyes. 'You can be the mother now and I'm the father,' said Veronika.

Malka nodded. She could understand a lot of German words, certainly enough for playing. Veronika couldn't speak Polish or Ukrainian, just German. It was a funny-sounding language, a bit like the one Malka's relations in Kraków spoke. Malka took the romper suit off Liesel so that the doll was left with the striped socks, green knitted pants and a white vest, and rummaged around in the box of dolls' things for something to put on her.

At that moment Mrs Schneider came into the room. 'Malka,' she said, taking a couple of quick paces towards her and lifting the child up. 'Malka, you have to go home – you can't stay and play here.'

Malka stared at the woman. Suddenly her freckled face didn't look at all friendly any more, and her gingery eyebrows practically met over the bridge of her nose.

'Malka,' Mrs Schneider said again, and this time her voice was a little gentler. 'You can't, not today. Run off home to your mama.'

Her upper lip was slightly raised and you could see her uneven teeth. Veronika lifted her head and looked at her mother with astonishment, but she didn't make any protest and just carried on playing. Mrs Schneider pushed Malka out into the hall towards the back door. The sun shone harshly into Malka's face when the door opened, and then she was standing outside. 'Hurry up,' said Mrs Schneider again. 'Off you go now, run.'

But Malka didn't hurry. She walked slowly up the street with her head down. She was hurt and angry and kicked out at a stone. Only when it hit the door of the Kronowskis' house with a bang did she feel the pain in her toe. Tears came into her eyes. Why hadn't Veronika said, 'But I want Malka to stay?' It must be because of that stupid star that Mrs Schneider had sent her away. Ever since she had been made to wear the star, the Polish and Ukrainian children hadn't wanted to play with her any more. They pointed at her and shouted, 'Jew-girl, Jew-girl' after her. Now she could only play with Veronika or with Chaya, the daughter of the kosher butcher. Chaya wore a star herself.

Malka bent down to rub her stubbed toe. At that moment, she noticed that she was still clutching Liesel's arm. She looked around quickly, and then stuffed the doll into the pocket of her dress.

When Hannah Mai left the house to look for Malka, who had disapppeared without telling Minna where she was going, she heard a horse galloping towards her down the slope of the hill. She looked across. The woman on the horse raised her arm and waved. Hannah stopped. Only when the horse came closer was she able to recognize the rider. It was Mrs Sawkowicz, the wife of a farmer from Kalne. The horse snorted and there was foam on its mouth when Mrs Sawkowicz reined in just in front of her and dismounted. 'Doctor, you must come to my husband, he's hurt his leg chopping some wood – it's a serious wound. Please, doctor. You take the horse and I'll come after you on foot. Please come quickly, it's urgent.'

Hannah knew at once what she had to do and didn't

have to waste time thinking about it. Making decisions quickly was one of her strong points, and secretly she despised people who were slow and hesitant, like her sister, for example. And her father.

'Please, doctor,' said the woman.

Hannah gave her an encouraging smile – a professional smile that came easily to her, whatever she was really thinking. Of course it was her duty to look after someone who had been hurt – and it wasn't just duty. She loved her work and enjoyed being needed. But today she felt that Mrs Sawkowicz had been sent to her as a gift from heaven. Kalne was the answer. Kalne was a much better idea than hiding out with neighbours for the afternoon. She would go with Minna and Malka to Kalne and stay there until the air had cleared in Lawoczne – if necessary, until tomorrow or the day after. The village was no more than a mile or so away, a distance that even Malka could manage easily on foot.

'Just a moment,' Hannah, and she ran into the house and told Minna to find Malka and come to Kalne with her. 'Take your jackets, because we may not come back until late this evening or even during the night.'

Then she went into her surgery and, before picking up her doctor's bag, opened the desk drawer. She didn't want to leave her father's letter with the photos in the house, because she had a sudden notion that the Germans might search the house and find the letter, and she didn't want that to happen. Her papers were in the drawer as well. On a sudden impulse, she tucked her children's birth certificates and her medical registration document into the inside pocket of her jacket with her passport, which she always carried with her.

As she left the house Malka came round the corner.

She looked depressed, but at that moment Hannah couldn't think of anything except her marvellous plan. 'Please would you take my children with you to Kalne,' she asked Mrs Sawkowicz, and jumped on to the horse. She saw Minna forcing her reluctant little sister to put her jacket on, and heard Malka's furious, 'No! In this heat? You must be crazy!' and saw Minna raise her hand. But she didn't see whether Minna really gave her sister a smack or not, because by then she had ridden off.

The wounded man was lying in bed on the first floor. He had pulled the covers only part of the way over himself to leave the injured leg free, and it had been raised up a little by having folded towels put underneath it. There was a white, clean-looking piece of cloth wrapped around it. The great red stain and the blood-soaked cloths lying on the floor by the bed showed that the wound hadn't stopped bleeding.

Hannah Mai took the disinfectant out of her bag, scrubbed her hands in the basin of water that stood ready beside the bed, and rubbed disinfectant into them before she peeled the makeshift bandage – which had stuck at the edges – away from the wound.

The axe had gone into the upper thigh just above the knee. The wound was a gaping one, and was beginning to form a scab at the edges, but in the middle it was still bleeding. Hannah cleaned the wound and the area around it carefully with iodine. The farmer groaned, but held his leg still.

'It will have to have stitches,' said Hannah. 'Can you cope with that?' The man's face was grey, in spite of his sunburned skin, but he nodded and she put in nine stitches to close the wound. He didn't cry out, although the sweat poured from his forehead and his eyes looked as if they were bursting from his head. Once she had bandaged up his leg, he grabbed her hand and kissed it in gratitude.

It was only when all the excitement was over that Hannah heard through the open window the sound of voices – orders given sharply and loudly in German, a lot of footsteps, a scream, a child crying. She ran to the window. Further down the street, on the square in front of the church, a group of people were milling around a horse-drawn cart. They were Jews – at least five or six families; men, women and children weighed down with bundles of all sizes. The first of them were just getting on to the cart, which was really too small for so many people. Some German soldiers were supervising all this, and making them hurry.

Two officers were standing nearby, and Hannah knew one of them. His name was Pucher and he was an officer in the border-control unit. He suffered from furunculosis, and during the winter she had, on several occasions, had to remove boils from the back of his neck. She was sure that he would be on her side. She ran quickly down the steps.

Malka was tired and thirsty by the time they got to Kalne. And she was furious at Minna for making her come all that way in the heat. On the walk over she made such a fuss that Minna had lost her temper and smacked her. After that she hadn't said a single word and had just trotted crossly along behind Minna and the farmer's wife. Only when they had gone through the wood did she pick a little bunch of wild flowers from the side of the path for her mother.

The village was strangely quiet, without a single soul on the street. The farmer's wife stopped, looked around, and then went on more quickly than before. Malka had to run to keep up with her and Minna. When they turned the corner just before the square by the church, they saw the cart with the Jews silently climbing on to it. All that you could hear were the voices of the Germans, and now and then a scream, when one of the soldiers hit out with the butt of his rifle.

Mrs Sawkowicz grabbed Malka's hand and pulled her past the two horses and the cart. Behind them, Malka saw her mother by the side of a house talking to a German officer. She pulled away, ran across and stood behind her mother. No one took any notice of her.

'Everyone is being moved,' the German officer was saying quietly to her mother. 'All the Jews in the region are being resettled.'

'Even those who work for the Germans?' asked her mother.

He nodded.

'Me too?' Her mother's voice sounded different to Malka – oddly high and strained.

The German nodded. 'Jews are Jews, no distinctions are being made.' Then he said very loudly, so that the other soldiers would certainly hear him: 'Go and see to your patient, doctor. We'll come and fetch you later.' And then he added very quietly, 'Get away from here, doctor, right now. You must get across the border.'

Her mother nodded, turned round and almost fell over Malka, who was standing behind her and holding the wild flowers out to her. They were already drooping because of the heat. Her mother tore the flowers out of Malka's hand and grabbed her by the arm. 'Come on,'

16

she hissed, and pulled Malka behind her up the street. She just dropped the flowers.

Malka didn't dare to protest – her mother's grip was unusually hard, her hand hot and wet. She pulled Malka into the house and upstairs to the sick man's room, and went and stood at the window. Malka stood by the door and stared at the man, lying in bed in his undershirt, the cover pulled halfway up his chest. His arms, lying on the blue checked bedcover, were sunburned to the middle of his upper arm, and so were his face and neck. The skin on his shoulders and chest was white, like dough, and there were little strands of grey and brown hair poking over the top of his olive-green undershirt. That looks horrible, thought Malka. The German officer looks much nicer in his uniform with the buttons all done up to the top.

Her mother stood at the window and twitched the dark curtain to one side – just enough to be able to look out without anyone being able to see her from below. A ray of sunshine fell on her face and divided it in two. Malka wanted to run across to her mother and press herself against her, but a violent gesture from her mother's hand kept her back from the window.

Malka looked round. Over the big bed hung a cross, black with gold around the edges, and on one of the two bedside tables lay a small book bound in black leather. On the chest of drawers with the mirror there was a washbasin and a water jug made of white china, with a comb lying next to them. The space between the window and the wall with the door in it was filled by a huge wardrobe made of light wood with a yellowish grain. The farmer was certainly pretty well-off. Malka knew the difference, because in the days when they had still had maids, she had often visited their parents' houses with them, and the houses weren't much more than wooden huts, sometimes with just one single room. She had never seen a bedroom like this in any of them, not even at the Wolynskis' home – Zofia's parents – and they had a proper house, made of brick.

Outside, you could hear a loud rumbling, horses' hooves clattering on the cobblestones, the crack of a whip. Her mother let go of the curtain and the ray of light passed from her face down across her neck and on to her blue dress, and then disappeared. 'They've gone,' she said to the man in the bed. 'We have to escape to Hungary. How can we get across the border?'

The farmer looked at her mother for a long time. Malka looked from one to the other and felt the tension in the room. She had heard the desperation in her mother's voice and knew that she had better keep her mouth shut.

'There's a young Ukrainian who works for me,' said the farmer at last. 'He'll take you to the border.'

Malka ran her hand over the pocket in her dress. Liesel was still there.

They walked along behind Ivan, the young Ukrainian. Minna was crying softly. Hannah gave her a sidelong look. Clearly her elder daughter was gradually realizing what was in front of them. Hannah could not think of anything comforting to say to her, and she was so agitated and afraid herself that she just snapped at her and told her to pull herself together. But then she saw the horrified look on Malka's face and thought: damn, I'm the one who has to pull herself together; I'm the last person who's allowed to crack.

Hannah kept her eyes fixed on Ivan's back. The arms of his jacket were too short for him and it was too tight across his back, so that the shoulder-seams were already tearing and you could see a bit of his light-brown shirt. His shorts were too long and came down below his knees. He was barefoot, but in spite of that he walked quickly, putting one foot in front of the other in such a regular rhythm that Hannah wouldn't have been surprised to see pads of hard skin on the soles of his feet, just like an animal's. She tried to take up his rhythm, but she was wearing light summer shoes with a medium heel and kept tripping. Besides, Malka, who was walking next to her, was getting slower and slower, so Hannah slowed down as well. By now the little girl could hardly lift her feet from the dusty track, and stumbled more than she walked. She's got the wrong shoes on, thought Hannah. We both have. It's only Minna's shoes that are more or less right. How on earth are we going to manage? But there was nothing for it; they had to keep going.

Hannah brushed the hair out of her eyes. It was so hot that she felt as if she was melting. Sweat fell from her forehead and ran into her eyes, making them burn; great streams of sweat poured down her back and from her armpits. What a rushed and unplanned escape, she thought. But Pucher's face, even more than his words, had convinced her of the seriousness of her situation. They were in danger – maybe in danger of their lives, if there was anything in the rumours that she had heard so often and never believed.

She blamed herself for not reading the situation properly, and for the fact that they hadn't escaped before this, instead of nursing a false sense of security and thinking that everyone else was in danger except them. But then, when she imagined herself having to carry a rucksack and other baggage up the mountain, she was almost relieved that they had fled without any luggage at all. Even this relief was shortlived, though, as she wondered how she was going to get her children through. All she had, after all, was a little money, which the farmer had given her in payment for her help and for her doctor's bag and its contents. This is not the right time to think about all that, she told herself. It will have to wait until later. All that was important now was to get to Hungary. Everything else could wait.

At last they reached the forest, and now that there was shade, Malka became more like her old self again, especially as the path was less steep. The little girl looked around with interest. She stopped by a low bramble bush, picked a few ripe blackberries and popped them into her mouth. Minna did the same. Now Ivan stopped as well. He watched sullenly as Malka and Minna picked black-berries and stuffed them into their mouths almost joyfully. Even Hannah ate a few, and laughed when the blue juice ran down Malka's chin.

Suddenly Ivan made a hissing noise and put his finger to his lips. The three of them stopped in the middle of what they were doing and stood there just like children playing statues, Minna with her mouth wide open and Malka with her hand outstretched.

Ivan moved his head slowly from one side to the other, his eyes darting around and his nose twitching like a dog's. Then he said, 'It was just some animal or other,' and walked on again.

Malka's cheerfulness had gone, as if it had been wiped away. She pulled on Hannah's arm and said, 'I want to go home. Why don't we go home?'

Hannah didn't know how to explain to her that they didn't have a home any more, so she just said, 'We're going on a little trip to Hungary. It's a long way and you've got to be a big, brave girl.'

Luckily, Malka seemed to be satisfied with this answer.

Malka's feet hurt. All she really wanted to do was sit down on the ground and cry, but her mother pulled her relentlessly on whenever it looked as if she was falling behind. Minna, who was a few paces ahead, stopped and waited for them. 'Why didn't we go through the tunnel?' she asked. 'Hungary starts just after the tunnel.' She sounded anxious and reproachful.

Her mother shook her head. 'First of all, we didn't know all this when we were still in Lawoczne, and anyway, the border guards will be watching the whole place, especially the tunnel.'

'It's all your fault,' said Minna furiously. 'If we'd gone with Papa when he left, none of this would have happened.'

'Shut up!' her mother snapped back at her.

'You always know better,' said Minna. 'I remember when Papa said—'

'That's enough, Minna,' interrupted her mother. 'Stop it, or there'll be trouble.'

Minna heard the threat, pressed her lips together and lowered her head.

They went on in silence. The sunlight was slanting through the trees. Malka was hungry. Apart from a slice of bread and butter that Mrs Sawkowicz had given her, she hadn't eaten anything. She thought about Veronika, who right now might be having a glass of milk and a piece of cake. Mrs Schneider often baked cakes – yellow

21

cakes with pieces of dark chocolate or raisins in them. 'Cakes for afternooon tea', her teacher, Miss Lemberger, called them. Civilized people take tea and cake. 'We didn't tell Miss Lemberger that I wasn't going to school today,' said Malka suddenly. 'She'll have been waiting for me.'

Her mother didn't answer, just shook her head, but Minna said, 'You don't have to worry about that. Miss Lemberger won't have been worrying about you. She's probably been taken away.'

'Where to?' asked Malka.

Neither her mother nor Minna answered.

Ivan had left the track and was leading them through the forest. The trees were so close together that the sun couldn't penetrate the canopy of leaves. Shadows crept out of the undergrowth and the trees threatened them with knobbly arms. Their footsteps seemed loud and echoing, even though they were walking over the soft forest floor, and in the distance was the sound of soft thunder.

Malka gripped her mother's hand. She hadn't often been in the woods as late as this – perhaps never at all – and she didn't like it one bit. She was tired, her legs ached, the soles of her feet were burning and the laces on her sandals were cutting into her. 'Mama, carry me,' she begged.

Hannah picked her up. Malka put her arms round her mother's neck and pressed her face against her shoulder so she couldn't see anything. After a while her mother stopped, put her down and said, 'I can't manage it, Malka. You're too heavy, you'll have to walk.' By now they had left the forest behind them and in front of them were gentle rolls of meadow-land stretching down to the valley.

It was lighter here than it had been in the forest, and the tops of the trees below them were already turning the yellow and russet colours of autumn.

Her mother pointed at a wooden cabin, some distance away on the hillside and only just visible. 'That's where we'll go,' she said. 'A woman I know lives there. Her mother was a patient of mine. I'm sure she'll help us.'

Hannah had spoken quietly, but Ivan, who was walking a little way ahead of them, had heard her. He stopped. 'This is far enough,' he said sullenly and stuffed his hands into his pockets. 'I've got to get home now, I've got a long journey back.' He took one hand out of his pocket again and pointed to the mountains on the far side of the broad valley. 'The border is over there somewhere. If you stay overnight here, maybe you can make it there tomorrow.' He turned round and had soon vanished into the shadows between the trees.

Hannah sat up suddenly. Minna and Malka were lying in the grass near her. They had only intended to rest for a little while, but they must have dozed off, because when she opened her eyes only the tops of the mountains on the far side of the valley were still lit by the setting sun. It had become noticeably cooler. Twilight had reached the valley already. It looked as if it was flowing out of the woods and down the slopes, filling the valley and rising higher and higher. They would have to hurry if they wanted to reach the hut before it was completely dark.

Minna got up right away and brushed dirt and grass from her skirt, but Malka just would not open her eyes. Minna looked from her mother to Malka, then across to the hut, which was barely visible in the twilight so that they had to guess where it was. Then she bent down and picked up her little sister. 'I'll carry you for a bit,' she said.

Malka slept on against Minna's shoulder. She didn't notice when, after a while, her mother took her back, and then Minna again. Progress down to the hut took a very long time, and it was already dark when they went in through the gate to the yard.

Hannah hesitated for a moment. She didn't know Mrs Kowalski particularly well – just knew that she had been widowed while still young, though she couldn't remember how the woman had lost her husband. It was already two years since she had treated the mother, a tough, strong-minded old lady who refused to let go. She pitched herself against death and didn't give up the struggle until she was as thin as a skeleton. Hannah's impression of the daughter was that she had been caring towards her mother and friendly, but at that time the whole basis of the relationship had been the other way round, and it had been the woman who had needed her and wanted something from her.

Hannah reached out and knocked at the door. Immediately, she heard steps from inside, a bolt was drawn back and the door opened. Mrs Kowalski was taken aback, but then she recognized Hannah. 'Doctor,' she said, with a questioning note in her voice. 'Doctor?'

Hannah could hardly speak. She raised her hands helplessly, swallowed and only then regained control of her voice. 'We need help,' she said. 'The Germans . . .'

Mrs Kowalski nodded and led them into her kitchen, which was lit by an oil lamp, though not very well. Minna was still carrying the sleeping Malka, and one blonde plait hung over the arm of her blue jacket. Hannah noticed how the peasant-woman's eyes became gentle, and she saw how tenderly she took the child from Minna's arms and laid her down on the bench by the stove. My beautiful daughter has done it again, thought Hannah, and sat down by Minna at the table. Malka seemed to feel this unknown woman looking at her, because her eyelids twitched and then she opened her eyes fully.

'What a lovely little girl,' said Mrs Kowalski, and held out her arms. There was the sound of a cow mooing in its stall.

'I'm hungry,' said Malka, and sat up.

Malka sat at the table. The oil lamp, which was hanging from a hook in the ceiling, threw strange shadows on the woodwork – shadows which looked like people swaying backwards and forwards, and changing all the time. Mrs Kowalski opened a cupboard, bent down and disappeared in the darkness. When she emerged again she put a dish and a jug of buttermilk on the table, then fetched from another cupboard a colander piled high with brown- and black-skinned boiled potatoes, sat down, took a little knife out of a drawer and started to peel them.

Her hands were round – in fact, everything about Mrs Kowalski was round. Malka couldn't take her eyes off those round hands, which wielded the knife quickly and expertly as the peel came away. She saw the potatoes come out from their skins, pale and with black eyes still in them. At home Minna always took the eyes out of the potatoes, but Mrs Kowalski left them in. Her round hands put potato after potato into the dish, then poured the buttermilk over them and fetched three spoons from the drawer. The spoons were made of aluminium, slightly bent and with dull, white patches on them.

Malka picked up a spoon, leaned forward and started to eat straight away. She was surprised that the potatoes were cold, but she was hungry so she chewed and swallowed and chewed and swallowed and felt how her stomach calmed down. Not until then did she raise her eyes and see her mother's hand coming into the light again and again, and disappearing into the darkness with a spoon piled high. Minna's hand hung motionless over the table. Only when her mother said, 'Come on, Minna, eat. You have to keep your strength up,' did she lower the spoon, mash a piece of potato and put it into her mouth.

By the time the dish was empty, Malka was full up and feeling much better. She was happy to let this stranger stroke her hair, and when Mrs Kowalski lifted her on to her lap, Malka laid her head against the round shoulder, which smelled of cows and hay and sweat, and closed her eyes. She was aware of the woman lifting her up and carrying her through the kitchen, and then she fell asleep.

Hannah lay on the bed which Mrs Kowalski had made up for her and Minna in the other room – a simple and not even particularly well-filled straw mattress with a woollen blanket over it. Minna lay by Hannah's side, nearest to the wall. She wasn't moving. Hannah could hear by her irregular breathing that her daughter was fighting back tears, and she stroked her face. Minna turned over and put her head on her mother's arm and pressed against her, just as she used to do when she was a little girl.

Hannah lay on her back, feeling her daughter's warm breath on her neck, and looked through the open window in the wall facing her. The sky was so clear that she could see a few stars. That evening, as they had climbed down to the hut, she hadn't noticed the moon, but it must be full or nearly full because the pale light that fell into the room through the window was so bright that if she turned her head she could see the bed in which Malka and the peasant woman were sleeping. The woman had really taken a fancy to Malka. And no wonder – Malka, with her golden-blonde hair and her big brown eyes, really was strikingly pretty. Even tonight, exhausted and not very clean, she had looked like an angel as she sat in this gloomy kitchen. Or like a princess on a dungheap.

Pressed close to her mother, Minna was now breathing gently and regularly, fast asleep. Hannah could not get to sleep – she was far too worked up. She thought about Chaya, the kosher butcher's daughter with whom Malka often used to play. She pictured the girl's face, freckled and with a mop of ginger curls, and she remembered how ill Chaya had been last year during the flu epidemic. She had almost given the girl up, and was already working out how to prepare the parents for the fact that they might lose their only child, but Chaya's will to live had triumphed and she had suddenly taken a turn for the better. Would that will to live help her when she got to wherever the Germans were taking them? Chaya was a late child, her parents were older than most and they wouldn't have dared to try and escape. Hannah reproached herself for not having sent Mrs Sawkowicz back to Lawoczne with the horse to ask the neighbours if she could take Chaya with her. They wouldn't have let her, of course they wouldn't, but she should at least have asked.

Minna snorted in her sleep, turned over and slipped down into the hollow between the mattress and the wall.

Hannah could at last pull her arm away and stretch it out. Some nocturnal bird was calling, and a dog was howling a long way off. Gently, she moved Minna a little closer to the wall, turned on to her side and closed her eyes. She had to sleep, she really had to, because who knew what the next day might bring? One thing was certain: they had to move on. They were still in Poland, right at the edge of the region she had covered as a doctor. Her hope was Hungary.

Mrs Kowalski woke Malka. It was still early, and the room was not quite light yet. 'Where are Mama and Minna?' asked Malka, frightened to find herself alone in the room with the peasant-woman.

'They're already in the kitchen,' said the woman. 'Come on, I'll help you dress.'

Malka let her help, even though she hadn't needed any help in getting dressed for ages. Then she allowed herself to be led into the yard, to the pump with the long metal arm, where the woman washed her hands, face and feet before she could put her shoes on again. After this she even let the woman plait her long hair. While Mrs Kowalski was combing it with a coarse-toothed comb, Malka looked around.

They were in an unflagged yard, with the only paving stones making a path from the door of the house to the pump, around which there was now a large puddle. The sun was rising behind the low animal shed, and you could already feel that it was going to be another hot day. Hens were scratching around the dungheap, picking at the earth with their yellow beaks. There was no sign of a cockerel, but there must be one because Malka remembered hearing him crow at dawn before she had gone back to sleep again. Mrs Kowalski combed carefully, holding the thick hanks of hair close to Malka's head with one hand while she drew the comb through the tangles. Not until she had finished the two plaits did she take Malka into the kitchen, where her mother and Minna were sitting eating thick slices of black bread.

Malka noticed right away that the bread was spread with dark plum jam and was very happy about that. Mrs Kowalski poured her a cup of milk, and spread some jam on a slice of bread for her. Then she fished some of the thick cream out of the milk-can and put it on top of the jam, and when Malka started to eat she sat down at the table too.

Malka's mother was drinking ersatz coffee made from barley – Malka recognized it from the colour and the smell – and in front of Minna was a full cup of milk with a small dirty smear just under the rim. Malka knew that Minna wouldn't touch her milk. Malka drank her own milk, and when the woman got up to pour some more coffee for her mother she quickly pushed her cup across to Minna and took her sister's full one. Her mother saw her do it, wrinkled her brow and gave her a sharp look, but Minna smiled gratefully.

'What do you plan to do now, doctor?' asked Mrs Kowalski.

Her mother drank some more coffee, put the cup down and said, speaking hesitantly as if this was the first time she had given it any thought, 'Down in the village there's a farmer I once treated. He lives in the house right next to the graveyard. I'll ask him if he can help us get further.'

Malka was aware of how tired her mother looked. She was pale, and the fine lines from her nostrils to the corners of her mouth suddenly looked like real age-lines.

Mrs Kowalski got up. 'That's old Anton,' she said. 'He's a good man. I'll go and fetch him so that nobody in the village sees you. You've got to be careful, doctor, there are people everywhere who would give you away.' Then suddenly, as she was knotting her scarf over her head, she asked, without looking at Hannah, 'Why don't you leave the child with me? She's too small for such a long journey. I'll take good care of her.'

It was a shock. Malka stopped chewing and stared at her mother. The sweet mixture of bread, jam and cream seemed to expand in her mouth and fill it up completely so that she started to choke. She noticed, too, that the plum jam was a tiny bit burned, not much, but you could taste it. Then her mother shook her head. 'No, there's no question of that, we'll stay together. Either we all make it or none of us.' Minna nodded and at last Malka was able to swallow her mouthful.

The woman looked disappointed. 'I'll go now,' she said, and she had already opened the door. 'You ought to take that star off yours and the girls' clothes. People don't need to know right away.'

Malka was no longer hungry. She went to the window and watched as Mrs Kowalski hurried down the slope. In spite of her bulk she moved as quickly and neatly as a mountain-goat and soon disappeared behind a ridge. Malka watched a couple of birds swooping in great arcs over the valley. After a while she got bored and went out into the yard. Her mother and Minna followed her and sat down together on the wooden bench by the door, from where they could look out over most of the valley.

Malka had a look at the hens first, and then she went to the animal shed between the house and the barn. Through a window she could see two fat pink pigs. They were moving around in separate sties and rooting in the straw. One pig raised its head, blinked its little eyes and twitched its comical round snout. Through the open window the smell of fresh dung reached Malka's nose.

Behind the pigsties, in a fenced meadow, a cow and a calf were grazing and there was another cow standing by the fence. Malka pulled up a handful of grass and offered it to the calf, but it wouldn't come. Its mother took no notice, and didn't even raise her head. Malka went and stood in front of the other cow and looked into its great brown eyes, which were unwaveringly fixed on her, although she didn't feel at all as if she were being looked at. She shook her head, but the cow didn't react, and when she started to jump up and down it still didn't move either its head or its eyes. Malka waved her arms about, but as far as the cow was concerned she was just part of the scenery.

The sun had reached the top of the birch tree behind the pigsties when the woman came back, accompanied by an old man who was just as round as she was. He had a red face and the long walk had made him cough. His grey hair stuck out from beneath his cap, but the most striking thing about him were his eyes, which were blue and round, like marbles. He greeted her mother, sat down on the bench next to her and had a few words with her. Minna sat there silently. When Malka came nearer she heard her mother ask, 'When?' He raised his head. 'Preferably right away,' he said, and stood up.

Mrs Kowalski wrapped a chunk of bread and a piece of smoked bacon in a cloth for the journey. Malka saw Minna pull a face, but her mother thanked the woman effusively, especially when Mrs Kowalski also brought out a horse-blanket and a thick grey pullover that smelled of mothballs. 'The nights are cold in the mountains,' she said. 'The child mustn't freeze.'

When they said goodbye the old woman's eyes were wet as she hugged Malka, kissed her on the cheek and quickly and secretly made the sign of the cross on her forehead.

The round old man with the eyes like marbles, whom her mother called Mr Anton, led them in a wide detour past the village, first down the hill, then along the flat part of the valley and up the slope again. Flowers were blooming in the meadows – blue, yellow and white ones – and Malka would have liked to pick a bunch, but her mother wouldn't let her. 'Later,' she said. 'Just let us get to Hungary and then you can pick flowers again.'

It was a good while after they had heard the bells for midday ringing out in the church down in the valley when the old farmer said to them that he couldn't go on any more. Hannah had seen this coming for some time. It hadn't escaped her notice that his puffing and panting was getting louder and more rapid, and she had seen with some consternation how a couple of times he had put his hand over his chest. *Angina*, she thought. He wasn't exactly a young man, either, and even for a healthy man of his age, climbing in this heat wouldn't be all that easy.

In fact, she was relieved when he gasped out that he couldn't make it any further, because without any glyceryl trinitrate, how would she have been able to help him if he collapsed? She couldn't even have checked his blood pressure. He took his leave of them, and she thanked him and told him that it would be better if he tried to eat less but more often, and to give up salt altogether.

Then she watched as he set off down the hill with drooping shoulders and his head bent, but, in spite of her relief, she felt strangely as if she had been abandoned.

Malka was crouching down in the grass with a shiny green beetle in her hand, and was clearly trying to feed it with a blade of grass. Minna was sitting sulkily beside the path and made no move to get up. 'I'm not coming,' she said. 'I hate the mountains and I hate Hungary and I hate—'

Hannah didn't argue. She just said, very firmly, 'Stop making a fuss and come on.'

'Everything always has to be the way you want it,' snapped Minna. 'I don't want to go to Hungary. What am I supposed to do in Hungary?'

Hannah lost her temper. 'Can't you just behave like a normal human being for once?' she shouted.

'What about you then?' said Minna.

Hannah leaned forward and smacked her on the side of the face.

'Stop fighting,' whimpered Malka. 'You two are always fighting.'

Minna rubbed her face and Malka started to cry. 'I don't want to go to Hungary either,' she said. 'I want to go home.'

Hannah shook her head helplessly. At last Minna stood up and they walked on. Minna kept up a hurt and reproachful silence, and Malka, too, didn't say a word.

The path led through dense undergrowth to the edge of the forest. In front of them was a flat terrace of fields, with people working in some of them. Mrs Kowalski's comments about people giving them away had made Hannah realize that they should hide from strangers and only ask for help under cover of darkness. 'Come on, let's have a rest here for a while,' she said to her daughters. She didn't want to admit how helpless and lost she felt.

She had felt like this once before, when, as a child, she had been with relatives in the country one summer and had lost her way. She had wandered around for hours before someone had found her and brought her back to her relations.

'I'm hungry,' said Malka. Hannah broke off a piece of bread for each of them and unwrapped the bacon. Malka took a bite straight away, but Minna refused to eat and certainly wasn't going to touch bacon. Even Hannah felt a strong resistance to eating it. She had long ago distanced herself from the religious practices of her parents' house, she hadn't brought up her children to be religious, and she hadn't kept a kosher kitchen, but it still didn't come easily to her to eat bacon. She only did it because it was clear to her that from now on she had to eat whatever she got, whenever she got it. It was high time that Minna realized that too, but at the moment Hannah felt just too exhausted to start another argument.

Minna took the blanket that Mrs Kowalski had given them, went a little way into the trees, lay down on the blanket and pulled a corner of it over her head. She fell asleep, or at least pretended to be asleep. Malka ran around, collected stones, bits of wood and grass, and made a house and garden, into which she put a doll with striped socks, green pants and a white vest. 'Where did you get that doll from?' asked Hannah in surprise.

Malka coloured. 'It's Liesel,' she said. 'Veronika lent her to me.'

Hannah could see perfectly well that her little daughter wasn't telling the truth – her voice was too high, almost shrill – but she didn't have the energy to worry about a doll. Never mind where the thing came from, it was good that the little girl had something to play with.

Hannah looked out across the fields, behind which the mountains rose up again. In one of the meadows a farmer was working with a scythe – a very big, broad-shouldered man with a peaked cap on his head. He looked familiar. She shaded her eyes with her hand to get a better look, and then stood up. 'No, not you,' she said sharply to Malka, who had jumped up and wanted to come with her. 'You stay here with Minna. I'll be back in a little while.'

She moved closer to the farmer, walking in a wide curve. She really did know him – she had looked after his father when he had been kicked by a horse. A broken tibia and fibula which hadn't healed particularly well, and the old man had limped ever since. She got closer to the man and called out softly, 'Wlado!'

He knew her at once and was clearly pleased to see her. Without hesitating for too long she told him that she and her children were trying to escape across the Hungarian border. He nodded and asked no questions. Presumably he knew about the Germans and their operation.

I can't take you all the way to the border, doctor – I've got to be back for the milking,' he said, 'but I'm sure we'll make it as far as the forester's house. The forester and his wife are good people – they'll help you get further.'

Malka looked at the man called Wlado. He was big and broad, with a suntanned face which made his eyes look very light, almost colourless. She looked further down, to his chest, to the naked triangle at the top of his open shirt. He had dark, curly hair on his naked skin too, but the skin was brown and the hairs didn't look as horrible. He smiled at her, and she turned her face away quickly, as if she had been doing something that wasn't quite proper.

Wlado hid his scythe in a bush that had red berries, which Malka knew were poisonous, and then he led them on a roundabout way through the forest, so that the people working in the fields wouldn't see them. When he noticed that Malka was finding it hard going, he offered to carry her on his shoulders. He folded his arms and bent down so that she could climb on. Her mother nodded her agreement.

At first Malka found it unpleasant, riding on the shoulders of this stranger, and she held tight to his head and let her bare legs dangle over his chest. But then he started to sing softly, in a fine deep voice which sounded strange, unfamiliarly masculine, and her mother hummed along with the tune. Only Minna walked along a few paces behind them, still angry and glowering. Malka felt as if she was sitting on the top of some great tower looking down on the world. The sky was nearer to her than the earth, and she followed the flight of a crow when it rose up, cawing noisily, from one tree and disappeared again behind another one further away. The man's steps rocked her from this side to that, from that side to this, bumpy and gentle at the same time. She picked a yellow and green jagged maple leaf from a branch and put it on his head.

When they were going along a track that was too narrow for Malka to avoid the branches and twigs sticking out from the trees, she had to get down, but he held her hand and sang, and she hummed the tune with him and hardly noticed any more how much her feet were hurting and how deeply the red laces of her sandals had cut into her legs. Then, after a rather steep climb, the path broadened out again and he took her back on to his shoulders. From her vantage point she looked down at her mother and sister. By now both of them were walking slowly and painfully, with their heads lowered – dragging themselves on with great effort. Malka bent over, took the maple leaf off Wlado's head, planted a kiss on his hair and then put the leaf back.

When a fairly large wooden house came into sight in the distance, Wlado stopped and lifted Malka down from his shoulders.

'Well,' he said, 'now I've got to go back.' He saw the tears come into Malka's eyes, and he quickly went on talking: 'The cows have to be milked, otherwise they'll get ill. You can ask your mother, she'll explain it. Cows that aren't milked can get infected udders, and then next winter we wouldn't have any milk or butter and we'd be very hungry.'

Hannah took Malka's hand. 'Let him go,' she said. 'He really does have to go home.'

They watched as Wlado left. He turned around once more and waved, and Malka was suddenly so sad that she couldn't stop herself crying. 'I want to go home too. I don't want to go to Hungary, Please, Mama, let's go home.'

'It's impossible,' said her mother. 'We can't go home any more.'

'Never?' asked Malka, very shaken.

Her mother shook her head. 'No, never.'

37

'And my room and my bed and my raincoat and my dressing-up clothes and my schoolbooks?'

Her mother shrugged. 'Gone, finished.'

'And Chaya and Veronika and Miss Lemberger and Yankel and all the others?'

'They stayed and we left.'

Malka was quiet. Without a word she walked along by her mother and sister until they reached the forester's house.

She didn't say a word for the whole evening. She hardly looked at the forester's wife when she gave her a bowl of soup and cut a slice of bread for her. She ate listlessly, and then only because her mother made her eat. Later on, when they were bedded down in the cattle-shed, in the hay, she turned her back on her mother and Minna, buried herself deeply into the hay and pressed Liesel against her face.

She felt betrayed. Her mother had lied to her. This wasn't just a trip to Hungary. What it actually was, however, she could not understand at all. And why Hungary? She didn't know anybody in Hungary. A woman and her daughter had stayed with them once, for quite a while, waiting for someone to take them across the border. The woman had been Hungarian and she and her daughter had only spoken Hungarian. Malka hadn't understood a word. How could she live in Hungary when she didn't know the language and didn't have any friends to play with and didn't have her own room and her own bed? What did Hungary look like, anyway?

In the middle of the night – it was still pitch-dark – the guide arrived who was to take Hannah Mai and her daughters through the forest and across the border into the Hungarian-occupied part of the Ukraine between Poland and Hungary. The forester, who clearly couldn't get rid of these unbidden Jewish guests quickly enough, had arranged for him to come. He was a man in his fifties, small and wiry, with a sallow face and crafty, yellowish eyes. Probably a heavy drinker with cirrhosis of the liver, thought Hannah. He looked almost comically like one would imagine a smuggler to be, sly and cunning, and he demanded money. Hannah was reluctant to part with the little she had, and offered him instead the gold wristwatch that her husband had given her on their wedding day. He examined it carefully, then put it in his pocket and nodded sullenly.

Clouds had gathered during the night, and the moon couldn't be seen – just a slightly lighter patch in the sky. It was so dark that Hannah could barely keep sight of the guide, even though he was only a short distance in front, and Minna, who had draped Mrs Kowalski's blanket over her shoulder, looked strange and almost sinister from behind.

Hannah had thought that the darkness would be an advantage, but she soon realized how hard it was to walk when she couldn't see where she was going. In her light shoes she slipped, stumbled, stubbed her toes against stones and scraped her leg against a low branch that she hadn't noticed. She was dragging Malka along behind her, half-asleep and clearly not feeling any better. The little girl kept complaining loudly until the guide stopped and snapped at her to shut her trap if they didn't want to get caught by the border guards or the Hungarian police. After that Malka didn't make another sound, and in the grey pullover that she had pulled on over her dress and jacket she looked even more lost than ever.

Apart from their footsteps, the rustle of the under-growth and the snapping of twigs as they stepped on them, there was hardly a thing to be heard – just the wind in the tops of the trees, and now and then the sound of some nightbird. Hannah got goose pimples when she heard those eerie cries, but maybe it was the cold as well, because her jacket wasn't warm enough for a night in the mountains. She thought ruefully of her warm coat, hanging in the wardrobe at home. And more than any-thing else she thought of the shoes and woollen stockings. Her feet were so cold that she could barely feel her toes.

In the forest the darkness disappeared much more slowly than in the open fields, and it was a long while before Hannah noticed that it was getting close to morning. Now she could distinguish the tree trunks, dark bushes and grey rocks. When they turned off to the left down a track, she could see the pale grey of dawn in front of her at the edge of the forest. Then at last they had the trees behind them and in front of them was a valley. In the grey light of dawn the woods shimmered like dark lakes between the lighter-coloured fields. Hannah couldn't see any villages, nor any individual houses – not even a hut. It looked as if there wasn't a living soul for miles around.

'We are in Hungary,' said the man. He raised his hand and pointed down into the valley. 'The border controls are still very tight here and it is very dangerous for you. Things won't get better until you are out of Hungarian-occupied territory and actually in Hungary itself, but even there you'll have to watch out. The Hungarian police amuse themselves by sending Polish Jews back to Poland, so I've heard. But if you carry on downwards, and then go westwards up the next valley, then turn south again when you get to the top, you should be able to make it.'

Hannah tried to memorize his exact words. After all they had gone through so far, she now felt something almost like confidence. At least they were no longer in Poland, which meant that they had escaped from the immediate clutches of the Germans. 'You were going to take us to a village,' she said.

'There's a village down there, just behind that little wood. Keep to the left and follow the stream.'

Hannah thought for a moment. At the start of their flight she had been able to turn to people that she knew, former patients or their relatives, but not any more, and here she no longer knew whom she could trust. 'Are there any Jews in the village?' she asked.

The man gave a derisive snort and spat on the ground. 'There are Jews everywhere.' He looked straight at Hannah, who met his gaze. After a while he said reluctantly, 'I do know one Jew down there – Shimon Bardosz. He's a cigarette smuggler. He lives in the last house on the right on the main street. It's sort of hidden behind a hedge, but you can't miss it.'

Hannah wanted to thank him and held her hand out to him, but he ignored the gesture and turned his back on them.

They stood there for quite some time, Hannah and her two daughters, looking down into the valley. It got lighter, though the sky was so overcast that there was no sign of the sun. Three deer trotted out of the wood below them and into the meadow.

'Hungarian deer,' said Malka with a note of awe in her voice. Then she looked at Hannah and asked, 'Do they ever go across the border?'

It was Minna who answered her, in a tone of voice that was still argumentative. 'Yes, but not in secret.'

'If only we were deer . . .' said Malka, but Minna snapped at her. 'Just shut up, will you!' Hannah didn't intervene, afraid of another angry outburst from Minna.

The deer grazed peacefully. Clearly, the wind wasn't blowing in the right direction for the animals to get any scent of them. What a pretty picture, thought Hannah. It's a shame that I never went for a walk in the woods in the early morning.

She would have loved just to stay there. It would have been the perfect place to sit and reflect, to watch the deer and see the daylight slowly filling the whole valley. But there was no time and it was too cold.

'Come on, we have to move,' she said.

It was a two-storey house, wooden and painted green, with yellow edging around the windows and yellow flowers on the window sills. It lay a little way back from the road, protected from prying eyes by a hazel hedge. The hazelnuts were light green, still completely enclosed in their pale husks, and it would be some time before they were ripe. That's a pity, thought Malka, and walked behind her mother and Minna up the four steps to the front door.

Her mother knocked. A portly, no longer particularly young woman with her hair combed severely back half-opened the door – and almost looked as if she wanted to shut it again. 'We'd like to see Shimon Bardosz,' said Hannah quickly. 'Someone told us he lives here.'

The woman glanced around the yard and over the hedge into the road, then opened the door properly and drew the three strangers into the shadowy kitchen. 'My husband isn't here,' she said in halting Polish with a lilting Hungarian accent. 'He's away on business. But please come and sit down.'

While Hannah explained where they had come from and how they had managed to get across the Polish border, the woman boiled water on a Primus stove and made some tea, laid the table and put out bread, butter and fresh, soft, cream cheese. 'It's nice to sit at a really clean table again,' Hannah said.

Malka drank the sweet tea and ate the bread and cream cheese until she was full up, really full up, just like at home.

'And where is your husband?' asked Mrs Bardosz.

Hannah hesitated, but Minna said quickly: 'Our father is in Palestine, in Eretz-Yisrael. He's been there for five years. Maybe we can make it that far and join him.'

Malka looked at her sister in astonishment. Her mother held her cup in both hands and took sips of tea, her eyes down. Mama didn't say anything about going to join Papa, thought Malka, she only talked about Hungary.

Mrs Bardosz sighed. 'Palestine is a long way off, a very long way. May God protect and help you in these difficult times.' She poured out more tea and pushed the sugar bowl towards Malka. Malka took three spoonfuls and might have taken even more if her mother hadn't put her hand on her daughter's arm. Malka hung her head. She knew you ought not to be greedy when you were someone's guest; it wasn't polite.

'Our father comes from Danzig,' Minna went on. 'He can't get a visa to come to Poland very often, and that's why we haven't seen him much. But he wrote to us from Palestine that we should come and join him. He lives on a kibbutz.'

Minna talked and talked about their father's last visit, but Malka couldn't remember him at all. For her, he was just the man in the photos that her mother showed her sometimes and which were all left behind in the house in Lawoczne. She didn't know anything at all about Palestine or the land of Israel, only that it was a country a very long way away, somewhere near where the sun rose, and that her father lived there. So she put her cup on the table, slid down off her chair and looked around curiously.

The kitchen wasn't very light. The window, high up in the wall, which let in the pale light, was very small. Just as in most of the Polish houses on the other side of the border, almost half of the kitchen was taken up by a huge, tiled stove, but now at the end of September it was not lit. Down at the bottom was the fire-damper, and in the middle there were the cooking plates; on top of the stove there were sleeping places for when it was very cold. A bench with coloured cushions ran around two sides of the stove.

Right at the back of the room, in the shadows between the wall and the door, something moved. Malka took a few steps in that direction. It was a cat, black with white patches. Its head was black, its face white up to the eyes, and it had a white, pointed blaze reaching up on to its forehead. Malka sat down next to it on the bench. The cat stood up, stretched, arched its back and cautiously raised a black front paw tipped with white. The paw stayed in the air for a long time, bent back, stretched, then bent over again. The cat's eyes, which were green and wide-open, were fixed on Malka. At last it made a soft noise, lowered its paw, jumped on to her lap, and curled up. Malka stroked the cat's black back and its

44

white front, and felt its body vibrating even before she heard it purring.

The women had stopped talking and looked across at her. In the sudden silence the purring sounded very loud indeed, as if the whole kitchen were full of purring cats. Malka laughed in delight.

'She loves animals,' said her mother. 'She loved animals even when she was tiny. I remember when she had whooping-cough – the only way I could be sure of calming her down was to show her our neighbour's baby rabbit. And when we went to stay with relatives in Skawina I could hardly get her away from the sheep.'

'Be careful,' said Mrs Bardosz. 'The cat's going to have kittens soon. You can feel the little ones if you put your hand on her tummy.'

Malka supported the cat's back with her left hand and pushed her right hand under its belly. She spread her fingers out very carefully. But she couldn't feel anything, just soft fur.

Later on, Mrs Bardosz led them up to a bedroom with four beds in it. 'Lie down and sleep,' she said. 'In a few days, when you've had a proper rest, Yossel, my eldest boy, will take you to a hut up in the mountains and show you the way from there.'

Malka's mother, who had just started to take off her shoes, stopped and asked in a worried tone who lived in the hut.

'Nobody,' said Mrs Bardosz. 'It belongs to a farmer from the village. Sometimes one of the maids used to sleep there when she had taken the cows up to the mountain pastures. But no one has done that for years, because these days the farmer is worried about the cows. You can sleep there for a night and then set off down the mountain. From the hut it isn't far down to the valley. You're not the first refugees from Poland. My husband and Yossel have taken plenty of people up there already. And in the valley, not far from Pilipiec, there's a Jew who lives in an old, disused mill – Chaim Kopolowici, he's called – and he helps refugees. Mind you, he wants money for it.' She clicked her tongue. 'He's one of those who exploits other people's misery. There are lots of them around here, too.'

Minna had already undressed and got into one of the beds. After her sudden burst of talking in the kitchen she had gone very quiet and hadn't said another word, but given the circumstances she looked content enough. Her mother took off her own dress.

Malka was still standing undecidedly by the child's bed that Mrs Bardosz had led her to. She was tired, but it didn't seem right to go to bed in the middle of the day. 'Wait a moment, I'll help you,' said Mrs Bardosz. She pulled Malka's dress over her head, then sat her down on the bed and lifted up her feet. 'That looks pretty nasty,' she said in a shocked voice when she had undone the laces of Malka's sandals, and had run her hands over the bloody weals.

'It hurts, too,' said Malka, and started to cry. She was tired and she wanted to go home, to her own bed. She didn't want to be in Hungary; she wanted to go back to Lawoczne. And she never wanted to climb another mountain ever again. The woman's hands were gentle, but they still hurt her. With her eyes tight shut and her lips pressed together, she let her mother and the woman, who had brought a bowl of warm water from the kitchen, clean up her legs, put some foul-smelling ointment on the wounds and then wrap bits of cloth round them.

'You can't get shoes in Poland any more,' said her mother. Her voice sounded as if she were blaming herself. Serves her right, thought Malka. Why did she ever have to bring us to Hungary?

After a while Mrs Bardosz said, 'I'm afraid I haven't got any more children's shoes.'

Malka's eyes were still shut. She heard Mrs Bardosz go out of the room and close the door softly, and she heard her mother get into bed. The wooden bedstead creaked, the cover rustled. 'Do you want to get into bed with me?' asked her mother.

Malka turned to the wall and didn't answer. She didn't know herself what she wanted; her legs hurt, the soles of her feet were burning. She was angry with everyone, even her mother. She was angry with the whole world – except the cat, who was asleep downstairs on the bench by the stove, waiting to have its kittens.

OCTOBER, 1943

Hannah Mai woke up when it was still dark in the mountain hut. She could hear by their regular breathing that Minna and Malka were still asleep. She lay there for a while staring into the darkness and waiting for sleep to come again, but it wouldn't. She was shivering. Yesterday evening she had let Minna and Malka have the two blankets that she had found in the hut, and the horse-cloth that Mrs Kowalski had given her was too dirty to cover herself with and could only be used as an under-blanket. She propped her head on her arms and looked at Malka, tightly rolled up in the blanket on the camp-bed next to her.

Hannah had no idea what time it was, and since she had given her watch to the smuggler she had to go by the position of the sun and her own instincts, but she was wide awake. And no wonder, since she had slept through the entire afternoon before Yossel Bardosz had led them up here. She got up and went outside the hut.

The sky was a grey dome over her head. The moon had gone and only a few isolated stars were left. To the south-east a range of mountains was visible on the horizon. The mountain tops were a soft, dark outline against a strip of lighter sky. Hannah sat down on the wooden bench in front of the hut and put her hands in her lap. It was still chilly up here, and her feet were wet with dew. She stretched her legs so that only her heels were touching the grass and wriggled her toes. The air did her sore feet good, in spite of the cold and wetness. Gratefully, she pulled more tightly round herself the woollen cardigan that Mrs Bardosz had given her yesterday evening, together with a worn pair of low shoes which were a bit too big and had to be padded with cotton wool, but which were at least better than her summer shoes with the heels.

There hadn't been any shoes for Malka, but they had wrapped cloths around her feet and instead of soles they had sewn on strips of oilcloth using big stitches.

'They won't last very long,' Mrs Bardosz had said. 'A couple of days at most, no more than that. I've tried it.'

Hannah massaged first one leg and then the other. Her calf and thigh muscles hurt – perfectly normal after such a long march – but she still felt curiously relaxed. The children were asleep, and for the first time since they had begun their escape she was sitting quite calmly without having to think out what their next step should be. The next move was clear. They would have to go down into the valley in which the mist was just rising, grey and thick, like a mirror image of the sky, only lighter.

If she listened very carefully she could make out the rushing sound of the river down in the valley; maybe there was a waterfall. Go across the meadow down to the river, Yossel Bardosz had told her yesterday in his funny-sounding Polish, and then follow the river into the valley in the direction of Pilipiec. In between there were only a few isolated farms and a couple of tiny hamlets. And just before you got to Pilipiec, when the valley had already broadened out and you could see the houses in the distance, that was where the mill was. You couldn't miss it.

But even there we won't be safe, thought Hannah. We've got to find a group we can join, that's what Mrs Bardosz said, because we won't get far on our own. The Hungarian police round up Polish Jews every day and send them back across the border. Not until Budapest, when they got to the city, would they be able to disappear into the crowd. You could only live without papers in a big city. But Hannah didn't want to think about that for the moment, not yet. The problems were down in the valley below her, and they weren't going to disappear.

The first birds were moving in the nearby trees – you could hear them whistling, twittering; strange little sounds in a huge world. At home the birds had often woken her up at dawn with their noise, but here they sounded lost.

I hope Minna comes through, she thought. The girl is so temperamental. Of course she's right when she says I'm making all the decisions, but who else should make them? Minna, maybe? Yesterday was the first time Minna had said what was going on in her head. She wants to go to Palestine, to the land of Israel. Maybe she'll make it – she's stubborn enough – she get's that from me. She's just not so ambitious. Maybe Eretz-Yisrael would be a possibility for Minna? Some time she would have to think hard about her elder daughter's future, but not now.

What mattered now was getting to Budapest. Minna was strong, she didn't need to worry about her, but Malka was another matter. She was only seven, even if she was big for her age. At home she had been the pampered little girl, the pretty one that everybody had to – and indeed wanted to – make allowances for; the little princess. Suddenly, she had become a real person, almost grown-up.

Why didn't the girls ask me anything the whole time? thought Hannah. Why hadn't they put into words their fears about the future? Or maybe they weren't afraid? I'm afraid. I'm very, very afraid. But I don't want to think about being afraid, because my fear would bring me down if I gave it a chance. Where were they going to live? How? What on? Hannah pushed these thoughts aside. Things would go on somehow once they were in Budapest. Maybe there would be a chance to emigrate to America – she'd prefer that to Palestine. But if there was no other possibility she'd even go there, just to survive.

Hannah wasn't particularly concerned about her husband, and their marriage had ceased to exist a long time ago. Actually, it had never really been a proper marriage, like her parents', or her sister's with her brother-in-law. Hannah thought of the man who was, after all, the father of her daughters, as if he were a stranger. To be really honest, she no longer knew why she had married him. Of course she had found him attractive, but she had found lots of men attractive. She had wanted children – she had hoped that children would help her to make her peace with her strict father. If there were other reasons then she had forgotten them. Her memories of other men, of other love affairs, were much stronger. Curious.

She wondered whether she would be able to work as a doctor in Budapest, maybe in a Jewish hospital or in a nursing home. But even if that didn't work out she was prepared to tackle anything else to earn enough to keep her daughters and herself. We're not the first Jews who've had to leave their home, she thought. And we're not the first Jews who've had to escape from Poland, either. Mrs Bardosz was right.

The sky was getting lighter, all the stars had faded. The mist was rising in thin strands out of the valley and drifting up the slopes. In the east there was a reddish band in the sky, the sun rose and the mountain tops stood out clear and dark against the light. The sun wasn't a ball of fire, as Hannah had expected, nor was it a glowing red disc, but more like a red patch of mist with a bright centre as it came up slowly behind the mountains. The red turned to violet, then to grey, and finally to a greenish blue. Perhaps it would be a fine day, even though she could see the clouds piling up in the west, grey and threatening.

Hannah didn't know how to gauge what the weather would be like here on the southern side of the Carpathians. Back in Poland she had been able to predict it pretty well, and it had often been important to look at the sky before setting off to see a patient, even if only to know what clothes to take with her.

She decided to wake the children. They would have to be on their way. The descent would be hard for Malka – her legs were swollen and the weals had become inflamed. But they couldn't stay here, however pleasant it might be. Perhaps she would be able to find a doctor in Pilipiec who would be prepared to let her have some iodine and a sterile bandage. When she stood up she noticed that in the corner, between the bench and the house, where a little clump of pinks was growing in the stony ground, there was a hedgehog, all rolled up. She would show that to Malka to cheer her up and give her some strength for the journey down to the valley.

When Hannah went inside the hut, Minna was lying on her bed with her eyes open, and smiled at her. Malka was still asleep with her cheek against the rag doll she called Liesel.

Hannah sat down on Minna's bed and took her hand. 'You've got to help me,' she said softly. 'I don't know how we are going to do it if you don't help me.'

The smile disappeared from Minna's face. She took her hand away and said, 'So all of a sudden I'm not a child any more, is that it?'

Hannah nodded and stood up. 'That's right,' she said. 'All of a sudden you're not a child any more.' She turned round and woke Malka.

Malka didn't know if she was awake or asleep when her mother touched her shoulder, because she was dreaming about her mother waking her up at home in Lawoczne. She sat up. In front of her she saw not her own window with the flowered curtains, but dark wooden walls with scraps of cobweb hanging from them. She thought she was still dreaming and rubbed her eyes, but that was her mother's face there in front of her – the new face with the two lines from her nostrils down to her mouth – and then it all came back to her. They were in Hungary. Yossel Bardosz had brought them up to this mountain hut yesterday from the house behind the hazel hedge.

'Will we get there today?' she asked her mother as she pushed away the coarse blanket and put her bandaged feet on to the ground. 'Mama, will we get there today?'

'Where do you want to get to?' asked her mother, giving her a piece of bread.

'I don't know,' said Malka. 'Somewhere.'

Going down through the dew-soaked grass was steep

and slippery. Malka did it practically on her knees, because the oilcloth soles kept making her slip. Although she didn't have the sandals with the laces on any more and her feet and legs were well bandaged, they still hurt more than yesterday, and the cloth soon got wet.

She wanted to cry, wanted to go back to being the child she had been before their escape, but deep down she knew that those days had gone. Something new had started – something that had to do with war, with the Germans, with the yellow star, and with words like 'army' and 'border guards' and 'resettlement' and 'operation', words she had only vaguely been aware of when she had still been at home. How long ago was that now? She felt for Liesel, who was in her jacket pocket, and slipped down again towards the broad band of bushes at the edge of the path. Don't think about how much it hurts. And don't think about home.

At last they got to the river, which up here in the mountains just looked like a broad stream with a fast current. There were big stones in the river that the water broke against, and on the slopes leading down away from the path there was high, thick grass growing, and sometimes a shrub, or a willow. The narrow path followed the river-bank. It was stony, it twisted when the river did, and in lots of places it was steep and impenetrable, but at least Malka found it easier to walk here than she had coming down through the fields. And the rushing noise of the river filled her head and made it easier not to think of home or of last week or of last month or of last year.

She tried to hear songs in the regular splash and rushing of the water – tunes that Olga used to sing to her. Songs whose rhythm would make it easier to walk along. But the sound of the river couldn't drown out the pain in her legs.

Around midday, when the valley had become a lot broader, they looked for a good place to stop and rest. They sat on flat stones by the river, protected by the riverside bushes from being seen from the path, and ate the last of their bread. They drank some water from a little stream, which was as clear as glass. It flowed into the river a bit further down, and it was so narrow that even Malka could have got across it with a big step. Minna and Malka would have liked to sit for longer, but their mother kept looking anxiously at the sky and made them move on.

The path by the river had merged with two other paths and was now an unmade road. When a cart came towards them they hid in the bushes until it had rattled past. After that they walked on for a while along the side of the slope beside the road, but it was such hard going that they made very slow progress, and Malka was crying because the pain in her legs was getting unbearable. Anyway, there was no one to be seen on the road, so they climbed down again. Minna took Malka's hand. Once they met an old woman leading a goat on a piece of string. The woman looked at them only for a moment and without any interest, and didn't even respond to their nods of greeting.

The sun had long since disappeared behind the clouds; the wind came up – a cold west wind which got sharper and sharper. Malka could hardly stay on her feet any more. Every time they saw a house, or a few huts clustered together, Malka looked at them longingly and hoped that someone would open the door and invite them in. But she never dared to say anything, because the faces of her mother and sister were now as gloomy and dark as the sky.

Here on their side of the river the valley was so broad that they were scarcely aware of the mountains any more, and the summits on the far side were hidden by heavy cloud. In the distance they could just see the outlines of houses and pick out church steeples. That must be Pilipiec.

'So where is the mill?' asked Minna. She had already asked a couple of times.

'Stop complaining,' said her mother. 'The mill won't be far.'

But then, with the mill still nowhere in sight, there was a flash of lightning. 'Quick,' said their mother. 'Hurry up. There's a bridge over there. We can shelter under it.'

They didn't make it. Before they reached the bridge a violent storm began with a cloudburst and torrential rain. Soaking wet, they huddled together under the stone arches. The thunder rolled and Malka could see the lightning through her eyelids even though she had shut her eyes tightly. She felt dizzy – her head hurt, her eyes hurt, and with every thunderclap she felt as if someone was bringing a hammer down on to her skull. And then suddenly she didn't care any more; she let herself fall backwards on to the ground. She sank down into a deep hole, sank as if into black cotton wool, and suddenly she felt completely light. She came to briefly when her mother put her hand on her forehead and held her wrist with the other hand, but she couldn't open her eyes.

'She's feverish,' she heard her mother say. 'She's running a high temperature. Minna, you stay here with her and I'll go for help.'

'But the storm . . .' objected Minna. 'The rain . . .'

What storm? thought Malka. What rain?

'I'm soaked anyway,' said her mother. 'Hold her close to you to keep her warm, if you possibly can.'

Malka felt her sister put her arm round her and pull her on to her lap, and then she sank back into the pleasant, black cotton wool.

Hannah Mai ran through the rain towards the town. She ran as if she wanted to kill her fear by trampling it underfoot. The little girl was ill – and no wonder, with dirt everywhere, and all the exertion. It had all been too much for a child, with the heat during the day and the cold at night. Maybe she should have left her with Mrs Kowalski, after all. She remembered Cella, the daughter of a Polish farmer; she had died of pneumonia when she was about the same age as Malka. She thought about the children who had died in the flu epidemic last year, children and old people; the former hadn't built up any reserves of strength yet and the latter had used all theirs up. Oh God, she thought, if you exist, you mustn't let my child die, not Malka, please, not my lovely Malka. She was crying although she wasn't aware of it, thinking it was rain on her face. The world was blurring before her eyes.

And then suddenly there was the mill in front of her. The first thing she saw was the huge, motionless mill-wheel.

Chaim Kopolowici was an Orthodox Jew with a long beard and earlocks and a black yarmulke on his grey hair. His gaberdine was worn and had a greenish sheen in places. He seemed to grasp the situation at once, because he took Hannah into the kitchen before she could even say a word. Two little boys clung to their

57

mother when their father came in with this unknown woman, and a girl of about Malka's age was chopping up vegetables – carrots, leeks and celery. Mrs Kopolowici was a good-looking woman with light skin and blue eyes. Her shapeless dress still allowed hints of a curvaceous body. She had a blue knitted cap on her blonde hair. Somewhat reluctantly she offered the stranger tea and something to eat, but Hannah didn't want to eat or drink anything. She just begged Kopolowici and his wife to help her get her sick daughter here, a child whose life was in danger if she couldn't be put to bed as soon as possible.

'Sick,' said Mrs Kopolowici in an accusatory tone, and opened her beautiful eyes wider. 'Sick, did you say? What if she's got something contagious?'

'I'm a doctor,' said Hannah. 'I was a regional medical officer in Poland. I can judge whether my daughter has a contagious disease or not. She's exhausted and she has open wounds on her legs and an infection, that's all. But if she stays where she is for much longer, she might catch pneumonia. Please help me – you have children of your own.'

Mrs Kopolowici hesitated, looked at her children and then nodded.

Chaim Kopolowici took a heavy overcoat from a hook in the hallway and put on a round, black hat. Off they went, fighting the wind and rain, until they reached the bridge. Minna was still sitting under the stone arch with Malka in her arms. 'She isn't moving,' she said. 'Mama, what's the matter with her?'

'Has she had any spasms?' asked Hannah.

Minna shook her head. 'She hasn't moved the whole time you were away.'

The storm had abated by now, but it was still raining.

Kopolowici took Malka in his arms and set off. Hannah followed him, dazed, unable to think clearly as she saw how her daughter's arm hung limply down and swayed from side to side with every step the man took. This sight shook her back to reality. She caught up with Kopolowici in a few steps and took hold of her daughter's hand. It was hot and didn't return her pressure.

'She will get better, won't she?' asked Minna beside her in a very small voice.

Hannah turned her head and faced her. 'Of course she'll get better,' she said loudly. 'She's caught a cold and there's that business with her legs. Those damned sandals. She'd have been better going barefoot from the start.' When she saw that her elder daughter was listening but with her head turned away, obviously fighting back the tears, she carried on speaking quickly, rushing the words to drown out her own fears: 'It was silly running away in summer clothes. But it was so hot and we didn't know we'd have to go across the mountains. The mountains are terrible – the sweat pours off you during the day so you think you're going to melt, then at night you nearly freeze.'

Minna didn't answer, and Hannah couldn't think of anything else to say. Luckily, there was the mill, just in front of them.

Mrs Kopolowici had made up a bed in an attic room that looked more like a cupboard and was reached by some open wooden stairs, but the bed had a clean sheet and a clean blanket. Hannah took Malka's dress off, eased the bandages from her feet and put her into bed. Malka came to herself and started to cry. Her skin was red, her eyes small in her swollen face. On Hannah's instructions Minna fetched water and cloths, and made compresses for Malka's calves. The child cried loudly as the cool water touched her hot skin. The weals on her legs did not look good – they were thick and inflamed – but luckily there was no sign of them turning septic. Hannah stroked her daughter until she stopped crying and went to sleep.

Only when she was breathing quietly did Hannah tell Minna to change the compresses in about half an hour. Then she kissed Malka and went downstairs. 'Is there a doctor in the town?' she asked Mrs Kopolowici, who was standing over the stove in the kitchen, stirring a pot. It smelled of chicken soup. Hannah's heart went out to her and for a moment she felt as if she were at home, like a child who has come in hungry after school.

'Didn't you say you *were* a doctor?' answered the woman suspiciously. Hannah explained that she had to get hold of iodine and dressings, that she had nothing with her and needed ointment for Malka, as well as something to bring the fever down.

The woman seemed satisfied with this, and told her how to get to the street and the house where the doctor lived, and Hannah set off.

Malka dreamed about Russians and Germans. She saw the backs of the Russians as they left Lawoczne to march towards the east while the Germans marched in from the west. But she couldn't see their faces, just their boots as they marched along in step, always up and down, and in her head thundered the rhythmic crack of their steel-tipped heels on the cobblestones. It got louder and louder, much louder than the storm, and Malka felt her mother pulling her away from the street and dragging her up a mountain. Then suddenly Liesel was walking along next to her, as big as she was herself, and she started to complain about being dragged to Hungary – especially as she was only wearing green pants and a white vest. 'Would you like to be seen on the street dressed like that?' she shouted at Malka. But the operation . . . there was a German operation going on – there wasn't any time. 'Who cares about the operation?' said Liesel. 'It doesn't make any difference to me. They can't do anything to me – I'm a German.' And then she started to scream at her, 'Jew-girl, Jew-girl,' just like Tanja and the other girls in Lawoczne had done, and she pointed a long, sharp finger at Malka, and then bent down, picked up a stone and threw it at her. The stone hit Malka on the head and she started to cry.

'Don't cry, Malka, it'll all be fine,' said Minna in a new and very gentle voice. She lay down next to her on the bed and pulled her closer. Malka pressed herself against her sister and slowly calmed down. 'When we get to Palestine, to the land of Israel,' said Minna, 'then everything will be all right. You'll see for yourself how beautiful it is there. We'll have to go by train first and then on a ship. The sun always shines in Eretz-Yisrael, or most of the time anyway, and oranges grow on the trees just like apples do here. Just think, Malka, if you want an orange you just go to the nearest tree and pick one. Or a lemon.'

'I don't like lemons,' said Malka. 'They're too sour. But oranges would be nice.'

Minna stroked her hair and her arms. 'Bananas grow in Eretz-Yisrael as well, lovely yellow bananas. Do you remember Papa bringing us bananas when he last visited us?'

Malka shook her head and snuggled closer to her sister. 'No, but go on telling me.'

'Papa lives on a kibbutz by a big lake called Kineret, the one the Christians call Genessaret. It's only friends who live together on a kibbutz, and they even call themselves that. You don't say Mr or Mrs Whatsisname, you say *haver* – that means friend – or if it's a woman you say *havera*.' Minna's voice in Malka's ear was like the gentle splashing of the stream in Lawoczne. She told her about communal work, about everyone eating together, about them all singing together.

'How do you know all this?' asked Malka.

'I used to go and talk to Zionists,' said Minna, 'three years ago, after we got that letter from Papa. Zionists are the people who want to found a state in the land of Israel for all the Jews so that they can get away from operations and resettlements and all that.'

'Does Mama know that you talked to these people?'

'No,' said Minna. 'You needn't tell her about it.' She stroked her sister again. 'Mind you, it doesn't matter much even if you do tell her. And now go to sleep, Malka. Sleep and get better.'

'I can only go to sleep if you go on telling me about it,' said Malka, and she let Minna take her on a trip through that strange country where oranges grew on trees, to show her the mountains of Galilee, and the wonderful Lake Kineret which had fish in it that tasted at least as good as the trout they had sometimes had at home, or like the fantastic carp that Aunt Feyge cooked for them when they visited her in Skawina. In the land of Israel there was a desert with mountains round it and camels going across it, and a huge lake called the Dead Sea. In the Dead Sea you didn't even have to swim – the water just carried you and you could just lie in it and read a book. 'Someone told me that the water is really warm and looks different from the water here, not clear and transparent, but more like mother-of-pearl.'

'How did he know that?' asked Malka.

'He'd heard about it from someone who'd been there.'

Malka's eyes closed. Minna's voice splashed on like the stream and carried her off into a country much further away from Lawoczne than even Hungary.

Hanna brought back a bottle of iodine, two sterile bandages and a little tube of quinine tablets when she returned to the mill. The Hungarian doctor had only given her these after she had shown him her certificate of medical registration, and even then he was reluctant and less than happy about it.

While Minna talked to the weeping Malka to calm her down, Hannah cleaned the wounds with iodine and bandaged them up properly. Then she dissolved a quinine tablet in some water and gave it to Malka. The fact that she swallowed the bitter-tasting drink without a murmur was a sign of how ill she was, even if the warmth and a couple of hours' rest had already done some good. Although she still had a high fever she was no longer so limp, and above all she was conscious. Now she fell back against the pillow and felt for Minna's hand. Minna took her hand and stroked it. Hannah was surprised, but said nothing. She just asked Minna if she would look after Malka so that she could go and talk to Kopolowici. Minna nodded, lay down beside Malka and put her arm round her.

Hannah found Kopolowici in the kitchen, sitting at the table drinking some tea. She asked him what chance she had of getting to Budapest. He looked at her first, then at his wife, and then finally he banged his cup down on to the table so hard that the china rattled. He took Hannah out of the kitchen to an out-building near the house. Amongst all the garden tools and piles of wood there was, in the middle of the shed, a chopping-block. With a wave of his hand he gestured to her to sit there, while he leaned against a sawing-trestle. She felt uncomfortable under his questioning look.

'Have you got any money?' he asked suddenly. 'Gold? Jewellery?'

She shook her head. 'Not much.'

He raised his eyebrows, pushed an earlock back behind one ear and looked as if he was going to get up, so she went on quickly and lied: 'But I've got cash in Budapest – I've got rich relatives there. I just have to get to Budapest and then I can pay you what you want.'

He shook his head. 'Budapest is a long way away, my dear lady. What use to me is your money in Budapest?' When she raised her hands imploringly he lowered his head again and said, 'I know where there is a group of Jews from Lawoczne waiting to be fetched. They want to get to Budapest. They prepared their escape well. Someone brought them here and someone is going to take them on to Mukačevo and there someone else will pick them up. You come from Lawoczne, don't you? Perhaps you can join those people. I'll speak to them.'

'Who are these people?' asked Hannah. 'What are their names?'

He shook his head. 'I don't know, and I don't want to know. Names don't interest me. In times like these it's better to ask as little as possible. Their leader seems to be a respectable man, educated, religious and with plenty of money, that's all I know. There are seven of them, four men and three women.'

Hannah pressed him to say where they were, so she could go and see them herself, but he refused. 'I'll speak to them first.'

They had already had an evening meal. Mrs Kopolowici had given them a small bowl of chicken soup and some bread to take up to the room, and Hannah had fed Malka, but the little girl hadn't eaten much and had gone to sleep again straight away. Minna lay on the bed next to her sister and Hannah was sitting by the window looking out when there was a sudden noise on the steps and Kopolowici knocked at the door. 'Come with me,' he told Hannah, 'right now.'

She looked questioningly at Minna. Minna nodded.

Hannah followed the man down the steps. He was carrying a lit storm-lantern – it was already dark outside – and led her through the yard, past the shed and up a slope. There, hidden behind some trees, was a small barn, built against the mountainside.

He unlocked the door. At the front of the barn was a stall with two cows standing in it. In the space behind them, bales of straw were piled up on the left-hand side, and there was a store of hay on the right. The smell was penetrating.

Kopolowici went to the wall at the back of the barn, bent down and lifted up two or three sacks, which could only have been filled with hay because they seemed to be so light, and exposed a door. He gave Hannah the lantern and took another key from his pocket.

'Why so much secrecy?' asked Hannah.

He looked at her. 'The Hungarian police make bets

with each other about who can catch the most Polish Jews and send them back to Poland.' He sniggered. ' "How many did you bag today? Twelve? I only got nine, but you wait, I'll beat you tomorrow . . ." Do you understand? It's dangerous for Polish Jews in Hungary, and it's dangerous for anyone who helps them. Do you think there are no anti-Semites in Hungary? We've got them too, more than enough, may their names be wiped out for ever.' He spat over his left shoulder. 'May the Lord punish all the enemies of Israel. The worst are the fascists, the Arrow Cross Party – you have to watch out for them.'

He opened the door, which was so low that they had to bend down, and led Hannah through it into a window-less cave cut into the mountainside, with only an oil lamp to give a little light. 'This is her,' he said loudly and raised his storm-lantern up in front of Hannah's face. The light dazzled her and she blinked.

'Doctor Mai,' said a woman's voice. 'Well, well, the great lady doctor, all of a sudden pretty small, eh?'

Hannah knew the woman right away by her voice and by her tone. It was Rachel Waiss, a rich Jewish woman from Lawoczne, with whom she'd had a few clashes in the past. A self-righteous, unpleasant person who behaved in a superior manner to all other woman, especially those that she reckoned to be less pious than herself. Her husband was a rich merchant and there was talk in the town that he'd got all his money selling contraband goods. Hannah would have liked to turn around and leave, but that was a luxury she couldn't afford – she needed the help of these people.

Kopolowici put down the lantern and Hannah's eyes adapted to the gloomy light, so that she could recognize the people. They were sitting on benches around the walls of the cave, and clearly they used them as beds as well.

It was Shmuel Waiss and his wife Rachel, Ephraim Kohen, a coal merchant and his wife, then another married couple, the Frischmans, who owned a small clothing factory where many of the women in Lawoczne worked. Mrs Kohen and Mrs Frischman were sisters. Hannah didn't know the last person, a young man in his twenties, and he was introduced to her as Reuben, just Reuben – no second name.

'And what were you thinking of, coming here with no money?' asked Shmuel Waiss, and his wife laughed sarcastically.

She's always had everything, thought Hannah, she's never had to work for anything. Her only misfortune is that she never had any children. But she's got a husband to look after her, and the two other women have got husbands too. It's only me that's alone and responsible for everything... She managed to suppress the hatred she felt welling up in her, and told them quickly about how she had had to flee from the Germans and their operation, and how she had crossed the Carpathians with her two daughters.

'Not bad going for a woman on her own,' said Mendel Frischman approvingly.

That bolstered Hannah's courage. 'Please take us with you to Budapest. I'll work and pay back anything I owe you. My daughter Minna can work, too – it's only Malka who can't.' And then she told them quickly about Malka's illness, giving an exaggerately optimistic version of events, saying that she was a tough child and had behaved well on the long march over the mountains. 'You should try it yourselves one day.'

But Mrs Waiss interrupted. 'Malka is a child and she's ill into the bargain. How can we take her with us? She'd hold us up, she'd make a fuss, she'd give us away. Children are dangerous.'

Her husband put his hand on her arm. 'Be quiet, Rachel, dear. Let's think about this. It would be a big advantage to have a doctor in the group, and you have to think things over before you decide.' He gestured to Ephraim Kohen and Mendel Frischman to join him, and the three men went into a corner and had a whispered discussion. Then they came back. 'The little girl could stay here with Kopolowici,' said Mendel Frischman. 'He's got children of his own. And when she's better we can have her fetched. We can pay him to look after her and bring her to join us by train when she gets better.'

Hannah shook her head. 'I'm not going without my child,' she said loudly.

'Don't get all worked up straight away,' said Shmuel Waiss. 'Lots of people leave their children behind, near the border. Nobody notices children, and once the parents have found somewhere to stay, they can fetch them. You have to think about yourself and your other daughter.'

Hannah felt numb as Chaim Kopolowici led her back out of the cave, locked the door and put the sacks in front of it again. A cow was mooing, a loud, dull sound. Still unable to think, Hannah followed the man down the slope, across the yard and into the house.

'Sleep on it,' said Kopolowici when she climbed the steps up to the little attic room. 'Good night.'

Malka and Minna were already asleep. Hannah sat down under the window and put her head on her knee. The suggestion was a tempting one. She could get to

Mukačevo with Minna – it would be much easier than taking Malka, especially with her inflamed legs – and everything would be less dangerous. She and Minna would escape and Kopolowici would bring the little girl afterwards. Malka would be spared the efforts of another march. Lots of people leave the children behind near the border, Waiss had said. It wasn't such a silly idea. After all, she didn't just have the one daughter – she had to think of Minna, too.

Malka woke up in the middle of the night, or at least she thought it was the middle of the night because it was completely dark, but then she saw a grey light at the window and knew that it must be dawn. Her mother and Minna were sitting underneath the window with their knees drawn up, and they looked like two black tents, their faces pale half-moons. They were talking together, so presumably it had been their voices which had woken her up. Malka listened without really understanding what they were saying, and the words just flowed through her head like the water over the river-bed – hitting against stones, going into whirlpools, lapping at the bank and flowing on.

'I don't know how long we'll need to get to Mukačevo – maybe a few days or a week,' said her mother. 'By the time we get there she's bound to be better and Kopolowici can bring her on to us by train – it's only a couple of hours. I know a doctor in Mukačevo, Doctor Rosner – we can meet up there.'

'What if they get caught?' asked Minna.

Her mother's voice had a comforting tone to it. 'They won't get caught. The Kopolowicis have a daughter who's roughly the same age and he can take her birth certificate with him. No one will notice that it isn't his child. And why shouldn't a father take his daughter to see relations in Mukačevo?'

'Are you really sure that leaving her here is the right thing to do?' asked Minna after a pause. Her trembling voice hovered in the air, then passed directly from Malka's ears into the pit of her stomach and filled her up so completely that she could barely breathe. She became dizzy.

Her mother started to cry. 'I don't know myself what I ought to do. We have to go on – we mustn't be found here. And she's ill. With that fever she has to stay in bed for a few days. You saw yourself that she could hardly walk. Nobody notices a child – a child will always make it somehow. It won't help if we all risk being caught. We can meet up again in Mukačevo, and from there things ought to get easier.'

Who are they talking about? thought Malka. What child? And where is the child supposed to go on the train?

She tried to lift her head, to show her mother and sister that she was awake, but she couldn't, because although it was still dark there were strips of light spinning round in front of her eyes, getting bigger and bigger like the lights on a train. She saw steam rising, reddish steam with sparks in it and the steam was all around her and it picked her up and rocked her from side to side.

When she woke up again it really was morning. Her mother and Minna were sitting on the edge of her bed and by the door there stood a man she didn't know. That must be Mr Kopolowici, the one her mother had been talking about yesterday. 'Come on, hurry up,' said the man. 'The others are waiting for you both.'

'Malka,' said her mother, 'you will be staying here for a few days with the Kopolowici family. And when you are better, Mr Kopolowici will bring you to us by train. We have to go to Mukačevo, and you are too ill to come with us.'

It took Malka a long time before the words sank in, and even then they weren't very clear and she didn't really grasp what they meant. But 'you, here', and 'we, Mukačevo' made sense to her. She started to cry. 'I don't want to stay here,' she said. 'I can walk perfectly well. I'm not a baby any more.'

Her mother lifted her so that she was sitting up in bed, put her arms round her and hugged her. 'It's the only way. We have to do it – there's no choice.'

Malka wanted to beg, wanted to scream, but then she saw her mother's face, and saw that Minna was close to tears, and she understood that it really was the only way. So she swallowed the bitter taste that had risen up in her throat, and said nothing.

'Please come on,' said the man at the door. 'I've got Doctor Rosner's address and you've got my sister's address, and I'll bring the little girl as soon as she's better – you needn't worry.'

Malka looked at the man, who was staring fixedly at the little window on the other side of the room, through which the light was getting stronger and stronger. 'You go,' said Malka. 'You go, I'll stay here.'

Then she fell back, turned to the wall and closed her eyes, so she didn't have to see her mother and Minna leave the room. With Liesel pressed tightly against her face she first heard the loud footsteps on the stairs, then the banging of a door. Then the footsteps were less distinct, as if they were on grass or earth. And then finally there was nothing more to hear. Just the hens clucking.

Hannah walked along behind the others. They'd all welcomed her decision and had assured her that she was doing the right thing. She and Minna had been accepted almost as friends, and even Rachel Waiss had shaken her hand and welcomed her as a new member of the group.

Hannah was relieved that she didn't have to make decisions any more. She didn't have to think; she could just go along behind the others. Right at the front walked the guide, who only spoke broken Polish and who had introduced himself as Imri. He was good-looking man, perhaps in his late forties, with brown hair and a broad face with high cheekbones and a wide, full mouth. In different circumstances, this Imri would have been just the kind of man Hannah would have been interested in. But the idea was absurd, she knew – she only had to look at her dirty fingernails and her clothes, which by now had become somewhat dishevelled. Imri was leading a donkey on a length of rope, laden down with the packs belonging to the other refugees.

A comfortable escape, thought Hannah, well planned and with plenty of money. Again there rose inside her anger, fury, almost hatred for those women who were not on their own.

But even with money, escaping was far from easy. The three men, Shmuel Waiss, Ephraim Kohen and Mendel Frischman, walked closely behind Imri, then came their wives. Minna and the young man called Reuben had been walking for hours side by side. Obviously Minna thought Reuben was a better travel companion than her mother, who suddenly felt as if she were an old woman.

Their progress was no faster than Hannah had made with her daughters on her way across the mountains, because they avoided all villages and settlements, took detours around any house they saw, and kept away from the roads. They followed pathways through the forest, walking one behind the other in single file, they climbed up hills and down again, and once, on Imri's instructions, they had to crawl across a field so that they couldn't be seen from a village that was not too far away below them.

At midday they rested in a wood near a spring and ate the bread that Imri had brought along. Hannah was happy to be able to wash her hands before she ate, but when she saw how the others sat there, dirty and, exhausted, and just grabbed at the bread, she lost her appetite and had to force herself simply to eat. In spite of her relief at being part of this group, she still felt alone and deserted. Deserted even by Minna, she thought, and glanced over to the left, where her daughter and Reuben were sitting, quite close together, but not touching. Hannah would have liked to jump up and push the pair of them apart, because it all seemed so wrong to her. It should have been Malka sitting there next to Minna, not this young man. In his way he was quite handsome, though too delicate for her taste. She wasn't particularly keen on his slightly ethereal Jewish-ness with the smouldering almond eyes and dark hair. She preferred strong men.

Mendel Frischman had been watching her. 'Don't worry, doctor,' he said. 'As soon as we are in Mukačevo you'll get your little girl back. Kopolowici promised.'

Hannah nodded, and forced herself to smile.

'My husband, Ephraim Kohen and Mendel Frischman gave the man quite a lot of money to look after the child,'

73

said Mrs Waiss. 'You have every reason to be grateful to us, Doctor Mai.'

Hannah made an effort not to show her irritation. She put on a grateful expression. 'We'll pay the money back,' she promised. 'We'll get work in Budapest and pay it all back.'

Mendel Frischman made a conciliatory gesture with his hand, and Shmuel Waiss said to his wife that that really was enough, and she should be quiet.

Then they set off on their way again. Hannah kept her head bowed, and saw hardly anything of the landscape – just the earth as it slid away behind her and sometimes started to blur. Time and again she thought about whether her decision was the right one. But had it been a decision at all? Had she had a choice?

The war wasn't her fault; the present situation wasn't her fault. The most you could blame her for was for misjudging the situation, for living for too long in a false sense of security. But long-term planning had never been one of her strong points. She knew herself; she was one of those people who can react quickly in an unplanned way, but often with a sure instinct. She hoped that this time, too, she had done the right thing.

Malka slept the whole time. Occasionally, she woke up when someone held a glass of tea or milk to her lips and she would obediently drink a few mouthfuls, or when they fed her. Then she would chew and swallow what was put into her mouth without noticing what it was, and without opening her eyes. She didn't even open her eyes when she was lifted out of the bed and set down on a bucket to do her business, or when someone put ointment on her legs.

Often someone would speak to her, but she never answered. Very rarely she heard a girl's voice, but usually it was a woman's, saying, 'Here, eat,' or, 'There's a drink for you,' or, 'Come on, I'm sure you need to piss or to crap.'

She was surprised about those words, which she had never been allowed to use at home – only Zofia had talked about pissing and crapping. Both the woman and the girl spoke Yiddish, a language the meaning of which Malka had to guess at more than she understood.

And then – she didn't know how much time had gone by – she woke up and felt better. She was a bit wobbly when she got out of bed and went over to the little window in the back wall, and her legs were shaking – but they carried her and they didn't hurt so much.

The window was open and she could look down at a yard which ran into a meadow with fruit trees in it. At the back of the yard, next to a shed, there was a brick well and a pump. There was no sign of any people around, just hens. The yard was full of hens, and suddenly she remembered that in her half-conscious state she had often heard the noise of hens without really being aware of what it was. She wondered how that could happen, that you could hear something and not really hear it, and only work out afterwards what it was that you had heard.

The sun was shining. Malka put her hand out of the window and felt that it really was warm. She stood there for a long time, watching the hens and listening to their cackling. Most of them were white with red crests and wattles, but there were brown ones, too, and some were grey with white markings. A cockerel was scratching around on the dungheap in front of some bushes. Malka could hear the rushing noise of the river, which must have been behind the bushes, though she couldn't see it.

She put on her dress but not the pullover, which lay folded on her bed, next to some new cloths to wrap round her feet and new shoe-ties. Then she sat on the bed and waited. She waited for a long time, wriggling her toes and humming to herself, took off Liesel's green pants and white vest, which by now had become grey, and put them back on her several times. And when still nobody came in, she put Liesel under the bedcover and cautiously opened the door. Some narrow wooden steps ran down steeply from a tiny landing. She went barefoot down the steps and found herself in a hallway with four doors leading off it. A small window lit the hallway, and in front of the main door there was a dirty cloth mat that you could wipe your feet on.

She opened the front door and went out. The sun was warm and pleasant and she felt a light wind on her bare legs. And suddenly it occurred to her how much she had enjoyed it every year when in spring she had been allowed to leave off her long stockings for the first time and wear knee-socks when she went out. What a wonderful feeling it was when you could feel the air on your bare legs after a long winter and the wind blowing under your skirt.

There were so many hens that she didn't even try to count them. They were running around in the yard, in the meadow next to it, on the dungheap and among the bushes that must have been in front of the river. Malka walked around the house, carefully avoiding the chicken droppings, and saw the mill-wheel. But it wasn't moving. This branch of the river, whose rushing she could hear, was dried up, but she could still see where it had been

76

by the indentation and by the particularly lush, light-green grass that grew there. The wooden channel above the mill-wheel had rotted; one plank had come loose and was hanging down, attached only at one end, and it was swaying back and forth in the wind.

Malka climbed up the slope and saw that on the other side of the house there was a fenced vegetable garden with a woman and a girl working in it. They were kneeling down between two beds, so close together that their heads seemed to be touching. The girl had blonde hair, the woman's hair was hidden under a dark headscarf. Malka slid down the slope, this time on the other side of the mill-wheel, and went up to the fence. The woman and the girl didn't notice her and carried on working quietly.

'Good morning,' said Malka politely, and put her hand on the fence.

The two heads bobbed up. The woman's face reddened in anger and she shouted furiously at Malka, 'Get back up to your room right now! What are you playing at? What if someone sees you?'

Malka backed away, turned tail and ran into the house. As she went round the corner she stumbled over a tin bucket that was lying there, trod in some stinging nettles and then in some chicken droppings, rushed into the house, wiped her feet on the mat, and ran upstairs. Later, as she sat on her bed, not knowing what to do, she was quite pleased that her feet and legs were burning right up to her knees, because it took her mind off everything else. She looked at the thick scabs that had formed over the weals on her legs, and picked at them a little.

The woman brought her some soup. She still looked very angry.

'Never let yourself be seen downstairs,' she said in a hard, cold voice. 'The police already suspect us of helping refugees.'

Malka shrugged and nodded, and only ate the soup when the woman had left the room. It tasted weak and it was lukewarm, but Malka was hungry and licked the bowl clean. When she was standing by the window looking down at the yard a little later, the sun seemed to her to have got duller, the sky wasn't as blue as before and the clucking of the hens was stupid and boring.

Later on three boys turned up, a tall one and two smaller ones, and went into the house. Malka could hear their voices but couldn't make out what they were saying. Towards evening, when the hen-house was already casting a shadow that reached to the middle of the yard, all four children went out to fetch eggs and put them into baskets, with layers of hay between them so that they didn't break.

Then the man came into the yard, not in his gaberdine this time, but with his sleeves rolled up and a leather apron round his waist. In one hand he had a little stool and in the other a knife. He put the stool down near to the well, went into the hen-house and came out with a white hen. He held it by the legs, sat on the stool, forced its head down between his knees and cut its throat. The hen carried on twitching for a long time, until all the blood had drained out of its neck. Then the man cut the chicken open and took out its insides, before passing it on to the woman, who had come out of the house. She washed the chicken in a bucket of water, and then put it down next to the well on the ground.

The man fetched another hen, and Malka went away from the window and sat on the bed so that she didn't have to watch the killing. Every time one of the hens screeched out in fear of death, she put her hands over her ears. Only later, when she had gone to bed and the hens were asleep, did she hear that there must be cows somewhere around, too.

The next morning she was woken early by loud shouting, and she ran over to the window. In the early morning light the people down in the yard looked like grey shadows, distinguishable only by their size. She could see Mr Kopolowici and his wife loading the baskets of eggs and two sacks, which probably contained the chickens that had been slaughtered, on to a large open-sided cart with long shafts.

The eldest son came round the corner leading a skinny horse on a rein. The girl brought a basket covered with a white cloth and put it on to the cart underneath the plank that served as a seat. The two smaller boys stood by and watched, and from time to time they nudged one another and laughed out loud, as if there was something very funny that Malka couldn't see from above.

The horse was harnessed and the man got up on to the seat of the cart, cracked his whip and off he went. Only then were the hens let out of their hen-house. Malka wondered for a long time whether the hens missed their recently slaughtered sisters, and she thought to herself that their clucking sounded different today – sadder, softer and less raucous.

She was given some breakfast and was bored. Apart from the hens there was nothing to see, just the sun rising higher in the sky and white clouds scudding across it. One looked like a ship. Maybe it was sailing to the land of Israel, she thought. She was sorry that she didn't have any paper or pencils, because she would have liked to draw a picture of that country of marvels and of the oranges that grew on the trees like apples did here.

Around midday, when the sun was high in the sky, Mr Kopolowici came back. The biggest boy took the horse out of the shafts, led it away across the yard and disappeared round the side of the outbuilding again while Mr Kopolowici was talking to his wife. The girl unloaded the egg-baskets, which were empty now, and the woman carried the sacks, now hanging down limply, across to the well. When Malka heard someone coming up the stairs, light steps which had to be the girl, she sat down quickly on the bed.

The girl held a plate out to her with potatoes and carrots on it. 'Here you are,' she said, and stayed longer than usual, standing there and watching Malka eat.

Suddenly she said: 'You've got to go. My Papa says there's going to be a raid.'

'What's a raid?' asked Malka.

'It's when the Hungarian police come and look for Polish Jews. Papa says you've got to go, or we'll all be in danger.'

Malka put her spoon down. Suddenly she wasn't hungry any more. 'And where am I going to go?' she asked.

The girl shrugged her shoulders. 'Just away. So nobody finds you with us. My father said he'd take you away right now.' Then the girl went out, taking the still half-full plate with her down the stairs again.

Malka wrapped the new foot-cloths round her feet, tied Mrs Kowalski's pullover round her waist, put on her jacket over her dress and tucked Liesel into her pocket.

She was ready to go. With any luck, her next hiding place would be less boring than this one.

They hadn't had much to eat. Imri, their guide, had only been able to get hold of a single loaf of bread in the village, which was by now a long way below them. One slice of bread per person, with a piece of the fatty salami that Imri had taken out of his pack. 'We'll get more this evening,' he promised them. 'Tonight we'll be staying with a forester.' And when Rachel Waiss had asked him in a tearful voice how much longer they would be walking, he had merely shrugged. Rachel Waiss was sitting with the two other wives under a tree. She had taken off her shoes and was massaging her feet and her swollen ankles. Hannah decided that in the evening she would make cold compresses for her and make sure that she rested with her feet up.

Minna plucked a few bright orange berries, the size of peas, from a thorny bush and showed them to her mother. 'Eat them,' said Hannah. 'Eat as many as you can – they're good for you.'

She was too tired to stand up herself, and stayed squatting down, rubbing her back gently on the trunk of a low, wind-blown pine tree. Avoiding the thorns and using the tips of her fingers, Minna picked one berry after another and put them in her mouth. Reuben got up and went and stood next to her. They were about the same height. Hannah noticed how the pair looked at each other. Minna stopped in mid-movement, as if the moment had been frozen in time, had stretched out and was getting longer and longer. Hannah stared at the pair of them; they noticed nothing, as if they were alone in the world. Then at last Minna moved her hand, picked a berry and held it to Reuben's lips. He opened his mouth without taking his eyes off her, and she put in the berry. Minna looked so strange, so different, as if she had no connection with the child that she had once been. Embarrassed, Hannah turned her eyes away. She felt as if she'd been watching something that was nothing to do with her.

She thought about her sister, Golda, who had married when she was barely older than Minna was now. They both had the same blue-grey eyes, which shone when they were happy and darkened when they were angry. Hannah smiled. She had inherited those eyes from her father too, just like Golda. Her eldest sister, Malka, who had died young, had had those blue-grey eyes as well. A family colouring. Only her own Malka, her daughter, had brown eyes. Hannah lowered her head.

Late on in the evening, when, after a long and tiring march, they had reached the forester's hut, they had mushroom soup, with a piece of dry bread. Minna turned away in disgust. She hated mushrooms. Malka liked them, but she never had; those spongy, slimy things, as she called them. Hannah suppressed the impulse to shout at her daughter and say that things were different now and would she kindly not make such a damned fuss, but instead she held out her slice of bread to her and said, 'I'm not hungry,'.

Later on, when they were lying in the barn with all the others, Hannah found it hard to sleep. She couldn't get out of her head the picture of Minna popping the berry into Reuben's mouth. There was something between the two of them that shouldn't be there, not yet. But then, why not? she thought. Just because it makes me feel older? Because my daughter is clearly growing up? She turned restlessly on to her other side. Minna had her back to her and her hair was tickling Hannah's nose. The girl was asleep.

She had been older, just over twenty, when she had had that love affair with the Polish aristocrat, a memory she tried to suppress because it was tinged with shame. Aleksander had been prepared to marry the Jewish girl he had loved. She had loved him, too – it was a crazy time. But she could never have coped with all the conflict, neither with her family nor with his. Besides, she was still a student, and she had other plans for her future which, if she were honest with herself, were more important to her than love. And when three years later Issy came along, handsome, blond, as tall as Aleksander, but Jewish, she thought that she would be able to have with him what hadn't worked out with the other man, whatever the reasons had been, and so she had grabbed him. At least she could bring him home to her parents; they would approve. Admittedly, he was an assimilated German Jew, not a Pole, but he *was* Jewish.

It's funny the way the past keeps coming back to you, thought Hannah; you just can't get rid of it. She hadn't thought about Aleksander for such a long time, and all of a sudden there he was again. But she'd be better off worrying about what would become of her daughter. When she had been about to send Minna away to a boarding school, the war had got in the way. But she had always found it convenient for Minna to be there to look after Malka when she had had to do a tour of her medical district, and would sometimes be away for a week or two. She wouldn't have been happy leaving the child just with the Ukrainian maids.

Was Malka sleeping? Had her fever gone away? Had

that women given her the dissolved quinine tablets regularly? When would she get her child back?

She moved closer to Minna so that she could feel the warmth of her daughter's body, and carefully, so as not to wake her, she kissed her hair.

Mr Kopolowici did not take Malka to a new hiding place, as she had expected him to do, but he took her along the street towards the town. Apart from a curt 'Hurry up,' he hadn't said a word to her. He walked fast, with long steps, so that Malka could hardly keep up and almost had to run. When the first houses were close enough for Malka to make out their windows and doors he stopped, lifted his arm and pointed to the town. 'You'll have to find yourself somewhere else, down there,' he said, so loudly that she gave an involuntary jump.

'And how will I get back to my mother?' she asked.

He shrugged his shoulders. 'Your mother will wait for you in Mukačevo and then she wants to go on to Budapest. You'll have to find someone else to help you – I can't do any more for you. And now off you go – I don't want anyone to see us together.' He turned round and walked away quickly the way they had come.

Malka stood in the road and didn't understand at first what had happened. Slowly, very slowly, it penetrated her consciousness. She was alone. Alone in a foreign country, alone on a foreign street. Strangely enough, she wasn't really frightened – on the contrary, she was relieved to have escaped from that boring room with the sloping roof and the little window. Now she had something else to see apart from the stupid hens.

She walked down the road to the town. She didn't dare look at the first people who walked past her, but lowered her head and pressed herself against the wall or into a doorway, but then she soon saw that no one was taking any notice of her. The words her mother had used that night came into her head and now she seemed to hear them properly for the first time: nobody notices a child – a child will always make it. 'That's right,' she said softly.

Pilipiec was bigger than Lawoczne, bigger and more beautiful, and there was a lot to see. Malka wandered through the lanes and alleyways, sometimes turning left, sometimes turning right, and soon had no idea where she was. She could never have found her way back to the mill. Bored, she thought up a new game for herself, a game she called 'collecting pictures'. If she saw something she really liked, so much that she wanted never to forget it, she looked at it for a long time, then closed her eyes and pretended it was a painting in a book.

On one page, for example, she put a green door with a coloured band all around it made up of red and blue lines and squares. In front of it was a stone step with two kittens playing on it. Their mother was sitting nearby washing her paws and pretending that they were nothing to do with her.

On the next page was a picture of a woman sitting on the pavement in front of an iron bucket full of hot coals, with a grill on top with yellow corn-cobs roasting on it. The woman was old and had a black fringed scarf over her head and shoulders. Malka watched as the cobs gradually browned. A man and a boy stopped and he bought one for his son. The smell tickled Malka's nose and taste buds, and she'd have loved to eat one herself. Saliva gathered in her mouth as she almost felt she could taste the slightly burned corn. But because she had no money she moved on quickly, and then put a donkey into her picture collection.

The donkey was standing at the edge of the road harnessed to an empty cart, with the reins looped round a post. The donkey stood there quietly, moving just its tail from time to time to keep the flies off its back. Malka leaned against a tree and watched the donkey. It was grey and bristly with a fat belly and a big head. On its forehead it had a jagged patch of lighter hair, which looked like a star. Maybe it was Jewish donkey? It looked at Malka with its brown eyes, patient, serious and unmoving, but when she stretched her hand out carefully and went to stroke it, it flared its nostrils, pulled back its upper lip and bared its long, yellow teeth. She pulled her hand back in fright.

The next picture was a little garden between two houses. In the garden bright blue flowers were growing and under a tree there was a bench, also blue, on which an old man and woman were sitting. They weren't speaking to each other but they were holding hands. Their serious, calm expressions reminded Malka of her grandparents in Kraków, whom she hadn't seen for ages, not since the war started. Her grandmother had died in the spring. When her mother told her she didn't cry, but now, months later, she was sad that she didn't have a grandmother any more.

She collected lots of pictures in her mind, so many that she would have plenty to look through if she ever had to sit in such a miserable room as the one at the mill. The last picture was of the sun going down behind the houses and casting a golden glow over the wooden roofs and walls.

But with the darkness came the cold. Malka untied the

pullover from round her waist and pulled it on over her dress and jacket. The sleeves were so long that she had to fold them back several times. She lifted her arm to her nose, and the smell of mothballs, which reminded her of Mrs Kowalski, had become weaker, but hadn't quite disappeared.

With the darkness came hunger as well. There weren't many people about on the streets now, and they'd obviously gone home to their evening meals, because coming from the houses you could smell soup, or cabbage, or boiled potatoes, or sometimes bacon frying. Now she was sorry, really very sorry, that she hadn't eaten up all her midday meal.

Malka got hungrier and hungrier and her feet were beginning to hurt. She came upon a square with a tree in the middle, and sat on the ground leaning against the tree trunk. But it wasn't her sore feet that kept her there, but rather the inn opposite, from which came loud music and laughter, and more importantly the smell of cooked meat. Whenever someone opened the door and someone came out or went in, light from the room fell on the pavement outside, the music and the voices got louder, and the smell of food got stronger.

Eventually she could no longer resist; she got up and went to the door. When two men came out, laughing and swaying slightly, she slipped inside the inn.

The room was large. The tables had been pushed together to form one long one which was laden with food. There were steaming dishes, plates of meat, cut bread and pasties, with glasses and bottles in between. At the table sat men in white shirts and women in coloured dresses, and in the middle was a man in a black suit next to a woman in a white dress, with a headdress of flowers. A wedding. The music came from a gramophone on a table in the corner. The people were speaking Hungarian – or rather, they were shouting – and there were a few children running around and eating bits and pieces given to them by different people.

Malka stood at the door for a long time and no one looked her way, not even the innkeeper, who was filling the glasses. There was a plate near her with pieces of roast chicken, and a basket of white bread. The chicken skin was nicely browned. Malka wondered if she couldn't just grab a piece of bread and run away, or better still a pasty or a chicken leg. But she didn't dare. No one was looking at her; it was as if she were invisible, as the people ate and drank without sparing the unknown child a glance.

Malka considered the wedding guests one after the other and then decided on an older woman with a broad face and a white scarf, who was sitting not far from the plate of chicken and who reminded her of Chaya's mother, the kosher butcher's wife. She stood next to her and waited. When the woman looked at her in astonishment she said: 'Hungry . . . hungry . . . bread,' and pointed at her mouth with both hands.

The woman raised her eyebrows, and then laughed, took a large, fat chicken leg and held it out to Malka. Malka took it and tried to run away, but the woman was already on her feet and sat Malka down on a chair and gave her a plate, on which she put some vegetables and potatoes. She spoke to her in a voice that didn't sound unfriendly, but Malka couldn't understand what she said, and shrank her head down to her shoulders. The woman put a fork into Malka's hand and indicated with a gesture that she should eat. Suddenly everyone was looking at her and Malka thought that she wouldn't be able to eat a mouthful with everyone watching. But the chicken leg in her left hand was so tempting that she forgot all these strangers and started to eat. When she had finished and had been given some tea to drink, two men got up and took her to the police.

There was one policeman on duty in the office. The two men who had taken Malka there talked to him in Hungarian, so she didn't understand what they were saying. The younger of the two, a man with dark eyes and a black moustache, stroked her hair and pointed to her, while a flood of incomprehensible words poured out of his mouth. Malka looked around. On the wall behind the policeman there was a small crucifix, and next to it a map with red, blue and green pins in it, but otherwise the room was almost empty.

The policeman was sitting behind a desk of light wood, on which lay papers, forms, pencils, an eraser and a pencil sharpener. At the side, right at the edge of the desk, was a black typewriter rather like the one her mother had, and which had been left behind in Lawoczne with all their other things. At that moment Malka was only worried about the fact that they had lost the typewriter, as if this was the worst thing that had happened to them. She stared at the keyboard with the letters and had to swallow, and when she wiped her eyes the back of her hand came away wet and shiny.

The young man with the black moustache stroked her hair again, said something, and left the room with the other man. Malka was left alone with the policeman. He asked her in Polish what her name was.

'Malka,' she said. 'My name is Malka Mai.'

'Are you Jewish?'

Malka nodded.

'And where are your parents?'

Malka shrugged, because she knew that if she said anything now she would really start to cry and she knew she mustn't do that, though she didn't really know why.

'Where are you from?' he asked, and when she didn't answer he put the question a different way: 'Where did you live before?'

'In Lawoczne,' said Malka. She noticed how strange her voice was sounding, as if it didn't come from her throat, but from somewhere outside herself.

The policeman shook his head and said a few words in Hungarian which sounded as if he was swearing. Then he put down the pencil with which he had been writing her answers, shook his head again and said, 'Come on.'

Malka stood up. He took her by the hand and led her downstairs into the basement. He switched on the light and Malka saw a door at the end of a corridor. The man unlocked it with a large key and pushed Malka into a dark room. Before he shut the door again she saw in the triangle of light that there were legs and feet on the floor. Then the bright triangle disappeared, the door clicked shut, the key was turned and it was completely dark.

'A child,' said a woman's voice in Polish. 'They've got no shame at all. Come here, child.' Malka felt a hand touch her leg and then feel around to take her own hand. She was pulled down on to the floor, and the woman said, 'Here's a bit of space – you can lie down here.'

Malka sat down. She was very tired. The floor, which was of beaten earth, was cold and rather damp. She stretched out, but then drew her legs back quickly when she bumped against someone, who shouted something out in Hungarian. She lay on her side, pulled her legs up to her stomach and pressed her head against her knees. Horror filled her and she went stiff.

'Go to sleep,' said the woman next to her. 'It's late, and sleep is the best thing for you.'

Malka lay there with her knees tucked up, staring into the darkness and unable to sleep. She sensed that there were more people in the room than the woman who had spoken Polish to her and the Hungarian man. She heard breathing; someone over to the right was snoring, and from time to time someone gave a groan. The room stank of filth and urine. Malka tried to hold her breath, but she couldn't. So she put her arm across her face and breathed in the smell of mothballs as deeply as she could.

To combat her despair and feeling of horror she thought about all the pictures that she had collected today. Where was the cat with the two kittens now? Had they gone in through the green door and were they lying comfortably on a bench around a stove? And the donkey – was he in his stable eating hay and thinking about the girl he met today, or had he already forgotten her?

The next morning she woke early from an uneasy sleep. Pale light was coming in through a window high up on the wall, only just below the ceiling. Shadows appeared and their outlines became clearer and clearer the lighter it got in the cellars she was in. The shadows turned gradually into people with bodies, faces and limbs, which stretched and moved, with hands that rubbed eyes and ran through hair – the shadows became men and women. There were two children there too, sitting close to each other in a corner; they reminded her of Shlomo and Yossel, two brothers she knew in Lawoczne. The older boy's face was a pale, shadowy disc, and all that could be seen of the other boy, who was lying with his head on the shoulder of the bigger one, was a mop of dark hair.

Shlomo and his brother Yossel lived with their uncle, the shoemaker Shmielevich, who lived on the other side of Lawoczne in the Jewish quarter, with its narrow lanes and little wooden houses, which she only visited three times a week when she went for lessons to Miss Lemberger. But of course she knew, as everyone else in Lawoczne did, that Shlomo and his brother had been visiting their uncle Yankel Shmielevich at the time the Germans had invaded Poland.

She had never understood why the two brothers couldn't go back to their parents. After all, she had been with her mother to Kraków around that time, visiting her grandparents and her Aunt Golda, and they had come back by train, a journey she remembered very well indeed, mainly for the bombing and the noise the bombs had made.

At all events, Shlomo and Yossel had stayed in Lawoczne, and the people whispered that Shlomo, the older one, was involved with smuggling, and that was the way he helped feed his uncle's big family. People said he used to smuggle cigarettes out of Hungary into Poland, and sell them for a good profit. Yossel, his brother, was a few years younger – a slight, dark lad, not much bigger than Malka, though he was two or three years older than her.

The grey square of the window got lighter and lighter; Malka heard voices, and people got up and went over to a corner where they did their business in a bucket, audible and visible to everyone, before sitting down again. Everyone was handcuffed. One man swore loudly in Ukrainian, and the Polish woman next to her, who looked older than Malka had expected from the sound of her voice, shouted to him that he should keep his dirty trap shut and would he mind at least turning around when he had a piss. And then Malka was quite sure that the two boys were Shlomo and Yossel.

The Polish woman put her handcuffed hands on Malka's leg and said, 'Keep your chin up, little one – just make sure you stay alive. Then the world will be different.' Her hair stuck out like a dandelion clock around her face, and looked very white, a strange contrast with the brown of her skin. The woman had lots of creases around her eyes, and two deep furrows from her nose down to the sides of her mouth and then further to her chin. When it got light enough, Malka noticed a small amount of hair on her upper lip, and curiously, this hair was black. The woman smiled at Malka and Malka smiled back, but she kept looking over at Shlomo and Yossel. They made her feel as if she was not quite lost and alone, because they belonged to Lawoczne, just like she did; they were a little bit of Poland in this foreign country of Hungary.

Hannah dragged herself along behind the others. Their escape wasn't a comfortable one any more, and she thought with a bitter smile about that word, which had come into her mind on the first day. No, not comfortable, but clearly well planned and paid for in advance. By now they had acquired a new guide, a Hungarian peasant-farmer, and now that the man with the donkey had left, the other refugees had to carry their own packs. And from here onwards, their guide had told them, they would have to walk in the evening and at night, and sleep during the day, so as not to be discovered, because there were known to be a lot of supporters of the Arrow Cross Party in this area.

When they had been down at the bottom of the mountain early on in the evening, he had told them that the climb would be a difficult one, and that anything they couldn't carry should be left in a hiding place here. He pointed out a hole in the undergrowth running through the thick roots of an oak tree into the side of the slope, presumably a disused fox's earth.

Hannah and Minna had no luggage, and Reuben's rucksack was small and flat and couldn't have had much in it. They had watched as the three couples unpacked silver candlesticks, cutlery, valuable bowls, clothes, high-heeled shoes, even a few books, and put them all into the foxhole. A lot of valuable items. The peasant covered up the hole with twigs and grass. He'll take careful note of where it is, that's for sure, thought Hannah. He probably picked it in advance, maybe even dug it out himself. Those things are a nice little extra to the money he's certainly already been given. But these thoughts left her indifferent. She no longer felt any animosity towards these rich people, neither envy nor anger, but she didn't have any sympathy or warmth for them either. And the thought that they had given Kopolowici money to look after Malka no longer weighed so heavily on her, since the stuff they were leaving here was worth a lot more than that.

One after another they went through the forest on the mountainside. Hannah had nothing to carry – just what she was wearing, and in the inside pocket of her jacket a few papers, which weighed very little – in contrast to her thoughts, the weight of which was nearly crushing her.

She should never have left the child behind, and yet it was a relief not to have her here for this difficult climb. She comforted herself with the thought that Malka was asleep in a bed, warm and with enough to eat. And in a few days, when she was better, she would have an easy train journey with Kopolowici to Mukačevo.

The path went uphill, always uphill. It was now so dark in the forest that Hannah couldn't see the others – only Minna, who was immediately in front of her. The girl was holding up well; she was a better walker than Hannah, who felt on the point of collapse. With every step the urge in her grew stronger simply to flop down. Once they were out of the forest, it was lighter. Now they had to climb up a narrow pathway with a vertical rock face on one side and a ravine on the other which dropped away so steeply that you couldn't see the bottom in the darkness. Hannah knew that one careless step could cost her her life.

Hannah stumbled, fell, grabbed hold of a small branch to steady herself, and went onwards on all fours. She could make out the silhouettes of the others and could see how Mrs Waiss was moving along, pressed against the rock wall, constantly encouraged by her husband, walking a few steps behind her. At one point, where the path widened out a bit, the guide stopped. They all leaned against the wall and looked up towards the top of the mountain. Nobody looked downwards into the ravine, the bottom of which was in darkness. They could hear a loud rushing noise, so there must have been a waterfall nearby. 'Come on,' said the guide, pointing at Hannah, 'come along by me.'

She got herself upright and walked past the others. The peasant smiled at her and took her by the hand. He led her onwards as if she were a child, shielding her from

95

the ravine with his own body. In front of them was a range of mountains, great black blocks against the night sky. From time to time Hannah looked round to try and pick out Minna in the group of people behind them.

At last they were at the top of the mountain, sitting on a flat, grassy area, coughing, gasping and trying to pull themselves together. Mrs Waiss was crying loudly, and her husband put his arm round her comfortingly. Mrs Frischman and Mrs Kohen were huddled together, with Mrs Frischman stroking her sister's hair.

Mendel Frischman cleared his throat, and then he said, 'And now we all have to tear up our passports and any other papers we've got that prove that we are Jews – even photos and things like that. It's time for us to turn into Christian Poles fleeing from the occupation of their country.'

One after the other they took out their papers, photographs and letters, and started to tear them up. In the first light of dawn the scraps of paper were shiny white, and soon the grass was covered with little white fragments that looked as if they were anemones. Hannah could see from the faces of her companions that getting rid of these things was much harder than losing the ballast of valuables that they had left down at the bottom of the mountain.

She took out her children's birth certificates, her passport and the letter from her father with the photographs. 'Here, have one more look at your grandfather,' she said to Minna before she tore up the photos, first the one of the stranger with the naked face and then her father with the beard and earlocks. As she did so she noticed how raw and torn her hands were, with broken and dirty fingernails.

She hesitated with her certificate of medical registration and, after thinking for a moment, she put it back into her pocket, where she also had just the small amount of cash that she had got from Sawkowicz. She couldn't part with her certificate of registration, whatever happened to her, because her work was her life. She had fought so hard to become a doctor, had given up so much to reach that goal, and this scrap of paper was worth more to her than any possessions. More than anything else it defined her identity, was a proof that she had the right to live her life the way she wanted, that she wasn't just a nobody, but a person who could command some respect. This scrap of paper was her link to her life so far, and at the same time it was her only hope for a new one, wherever it would be.

Reuben held out a photograph to Mrs Waiss. 'It's my mother,' he said. 'She doesn't look Jewish, does she? Don't you think I could keep that photo?'

'Yes, Reuben, you can keep that photo, it won't give you away,' said Mrs Waiss, her voice still sounding shaky from all the crying, but surprisingly gentle. Hannah suppressed the comment that the woman on the photo looked very Jewish, and that any idiot would be able to see that she was a Jew, let alone the anti-Semitic Arrow Cross lot. But anyone would be able to tell that Reuben was Jewish too, so it didn't matter what photographs he was carrying.

The guide pointed down into the valley. 'In the woods down there there's a little hunting-lodge. That's where we'll sleep through the daylight. Then we'll set off again when it gets dark.'

'Let me rest a little bit longer, said Mrs Waiss. 'Just a couple of minutes.' The man nodded.

Minna sat down next to Hannah and said softly, 'Malka would never have managed a climb like that.' Hannah took her hand and squeezed it.

Minna's words were intended to be comforting, Hannah knew that, but they gave her no comfort. Deep inside her was the nagging feeling that it had been a mistake to leave the child behind, however often she said to herself: she's in a bed. She's asleep. She's warm. She's had food. She's all right.

Hannah started at the rising sun. I ought to be inspired with sublime feelings, she said to herself, and to be having uplifting thoughts. But she was too crushed. And too completely exhausted.

On the fourth day two policemen came and fetched Malka, Shlomo and Yossel out of the prison. She had spent three days in the cellar next to the Polish woman with the white hair. Apart from herself, Shlomo and Yossel there had been two women and four men. She had looked at all of them and wondered why each of them was there, but she hadn't asked any questions. On the first morning she stood up and went over to Shlomo and Yossel because she wanted to sit with them, but Shlomo shouted at her to clear off. Shocked and hurt, she had gone back to the Polish woman.

The woman's name was Saskia and she was from Kraków. She told Malka about how she had come home from work one day and found that her mother and her three children had gone. 'It wasn't that long ago,' she said, 'and overnight my hair turned white. I'm not as old as you think.'

And when Malka asked where her mother and her children were, she said the word that Malka never wanted to hear again, 'There was one of their operations.' The woman pulled a face and spat on the ground beside her. 'The Germans took them away. They call it resettlement. But I don't believe a word of that. If you ask me, they want to kill us all.'

Malka had turned aside and had taken Liesel out of her pocket and was undressing and dressing her over and over again – the green pants, the white vest, the striped socks. Off, on. Off, on. The woman had barely looked at her again after that.

Twice a day they got something to eat, a kind of stew made of potatoes and vegetables, and with it a cup of some hot drink which tasted bitter and not very nice. A policeman came and unlocked the handcuffs of the prisoners before they gave out the food and another watched them with his rifle at the ready. During this time Malka suffered far more from thirst than from hunger, and when the mug was held out to her she drank it all down greedily. Often she was lucky, and the policeman filled the mug up again for her.

Once a day they would be taken out in twos and threes to the yard behind the police station, where they were allowed to exercise, walking round one behind the other. The sky was grey and overcast and the air was damp, but Malka was pleased despite that because she could leave the cellar and its eternal stench. She enjoyed the exercise and felt the blood moving in her legs again. The scabs on the wounds came off and the new skin underneath was white and sensitive. She spent hours scratching away the last bits of scab and running her fingers along the light lines they had left behind – first one leg, then the other. On her skin, which was still brown from the

99

summer, they looked like some kind of writing that she couldn't decipher.

When a policeman came along in the morning and signalled to her, Shlomo and Yossel to come out, she stood up in relief and pushed Liesel deeper down into her jacket pocket. Something was going to happen. Something. Anything was better than being here.

'God bless you, child,' said the Polish woman with the white hair. 'May the Eternal One protect you.' And then she wept.

Two policemen took them to the Polish border, because, as one of them said in broken Polish, they had some business there anyway. Shlomo still had handcuffs on. The two men chatted to each other in Hungarian, and once Yossel whispered to Malka, 'Maggi-Magyar catches flies in a jar.' Shlomo snapped at him to shut up.

Around midday they had a break. One of the policemen took some bread and a thermos flask of tea out of his pack and they ate. There wasn't enough tea, and at the next little stream, Malka kneeled down and drank like a dog from a bowl. The policeman laughed good-naturedly, and waited until she had drunk enough.

Although they were walking along the road like normal people, not like refugees, who had to keep out of sight, it was still hard going. Often the road became steep, and then it would wind down a slope again. Malka could hardly feel her legs any more, and her feet hurt, because the cloths which were all she had to wrap around them were worn through and she felt every stone and every thorn.

The policeman who was walking behind them, a great giant of a man, suddenly gripped her round the waist and swung her up on to his shoulders. She grabbed on to his hair in fright. She was scared to be up so high, but she was pleased as well that she didn't have to walk for a while. Wlado had carried her like that. When she thought of him she got a warm feeling. When that had happened – how long ago was it really? – she hadn't been on her own. Mama, she thought, Minna. She imagined the bowed heads of her mother and her sister. It's the wrong direction, she heard her mother say – Malka, look out, it's the wrong direction.

She closed her eyes and let herself be carried along. In the wrong direction.

Then she had to walk on her own again. The road wound its way up the mountainside. Suddenly, as they went round a curve they saw a small guardhouse stuck to the slope, with a huge black hole in the side of the mountain next to it. Rusty railway tracks came out of the hole and ran down the smooth part of the slope to a bridge. 'That's the border,' whispered Shlomo. 'Lawoczne is on the other side. They're taking us through the tunnel.'

The two policemen took their three prisoners up to the guardhouse, spoke to the soldiers, removed Shlomo's handcuffs and turned and set off back. The giant turned round once more and waved to Malka, and she waved back. A Hungarian soldier pointed to the bench in front of the little guardhouse and indicated that they should sit there. Shlomo rubbed his hands, flexed his fingers, clenched his fists and then flexed them again. The soldier brought each of them a piece of bread and dripping. The bread was brown, with a crust that was almost black, and it tasted good. Another soldier disappeared into the black hole.

Malka had eaten her bread long ago. She stared at the railway tracks and she was trying to follow with her eyes the two rusty-brown strips down into the valley when suddenly voices could be heard coming from the mountain. Shlomo nudged her and nodded with his head towards the tunnel. At first you could only see the light of a torch, and then the Hungarian came out of the hole, followed by two German soldiers from the border guards.

Malka, Shlomo and Yossel sat on the bench and didn't move. They watched while the Hungarian and German soldiers talked to each other, laughed, offered each other cigarettes, and smoked them slowly. One of the Hungarians took a little flask out of his pocket and passed it round. One after the other, each man took a drink from it, then wiped his mouth with his hand and passed it on.

Shlomo swore quietly. 'The bastards are taking their time,' he said.

If it had been up to Malka they could have taken all the time in the world, because she was scared of the road that led into the inside of the mountain and wouldn't have minded sitting there for the rest of eternity. But eventually they did have to go.

The further into the tunnel they went, the darker it got, with just the beams of the two torches dancing along the ground. They were walking one behind another along the narrow footpath beside the railway line, which hadn't been used for years because when the Russians had withdrawn they had destroyed the track and the station.

Broken ballast stones lay in the way and Malka stubbed her toes on them. The worn-out foot-cloths gave her feet hardly any protection now. Once she stumbled over a wooden sleeper that she hadn't seen, fell down and cut open her knees and her hands. She cried. The German who was walking at the front said something in a harsh and unpleasant voice, and Shlomo took Malka by the hand and pulled her along.

Eventually, a dark grey speck appeared in the blackness, and it got lighter and lighter until the end of the tunnel was there in front of them. Shlomo let go of Malka's hand and pushed her away. The sky was grey and overcast here, too, but after the darkness of the tunnel it seemed too bright for Malka, and she had to squint and shade her eyes with her hand.

They were sitting next to one another on a wooden bench in a room with a small window. Two Polish policemen came in with a soldier from the German border guard.

The German sat down behind the desk, took a sheet of paper and picked up a pencil, and the two Polish policemen stood in front of the children. 'Right,' said the German in a bored voice, 'let's start with the girl. What's your name?'

When Malka didn't answer right away, one of the two policemen repeated the question in Polish.

'Malka Mai'

'Are you Jewish?'

'Yes.'

'And who are your parents?'

'My mother is Doctor Mai.'

'And where is your mother now?'

Malka started to cry. 'Get on with it,' said the German impatiently, and the elder of the two policemen barked at her, 'Just answer when you've been asked a question.'

'Who took you across the border?' asked the German. 'It must have been someone from round here because you lot wouldn't have made it on your own. So who was it? I want names.'

Malka shrugged. She hadn't really understood what he had said, and his German sounded quite different from Mrs Schneider's and Veronika's.

'Answer me!' the elder of the two Poles shouted at her, and when she shook her head helplessly he strode towards her and slapped her face, once, twice, three times. She put her hands up to her face to protect herself and the German said, 'Leave her, let's have the other two.'

Malka cried and couldn't really understand what they were asking the boys, although when they were supposed to give their names, she heard that they didn't say Shlomo and Yossel, but gave different ones, saying they were called Andrei and Jurek Pollack. They also denied being Jews, and only when the German gave the order, 'Drop your trousers,' did Shlomo say very quickly, 'Yes, we are Jewish.'

Malka's cheeks were burning from the blows. She heard them hitting Shlomo and Yossel as well, and her surroundings disappeared behind her hands. Her cheeks stopped burning, but she felt numbed and deaf – as if her whole body were deaf and there was an emptiness all around her, just the roaring of a storm in her ears, or maybe it was herself crying. But she wasn't crying and no sounds came from her throat; she couldn't hear anything, and she only felt herself shaking.

Later on the storm abated, died down to just a wind and then stopped altogether. She was sitting on the bench again with Yossel and Shlomo. Yossel was holding her hand in his rough, dry fingers. Malka was very tired as she looked around her. They were alone in the room but Malka hadn't noticed the German and the two Poles leaving.

'Is that the first time someone has hit you?' asked Yossel. 'Because you got very worked up.'

Malka shook her head. No, it wasn't the first time, and her sister Minna had hit her often enough because she had always been strict with her. Even her mother had slapped her when she hadn't done as she was told. But this time it had been quite different. The blows hadn't been given in anger because she had been cheeky or hadn't done something. They were blows given in contempt. The way you hit a dog or kill a fly, thought Malka, but she didn't know how to explain that, so she said nothing.

'The Hungarians are nicer than the Poles,' said Yossel. 'They're not quite so quick to hit you.'

'Maggi-Magyar catches flies in a jar,' sang Shlomo softly. Yossel laughed and turned to Malka. 'All Hungarians have got red faces and big moustaches,' he said. 'And when they're not playing the violin they go and eat goulash or they catch flies. Honest, I've seen them myself.'

Malka didn't answer and she didn't laugh either, but she did move up closer to him.

'We're getting out of here,' said Shlomo suddenly. 'Through that window. I've worked it all out.'

'Why?' said Yossel in a very small voice. 'What if they catch us again?'

'They won't this time,' said his brother. 'We'll do it differently. We'll go through the forest, never mind how much of a detour we have to make, and we'll make sure no one sees us. And this time we'll go straight to a village where I know some people who'll help us. I'm not staying here for them just to shoot me.' He pretended to hold a gun in his hand and pull the trigger: 'Bang-bang, and that's it. Don't you want to get away?'

Yossel didn't answer, but Malka noticed that his body had stiffened. She understood him completely because she knew how hard it was to go across the mountains, just to keep going, on and on without a break, on and on even when you really couldn't go another step. But in spite of that she asked, 'Will you take me with you?'

Shlomo said nothing and nor did Yossel. By now it was dark in the room, and Malka noticed that it smelled of dust and ink. Shlomo said something, Yossel answered, but Malka no longer took it in. She didn't care about anything any more; she was tired. She flopped on to one side half across the arm of the bench, took Liesel out of her pocket, pressed her to her face and closed her eyes. She just heard Shlomo say, 'I'll think about it. What we're going to do is very dangerous.'

When Malka woke up the next morning, Shlomo and Yossel had gone. They hadn't taken her. She was alone. All alone again.

Hannah had blisters on her heels, and her toes were rubbed and raw. She was annoyed that she had no iodine, no tweezers and no dressings with her so she could burst and clean the blisters. They hurt like hell, but she didn't dare complain because the others were no better off, and everyone was exhausted, filthy and miserable. Mrs Waiss had blisters on her feet as well, as Hannah noticed when, after walking all through the night, they sat towards morning side by side at a stream. They had taken off their shoes and stockings and were cooling their feet in the water. It had been a brightly moonlit night, and they were hardly aware that it was dawn.

'Damn the Germans,' said Mrs Waiss. 'May they be

wiped from the face of the earth, and all their children, and may the memory of them be lost for ever.'

Hannah just nodded.

'You always got on so well with them,' said Mrs Waiss. 'Everyone knew that German officers used to visit you a lot.'

'I used to treat them – I'm a doctor,' said Hannah dismissively. She had heard the implicit reproach in the other woman's voice, reproach and condemnation. Oddly enough, it had never occurred to her at the time that people might talk about her. She wouldn't have cared anyway, because she had never paid much attention to things like that. She wasn't one of those women who saw their own happiness only in terms of their roles as wives or mothers or as the perfect housewife. She followed a different set of rules; she'd cut herself free from all that, and she'd always rather looked down on those other women.

'Yes, yes, of course, you're a doctor,' said Mrs Waiss. 'Of course. But all the same . . .'

All the same, thought Hannah later on as she lay on a straw palliasse in a hut listening to the breathing of her fellow refugees; all the same, even if I never wanted to belong to these people, I do now. Fate has caught up with me. Did I ever really believe I could be like the gentiles, just because I trained to be a doctor? And did I really believe that the Germans would behave any differently towards me just because I treated them when they were ill, and because I'm an educated woman who's read the German classics in the original language? An image of her father came to her, not the man with the naked face, nor the other one, the dignified one with the beard and the earlocks and the round hat on his head, but her father at an even earlier time, red-faced and shouting at her in fury. 'You'll do what I tell you! You are my daughter and you will obey me.' And then he had raised his hand.

She saw herself standing there – she must have been sixteen years old, Minna's age now – rigid, white-faced, her eyes dark with anger, and she heard herself saying, 'If I'm not allowed to study, I'll kill myself. And you will be responsible because you will have driven me to it.' Her father had lowered his hand. His arm had dangled helplessly at his side. 'What is it you want?' he had asked at last in a voice which betrayed his defeat. His defeat and her victory. 'I want to be a doctor,' she had said.

Father, father, thought Hannah now, I didn't imagine it would be like this. I wanted so much, and I accomplished so much, all to bring me back to a point where I am, after all, first and foremost a Jew. And the mother of Jewish daughters.

There was a great deal of fuss. Malka was asked over and over again how the boys had managed to escape. 'I don't know,' she said helplessly. 'I was asleep.' Then she was hit by the same man as on the day before. She cried, and the other one said, 'Stop that, can't you! If she was asleep she can't possibly know. And anyway, it's happened, and the two of them will be over the hills and far away by now.'

With that they stopped asking her. Malka sat for the whole day, sometimes in one room, sometimes moved to another, with no one ever speaking to her and without having any idea what the Germans were planning to do with her. Through the window she could see a tree, a beech tree with copper-coloured leaves. It's a Lawoczne tree, she thought, and when a squirrel ran along a branch she fished Liesel out of her pocket to show her the Lawoczne squirrel.

Eventually a Polish policeman came in, one she hadn't seen before, and quietly spoke a few words with the German who was keeping an eye on her. Then he came over to her and whispered, 'Don't worry – I'll get you out of here. I know your mother.'

And sure enough, the man appeared again a little later. The German picked up a couple of files and left the room. The man took a black headscarf out of his pocket and tied it round Malka's head. 'You must hide your hair,' he said. 'You are so blonde that everyone would recognize you by your hair.' Then he led her out through the back door to a fence which had a bicycle leaning against it. It had wooden wheels rather than rubber tyres, and the wood had a metal strip around the rim, just like the farmers' hay-carts. The man lifted Malka on to the luggage-carrier at the back and said, 'Hold on tight, and make sure you don't get your feet caught in the spokes.'

They rode through the side-streets of Lawoczne. Malka sat there on the back of the bike, shaken and rattled about, and saw all the houses she knew so well and all the familiar streets and alleyways. Most of all she would have liked to jump off and run home and into her own room. She would have got into bed and gone to sleep and the next morning told her mother and Minna about the horrible dream she had had, and her mother would have laughed and run her hand over her hair and said, 'You get that from me, Malka, love, I always used to dream a lot,' and Minna would have said something about a dream being like steam.

They rode on for a long time. Malka's bottom was

hurting from the bumping of the hard luggage-carrier that she was sitting on, and she fidgeted from one side to another until the man told her to sit still or they might crash. She clung to him more firmly. The last houses of Lawoczne had disappeared when they turned left off the asphalted country road that led to Skole and went along a track into the mountains. Whenever it got too steep Malka had to get off, and the man pushed the bicycle with Malka walking along beside him. At last they reached a remote house, really a hut, right at the edge of the forest.

The kitchen was big, much bigger than you would have expected from outside, and through an open door was another room with beds in it. The evening sunshine came in through a window and underneath it two boys were sitting at a table eating porridge. One was not much younger than Malka, the other at least the same age as Tanja's little brother. A third boy – going by his size, the middle one – was sitting on the floor by the table with a couple of wooden building blocks in front of him. He stared at Malka, who had stopped in the doorway, and a line of dribble fell from his mouth on to his pullover.

The man exchanged a few words with his wife. Her name was Teresa. She laughed in a friendly way and gave Malka a plateful of porridge too. Marek, the biggest boy, carried on eating. Julek, the smallest, could not take his eyes off Malka. Plainly he rarely saw anybody new. Zygmunt, the husband, the man who had brought Malka here from the border-control station, also started to eat. Teresa lifted the other boy from the floor, sat him at the table and fed him. The boy ate greedily.

'Your mother saved Antek's life,' said Teresa, and pushed another spoonful of porridge into the boy's mouth. 'In the spring he was so ill that we thought he would suffocate. Your mother came every day, twice a day at the start, and drew off the fluid from his lungs. We shall never forget that.'

Malka lowered her head over her plate. She was confused – it gave her a warm feeling but at the same time she didn't want to hear it. She didn't want to think of her mother, who was in Hungary with Minna and who had left her all alone at the mill.

'Antek is a bit different,' said Teresa. 'But he's a very good boy – he's something special. That's right, isn't it, Antek?' She leaned forward and kissed him on the cheek. Antek beamed at her, then he beamed at Malka; he beamed at everyone. His eyes became narrow bands when he laughed. Malka emptied her plate without saying anything, and nodded in relief when Marek asked her if she wanted to see the animals.

'Take her out to the shed,' said his father.

'Me too,' shouted Julek, as he slid off his chair and grabbed Malka's hand. He toddled along happily at her side.

Malka was happy with Teresa. In fact, she was very happy. At night Zygmunt and Teresa took little Julek into their bed to make a place for Malka. The child's bed was narrow and short, and if she didn't roll herself up her legs hung out over the end of the bed. On the first night she hardly slept because the bed was so short – and her bottom still hurt. Perhaps it also had to do with the fact that she was listening to the breathing of the others – Marek and Antek in the bed next to hers, and the parents and little Julek in the other one. Zygmunt snored on a deep, rumbling note; Teresa made high and loud puffing noises. Malka turned this way and that, rolled up in a ball, stretched out, opened her eyes and shut them again, and had the feeling next morning of not having slept a wink.

After Zygmunt had gone off on his bicycle, Malka got up and went out to the shed with Teresa. The three boys were still asleep. Teresa sat down by the goat and started to milk it. She sang while she did so. 'The goat likes it if I sing,' she said. So do I, thought Malka, and she laughed because Teresa had laughed. She hadn't laughed for such a long time. The goat's milk smelled strong and tasted odd, quite different from the milk Malka knew. All the same she drank the mug-full that Teresa gave her for breakfast. Then Teresa woke the boys and Malka helped to dress Antek and Julek, and to feed Antek.

Antek really was different, but when he put his arm round Malka's neck and pressed his face against her she knew exactly what Teresa had meant when she said he was special. When the sun was shining, Teresa would take him out into the fresh air to a little piece of field that had been fenced off with sticks. The fence was so low that you could step over it. 'But Antek can't get out,' said Teresa. 'He's safe here.'

Malka fetched the building bricks and laid them out in a row in front of the boy. They were polished and felt like silk. Antek laughed. He always laughed, all day long. Teresa laughed a lot, too. This was a new experience for Malka, because there had never been a lot of laughter in her family. She asked Teresa for some cloth and a needle and thread, and made a ball for Antek. She had learned how to do that from Tanja. Teresa kissed her when Antek laughed in delight and crawled after the ball.

Malka helped them gather eggs and helped in the garden, pulling up thick carrots, and, under Teresa's instruction, weeding. Teresa laughed out loud when she picked up a large worm that she had disturbed and carried it over on to another bed. Malka looked at her in amazement and she laughed too, even though she didn't know what the woman found so funny about that. But she was happy – it had been a long time since things had been so good. The feeling was so strong in her that she ran over to Antek, climbed into his playpen and tickled him until he crowed with pleasure and Julek called out to her, jealous.

In the evening, over the meal, Teresa said to Zygmunt,

'It's a pity we haven't got a big daughter. Life is a lot easier with a big daughter.'

When she was lying in her far-too-short bed, Malka decided that she would work very hard and be very helpful. She would have to make herself absolutely indispensable, so that Teresa would keep her because she couldn't manage the work by herself. Living with Teresa, Malka could even think about words like 'tomorrow' or 'the day after'. That night she slept better.

The days went by. Malka made herself useful. From dawn till dusk she kept her eyes open for any way she could find of helping Teresa. Together with Marek she looked after the animals. There was a big goat and a little one, and they would graze in a nearby field during the day. In the evening they had to be brought back into the shed. Marek would put a rope round the neck of the big goat and lead it to the shed, which was behind the house, and then the little goat would follow without being tied. In a run fenced off with wire netting there were hens. Clapping and shouting, Marek would drive them into a small, brick hen-house, and Julek would help him by running around and screeching. The hens fluttered about in fright, against the fence or the outside of the hen-house, but eventually they were all inside. Marek closed off the hole they had gone in through with a wooden flap. In a sty two pigs grunted and snuffled. In addition to all these there was a large black cat. Often, he would rub lazily against Malka's leg a few times and then disappear again.

Teresa showed Malka how to milk the goat; they washed clothes together in the nearby stream; they collected mushrooms in the woods and Teresa was surprised at how well Malka knew which was which. They cooked

114

together, and Malka felt as if she had been there for a very long time. From day to day she grew happier. She liked everyone, especially Antek, but most of all she loved Teresa.

All went well until the evening when Zygmunt came home very downcast and said that he would have to take Malka away. The people in Lawoczne had got wind of the fact that she was here and it was too dangerous for his own family. Malka stiffened, and when Teresa took her in her arms she started to cry.

'I can't do anything about it,' said Zygmunt. 'The Germans told me to get rid of her. Jews are Jews, they said, children or not, and it mustn't be said that they made an exception for the little girl. Schneider himself had a word with me. And we can't take any risks because of Antek – you know what they do with children like Antek.'

'You could take her into the forest to my sister and her family,' said Teresa.

Zygmunt shook his head. 'That would occur to the Germans too, and they'd only have to ask around long enough. No, I'll take her to Skole, to the ghetto. I know a Jewish family there and they'll take her, I'm sure. They'll have to – I once helped get the husband out of a bit of trouble, and he still owes me.'

'When, though?' asked Teresa.

'Tonight,' he answered. 'We'll have to set off after supper.'

Malka could hardly eat a morsel of the evening meal. Teresa's eyes were red, and Marek and Julek stared at Malka without saying a word. Only Antek laughed and beamed when Malka kissed him goodbye. He was a special child, but he didn't understand that Malka was

115

frightened, very frightened. When she was sitting on the back of the bicycle with the wooden wheels once again, she felt in her pocket and held tight to Liesel. Only then did it occur to her that for the whole time that she had been in the house at the edge of the forest she had not played with the doll at all.

Their guide had brought them to a barn, and was going down into the village to get some food for them. Mendel Frischman asked him to look up an acquaintance of his father's, a man named Hersh Rapaport, who lived around here, and from whom they hadn't heard for a long time. Hungry and tired, they sat on the straw, huddled together to try to keep a little warmer after the cold night; and they waited. Minna had put her head in Hannah's lap and gone to sleep. Hannah stroked her elder daughter's brown hair and thought about the blonde hair of her other daughter.

She found herself in a strangely distant frame of mind, more like an automaton than a human being, a bit like the clockwork monkey that Issy had brought for Minna on one of his visits when she was still very small. Malka hadn't yet been born. The little tin animal had just stood there on the table, in its painted suit, a drum at its front and sticks in each hand. But when you wound it up it started to work and beat the drum, and the movement of its arms made it move slowly across the table top.

The guide returned without any food, but with an invitation from Mr Rapaport. The gentleman would be delighted to receive the group in his home, he had said. Those very words. The refugees looked at one another in amazement and disbelief; these were words from another world, one that they had left behind long ago.

'It could be a trap,' said Mr Waiss, but his wife shook her head and said, 'A bed! A proper bed with a mattress and sheets and everything.' Tears ran down her face and her husband took her hand and squeezed it.

They didn't discuss the matter for too long; the longing for a proper room and a proper bed and a meal sitting at a table was etched on everyone's face. Minna, lying with her head in Hannah's lap, opened her eyes and said, 'And a bathtub.' Maybe she hadn't been sleeping at all.

Reuben smiled at her, and Hannah said, 'Possibly.'

The guide took them in groups of two or three at a time down to the Rapaports' villa, which fortunately stood at the edge of the village, and could be reached without too much risk of their being seen. The host and his wife, a dignified elderly couple, stood at the door to receive their guests formally in a touchingly old-fashioned way. They were so clean and well-dressed that Hannah shrank back involuntarily, because she felt herself to be so grubby and wretched. The others, too, didn't look much better, and they seemed to feel it as well, because they behaved in an embarrassed, even clumsy manner, as if they no longer knew how to wipe their feet or how to behave in a proper house.

They simply washed their hands before sitting down, dirty and ragged as they were, at a laden breakfast-table and starting to eat, first hesitantly, not quite believing, and then increasingly heartily. 'Herrings,' gasped Mrs Frischman. 'It must be ages since I last ate herrings,' and her host and his wife invited her over and over again to help herself to more. Then they were taken upstairs, where rooms had been prepared for them. Hannah and Minna were given a room with its own bath, and a maid brought up hot water from the kitchen. 'Underwear,' said Hannah to Minna. 'We absolutely must wash our underwear.'

They got into the bath together. They had never done that before. Hannah would never have thought it possible that she would be able to undress in front of her daughter, but the days fleeing from Poland had clearly put an end to any feelings of embarrassment. The water was warm, her muscles relaxed, and suddenly Minna began to cry, as if her spirit wanted to relax as well. She cried uncontrollably, like a small child, and Hannah put her arms round her and had no idea what to do. She would have liked to cry with her, but she was the mother – she had to be strong to comfort her child. But that was no help. This wasn't the real world – her world had never been like this. The one she had had was lost, and now they were just vagabonds.

They stayed for two days in the beautiful villa with the carved wooden furniture, the thick carpets and the tapestries. Two days in which they ate and slept and tried to behave like civilized human beings. On the first day, Hannah had asked for some iodine, had sterilized some tweezers and a small pair of scissors, and treated the blistered feet of her companions. She had cut away the dead skin to remove the possibility of bacterial infection and had cleaned the wounds. Mrs Waiss had cried when Hannah had to deal with a seeping blister on her right foot.

On the last evening, before they left, they talked with their hosts over the evening meal about the position of the Polish Jews, and Hannah became suddenly angry, without knowing what had caused it. Perhaps it was the conspicuous wealth of the Rapaports, the fact that they were untouched by all the misfortunes that had affected

Jews all over Europe. She saw Mrs Waiss, who had been rich herself once, sitting there with her head bowed; she saw Mrs Frischman, who had been looking after her sister solicitously for the last few days; and she saw the men, who had been respected members of the community, but who in these surroundings seemed humbled and pitiful. Just like us, thought Hannah. She looked at her scratched and uncared-for hands holding the cutlery, and she looked across the table at Minna's hands, which were cutting up a piece of meat with her knife and fork and doing so deliberately slowly, so as not to betray how hungry she was. Suddenly she was overcome with a great pity for her fellow refugees, for her daughter Minna, and for herself. And for her daughter Malka, who was somewhere amongst strangers, alone and frightened.

She almost wept tears of pity, but then that feeling turned to one of fury. Hannah couldn't control herself any more, and said in a rather sharper tone than she had intended, 'The Hungarians feel safe while Admiral Horthy is ruling the country. But the Germans won't spare them and Horthy is no real protection. The Germans still need him for the moment, and while they do they'll leave Hungary alone and Hungarian Jews are safe. But it won't last for ever. The disaster will hit everyone. No Jew anywhere within reach of Hitler is safe. It's stupid to think otherwise.'

Her companions contradicted her, especially Mr Waiss and Mr Frischman, and Hannah wasn't sure whether they were doing so out of conviction or politeness, but she felt their reproachful looks. Even Minna nudged her with her elbow. Hannah hung her head in embarrassment and was cross with herself for not keeping her mouth shut. She was no less grateful to her gracious hosts than the others,

119

and she wished them well – they should live long and happy lives, a hundred years at least. But damn it all, they shouldn't feel so *safe*.

It was different in the ghetto, very different from the house at the edge of the forest. For a few days Malka walked around in a daze. The Goldfaden family, to whom Zygmunt had brought her, did indeed, after a certain amount of resistance, take her in, and they put a thin mattress on the floor in the hallway for her so that she had somewhere to sleep. They gave her food, but beyond that no one took any notice of her. If she hadn't had Liesel, she would have been completely alone.

Mrs Goldfaden worked in a clothing factory in the ghetto. Malka had no idea what her husband did, but he was away during the day as well. The children, two bigger girls and a boy who wasn't much older than she was, hardly spoke to her unless it was to send her out to the pump with a bucket to fill with water because the water supply to the house didn't work. The house itself, right at the edge of the ghetto, was small and poor-looking, like the other houses along the unpaved lane. On the main street of the ghetto, which led to the square with the pump, there were bigger houses, several storeys high and with a courtyard or two, with other houses standing nearby. There were people everywhere, all talking, swearing, shouting, crying and sometimes laughing.

Malka tried to understand what all these people did and how they lived, but the ghetto remained a mystery, as strange to her as the Goldfaden family. Maybe it was to do with the fact that most of the people here spoke Yiddish – the women at the pump, the children on the streets, the men selling things, the boys offering cigarettes or the women selling bagels.

The food Malka got didn't taste good and there wasn't enough of it, so that she was always hungry. But the Goldfadens themselves, apart from the father, didn't have much more on their plates. Malka thought with longing of the potatoes and cabbage she had eaten at Teresa's, or the goat's milk and the bread that Teresa baked once a month and that she would toast on the hotplate when it was hard and rub with garlic, and of the porridge that made your stomach feel so full and warm.

It was far easier to think of Teresa than of her mother, because Teresa knew where she was, here in the ghetto with the Goldfadens. But how would her mother find her? She mustn't think of her mother. Something in her head and in the pit of her stomach told her that she would be better off keeping clear of words like 'Mama' or 'mother', because then her thoughts did funny things to her. If by mistake she thought 'Mama' or 'mother', then the tears came to her eyes and she felt helpless and defenceless. That wasn't allowed to happen, because it was important that she should be strong and always able to work out what she should do in every situation.

If anyone asked her – which didn't happen very often – who she was, she no longer said, 'My mother is Doctor Mai', but rather, 'I am Doctor Mai's daughter'. 'Daughter' was a harmless word, one you could think or even say out loud without it knocking the breath out of you. Doctor Mai was a stranger, a woman in whose house she had lived once, a long time ago. The woman for whom that German officer had once played the violin, and who was in Hungary now, a long way from Lawoczne, and even further away from Skole.

Doctor Mai and her daughter Minna were in Hungary and she, Malka, was in Poland, and in Poland it was better to think about Teresa. She liked thinking about Teresa, even if her longing still sometimes brought tears to her eyes. Teresa.

Often she thought about Mrs Kowalski, who lived in the mountains on the way to the Hungarian border, especially when it was cold and she wore the grey pullover on top of her dress and her jacket. It didn't smell of mothballs any more, though. Malka was sorry about that, and she would often sniff for a long time at the sleeve to see if there was anything left of that smell. She had come to like it because in some way it reminded her of Mrs Kowalski.

When at night she lay on her mattress and wrapped herself and Liesel up tightly in the blanket Mrs Goldfaden had given her, so tightly that not a single finger or toe poked out – because she had seen rats around the earth-closet out at the back of the house – then she sometimes thought that she would go to Mrs Kowalski if she couldn't go to Teresa.

In her mind she ran through woods and fields, saw trees go past her as if she were really running through a forest; she saw brambles and raspberry bushes with red fruit on them shining through the green leaves and she was cross with herself for not taking careful note of the way the Ukrainian had taken them when they first left Kalne. Why had she behaved like a silly child and just trotted along behind them? Then she pushed those thoughts out of her head. She wouldn't even be able to find her way back from here to Lawoczne. All she knew was how to get from Lawoczne to Kalne, to the farmer Sawkowicz and his wife. She would certainly have found her way back to Teresa if it had been possible, but she would be a danger for Antek.

A restless unease was spreading over the ghetto, something Malka felt intuitively rather than understood. She felt the fear like a buzzing in the head, a twitching of the nostrils. She could smell the fear flooding into the ghetto like a poisonous cloud, filling the streets. Fear spoke from the eyes and the voices of the people, and made some of them become louder and more energetic, others stiffer and quieter. An operation, that was the word; all the signs were that there was going to be an operation. Certainly you saw armed German soldiers in the ghetto more often than before, on foot with dogs, or in cars. Then the Jews all disappeared into their houses and it was so quiet that the motors roared and you could hear the crack of the Germans' boots on the pavement. But anyone who had work still went off in the morning and came back in the evening, though their faces were more serious and tense than before.

Malka smelled the fear and felt the same restless unease come over her. She asked Yankel, the Goldfadens' son, what they would do if the Germans really did mount one of their operations.

He put his finger to his lips and led her into the bedroom. He stopped in front of the wardrobe, which was really far too big for the small room in which all five of the Goldfaden family slept, opened the big double doors, pushed some coats and other clothes to one side and pointed to the base.

'You can lift that board up,' he whispered. 'My father has dug out a hole in the ground underneath it. We spent two days down there when they last mounted an operation.' He rolled his eyes. 'It's horribly cramped and nasty and dark down there. Only two people can lie down at a time, so we take turns. Otherwise you just sit there and nobody can say a word or you'll give yourself away. There's a pipe sticking out of the ground in the patch of nettles behind the bedroom wall so we can get air. But it's really horrible.' He pulled a face and snorted. 'Come on now, and don't tell them that I showed you it.' By 'them' he meant his sisters, who were out in the yard washing clothes, and who now shouted to Yankel and Malka because their buckets were empty and they needed fresh water.

The next day the German operation started. Early in the morning cars with loudspeakers on them drove through the streets, and thunderous voices ordered everyone to stay inside their houses, even the work-detachments. The Goldfadens ran around, gathered food together and rolled up their blankets. Malka stood and watched.

'We can't take you with us, said Mrs Goldfaden quickly, without looking at her as she spoke. 'You must under-stand – there just isn't enough room or enough food. Get out, do you hear – get outside and hide somewhere.'

And Esther, the elder daughter said, 'With your blonde hair you won't stand out as much as we do.'

Malka plunged her hand into her pocket and grabbed hold of Liesel. She looked from one to another, but they all looked away as Esther took her by the shoulder and pushed her out of the door.

There wasn't a soul in the lane, nor in the main street. Malka crept along in the direction of the pump, keeping close to the houses. Sometimes she heard a car coming, and then she disappeared quickly into a yard and only came out when it had gone. Then from somewhere came the sounds of screams, shots, dogs barking and suddenly the noise of a lot of boots.

Malka was standing pressed against the wall of a house and didn't know what to do. Just as she was about to duck into a courtyard in the hope of finding somewhere to hide, she noticed the open window of a cellar, down low on the wall, at street level. It was tiny and she had to squeeze herself in backwards, but her feet landed on a ramp and she let herself slide down.

Only when she got to the bottom did she see that she was in a wooden-walled part of a cellar, and that the ramp she had slid down was a wooden chute used for tipping coal into the cellar. There was no coal in there now, but the smell of coal dust hung in the air and there were a couple of empty coal sacks in the corner. It was very quiet down there. All that could be heard was the Germans' boots, coming closer and closer.

She stood by the window and looked out. There were lots of Germans and they had dogs with them. Malka jumped down, crept into the corner and pulled the empty sacks over herself. Shots rang out and she put her hands over her ears. Suddenly everything sounded duller and further away. Only when she could hardly hear anything at all did she stand up and go to the window again. The boots had disappeared. She poked her head out cautiously and saw that people were being driven towards the square with the pump, guarded by armed German soldiers with dogs. Every so often the soldiers would shoot into the air.

Malka went back to her corner. She hardly dared to breathe. She squatted there stiff and immobile and lost her feelings – even her sense of time. She waited for ages, and only crawled out of the cellar when it was completely quiet. Her hands were black and her jacket had black smears on it; the hem of her dress was undone and it hung down. One of her foot-cloths had come loose. She bent down and tied it back in place.

A man ran past her. She thought she knew him – one of the beggars who sat around the pump. He shouted at her, 'Get over on to the Aryan side, girl – quickly, run!'

Without thinking, she ran down the street which led out of the ghetto to the adjacent Aryan district. It was a wide street which crossed another equally wide one. Malka saw a group of Jews coming towards her, being moved along by German soldiers with their guns at the ready. She looked away quickly and ran diagonally over the crossing to the far side. Suddenly she heard shots and turned round. The Jews raised their arms and fell down in the street – just like that, as quiet as rag dolls – and all that could be heard was the rattle of the machine-guns. She panicked. Not far away was a church; she could see the tower. She ran on until she reached the church, stumbled in across the stone steps and threw herself against the door.

It was dark in the church. There was a priest standing at the altar giving the sermon, and in the first few rows there were people attending the service. Malka knew how to cross herself, and she even knew the words of the *Hail Mary* by heart. She had been taught it by one of their maids, who had often taken her to church with her. She genuflected by one of the pews, crossed herself and sat down. She was shaking all over and felt sure that everyone in the church could hear how loudly her heart was beating.

Now for the first time, in the silence – broken only by

the deep voice of the priest – she felt fear. Fear crept out of the shadows of the choir stalls and came towards her. It came with the smell of the incense and filled her lungs. It fell in blue stripes of light from the high windows and it merged with the image of people who lifted their arms up and then just fell, dumb, silent as rag dolls.

The people in the church, mainly women, stood up to pray, and Malka did the same. She crossed herself when the others crossed themselves and murmured to herself when the others murmured, kneeled when the others knelt, and bowed her head when the priest blessed the congregation.

She sat and watched the people leaving the church. They looked so untroubled and Malka couldn't understand it. Not far from here, something horrible had happened. Not far from here, Jews had fallen like rag dolls on to the street, and these people here were quite calm and even smiling. An old woman with a blue headscarf looked her up and down for a long time, and Malka shrank down and tried to look very small. Then the woman went on and Malka relaxed – until the woman suddenly took her hand. She must have come back without Malka noticing.

'Come on, little one,' she said softly, as you do in a church. 'Come home with me. I'll find you something to eat.'

Malka looked at her. The woman was old; she had a friendly face with friendly grey eyes, as far as she could tell, and her voice sounded friendly too. Malka stood up. She had no choice. She couldn't stay in the church for ever.

Hannah woke up suddenly, still caught up in her dream.

She no longer remembered exactly what it had been about, just that she had been wearing a formal gown, the brown velvet one she had had made for Minna two years ago and which now no longer fitted her. In her dream she was wearing the dress, but she didn't look like Minna – not just because she was darker than her daughter, but because she was different in a strange and not easily definable way. Even in her dream she thought herself arrogant; she didn't need to wake up to remember that. She was walking down the street with Aleksander, walking and walking, and they ought long since to have arrived somewhere, but the street was endless.

When she woke up, she couldn't get Aleksander out of her head, and the whole day he walked along beside her.

'Who *are* these people you're associating with?' he asked her in that superior tone that she used to find so attractive. 'They're really not your sort, you know. You just have to look at them – grubby Jews, vagabonds, cowards who are just running away.'

She looked at her fellow refugees, then she looked at Aleksander and she thought: I imagined it would all be so different. I tried so hard not to be like them, not like these women and not like the men either. And what has become of me now? What will happen?

'And the way they speak,' said Aleksander. 'Just listen to their uneducated language!'

She turned her head to one side, looked him up and down and said, 'Shut your mouth and just disappear. I don't want to see you again. Not ever.'

Aleksander raised his eyebrows and left.

The old woman took Malka by the hand and led her

through two or three streets until they reached a grey and ugly block of flats, and climbed up to the second floor. Her flat was very small, and consisted of a kitchen and a tiny bedroom, really just an alcove in which there was nothing more than a bed and a wardrobe. The woman asked Malka her name, and then told her that she could call her '*Ciotka*' – 'Auntie' in Polish.

While Malka sat at the kitchen table, Ciotka cooked potatoes and fried some bacon. She herself ate almost nothing, and when Malka had eaten everything on her plate she pushed her own plate, still half full, over to her. Malka ate – it had been a long time since she had felt really full up. Ciotka didn't ask her any questions; in fact she said nothing at all, just murmured incomprehensible words to herself. After the meal she put a parish magazine from the church in front of her on the table and said, 'I'll be back soon.' Then she disappeared.

Malka read without understanding any of the words, and waited. She had to wait for a long time, because when Ciotka came back it was already evening. She brought a loaf of bread and some sausage back with her, and cut a couple of slices of it for Malka.

After they had eaten she told Malka to take her things off, and gave her a lime-green flannel nightdress that was so long that she could only walk if she lifted it up at the front and dragged the back along like a train.

While Malka lay in the bed with the huge, heavy eiderdown, Ciotka washed Malka's clothes in the kitchen and hung them on a clothesline over the cooker. Malka heard from the bedroom how Ciotka ran the water and how she murmured to herself as she walked backwards and forwards.

Malka took off Liesel's by now grey vest, got out of

129

bed and held it out to Ciotka. Ciotka laughed, took it, washed it and hung it with Malka's things. Then she undressed and came to bed. Her nightdress looked like the one she had given Malka, except that it was light blue.

She was so fat that the mattress sagged under her weight and Malka slid towards her. She smelled of soap. Malka lay there motionless, but then Ciotka stretched out her arm and Malka laid her head against her warm, soft shoulder. 'Sleep well, child,' said Ciotka and stroked her hair.

It was an odd feeling, being in bed with the unknown woman – like with Mrs Kowalski, only different. With Mrs Kowalski she had only noticed in the morning where she was, and then it was time to get up. Malka lay there, stiff and unmoving, and didn't know what to do, then suddenly Ciotka gave her a kiss and pulled her closer. And then Malka started to cry. Ciotka asked no questions, just stroked her hair until she fell asleep.

Even on the next day Ciotka said little, and that suited Malka exactly because she was afraid of questions and didn't want to talk or even think about what she had seen. After breakfast Ciotka washed Malka's hair and combed it, although that wasn't too easy. The last time Malka had combed her hair was when she was with Teresa. It tugged at her scalp when Ciotka tried to get the comb through it, and brought tears to Malka's eyes. In the end Ciotka took some scissors and cut away some of the really matted parts.

During the daytime Ciotka was often away and Malka was left alone in the flat. To amuse herself, and also to stop herself thinking about what would happen if Ciotka never came back, she read a book of Bible stories that she found on a shelf in the kitchen, and that gave her something else to think about. But Ciotka always did come back, and every time she brought something for Malka to eat, once even a piece of cake.

One day there was an unexpected knock at the door. Ciotka pushed Malka into the bedroom and into the wardrobe. When the door closed behind her and she was in the dark she heard the key being turned, and all the fear came back. Malka pulled a winter coat over herself and squatted there in the darkness, rigid with fright. First she thought it might be a neighbour – one of the other women in the flats, visiting Ciotka – but the longer she sat in the wardrobe the more likely it seemed that it must be a German who had come to get her. It smelled of camphor in the wardrobe and the smell tickled her nose and throat until she needed to cough. She held her breath in desperation and swallowed down the cough, choking it back until tears came to her eyes. When Ciotka came in, a long time afterwards, and opened the door to let her out, all she could do was cry.

The day after that, Ciotka took her to the window. The sky was grey and it had been raining, so the pavement was still wet. Ciotka pointed to a grocery shop a few houses further along, on the other side of the street. 'We mustn't go out of the house together any more or people will get suspicious,' she said. 'Go down now and wait for me over there. I shan't be long.'

Obediently, Malka put on her clean jacket. Ciotka opened the door and looked around. As there was nobody to be seen, she ushered Malka out towards the stairs. Malka went down the stairs and out of the main door. When she crossed the road she had to force herself not to look up at Ciotka's window. She was freezing, because the rain had brought the cold with it. She pulled her jacket round herself more tightly, and was annoyed that she had left her pullover in the ghetto. It was on her mattress, underneath her folded-up blanket.

Then she stood in front of the shop with her back to the street looking in the shop window. The glass was broken on one side, with strips of paper stuck on to hold the pieces together. There wasn't much to see in the window. A couple of brooms, a drum of washing powder and a few dusters, piled one on top of the other. Malka raised her shoulders, then relaxed them again. She was clean and her clothes were washed, and Ciotka had even sewn up the torn hem on her dress, so there was no reason why she should arouse any suspicion. She was just an ordinary little girl. No one could see by looking at her what she knew, what she was thinking, what she was feeling. Or what she had seen.

Ciotka crossed the street and took Malka by the hand. She took her back towards the church. Malka only realized when they came round a corner and she saw the stone steps leading up to the church doors. She quickly lowered her head so that she didn't have to look down the street that led to the ghetto, but she had already seen that there were no people thronged together at the corner and no Germans with raised rifles standing there.

Malka stared at the ground, at the raised cobblestones, which were slightly bowed upwards in the centre. Some were broader and higher than others. They were still damp from the rain and shining a grey-blue colour as if they were reflecting the sky. The damp slowly seeped through her foot-cloths. Malka watched the cobblestones slip away behind her as she stared downwards; she saw Ciotka's legs, her feet in solid, brown shoes with the toes

132

worn down and the lace of the right one knotted several times.

Ciotka was wearing thick, dark-blue woollen socks similar to those that she had put on Malka that morning, before she had tied new foot-cloths on top of them. The socks were far too big for her feet, but they felt rough and warm and good. 'You'll have to turn the toe part up,' Ciotka had said, 'so that they don't get twisted and hurt the soles of your feet.'

Suddenly the brown shoes stopped, and the grip on Malka's hand relaxed and then let go. Her hand fell down limply and hung at her side, helpless and unwanted, and Malka missed the warmth she had been feeling. But then Ciotka took her hand again and Malka saw the lined hands that had washed, combed and fed her, put a rosy apple into her own hand and close her fingers round it. 'You can go home now,' said Ciotka. 'It's over. The ghetto is quiet again now.'

Malka felt Ciotka's hand stroking her hair once again, and then she saw the brown leather shoes from behind – the raised-up piece at the heel and over that the rolled-up, dark-blue socks, the creased, broad, dark skirt with her calves lighter beneath it – as Ciotka went up the steps. She saw the grey apron-strings tied across the broad backside, which moved as she walked. Her waist was invisible – and to see that, Malka would have had to raise her head. The church door opened, the shoes turned to one side, the skirt disappeared with a quick swing and the door closed.

Malka stood there alone, the apple in her hand, and only now dared to raise her head. Keeping close to the houses she moved along towards the corner of the street. As she went, she put the apple into her pocket and kept her hand protectively over it. It had happened on the other side of this street; here, in front of her and to the right, people had fallen and had just lain there. Don't look, she thought. Keep your eyes on the other side of the crossroads, on the street leading into the ghetto. And then she did look across.

There was nobody lying there on the street. A tall boy was going round the corner pulling a handcart with two sacks on it. Over there, too, the rain had washed the stones clean; the lines of earth between the slabs looked a bit darker than the others, but maybe that was just her imagination.

Malka crossed the street. Two German soldiers were strolling up and down on the pavement. Their rifles were hanging over their shoulders and they had cigarettes in their hands. They looked like perfectly ordinary men. Every so often they would stop and chat to one another. One laughed out loud, perhaps because his comrade had told him a joke. He looked, at least at first glance, a bit like Veronika's father, but he was an enemy. All Germans were enemies, though she hadn't known that before. Malka took a few steps forward, then stopped, but the Germans didn't look in her direction. She waited until they turned the other way and had their backs to her, and then she ran into the street that led to the ghetto.

The ghetto was like a ghost town. Just occasionally someone rushed across the street and disappeared into one of the houses. It was strangely, eerily quiet. If Malka stood still and closed her eyes she could still hear all the noises that had been there before, roaring in her ears – shouting, yelling, sometimes laughter – and then these noises died away, and there was only the sound of the

German boots on the pavements and a shot ringing out. Malka opened her eyes in fright, and there it was again, that eerie stillness. There wasn't even any birdsong – nothing at all.

Even at the pump, where women were usually bustling around with their buckets, there was no sign of anyone, just a couple of men standing by a doorway, down the road, talking. Malka couldn't understand them, because their voices didn't carry that far, but they were moving their hands, pointing in one direction, then in another, turning their heads away and then back towards each other. The arm of the pump, which was normally in permanent and noisy squeaking motion, was just hanging down. The stone basin in front of it was full.

Malka bent over and looked into the water. Her own face looked back at her. She put her hand to the edge of the basin and let it sink into the water. Circular ripples broke up the image of her face and tore it into pieces. Malka was frightened and stood up. She turned round and let her eyes wander over the whole square. There were no signs of the usual beggars, of the children who used to run around amongst the grown-ups – there was even no sign of the bagel seller, who always used to sit in the entrance to the big house right behind the pump. But who would she have sold her bagels to, when there was no one there?

Malka ran to the Goldfadens' house and was out of breath when she got there. The door was open, but there was no one in the kitchen, nor in the bedroom. She hesitated briefly, then, still hesitatingly, she stretched out her hand. The wardrobe doors creaked as she opened them. There were coats and dresses hanging on the hooks, just as they had been on the day Yankel had shown her the hiding place. The loose board was in place, just where it should be, and there was nothing else different.

She knocked on the board, as if she were knocking on a door, gently at first, then louder. There was no sound in reply. 'Mr Goldfaden!' she shouted. When there was no reply, she tried to lift the board but couldn't, either because it was just too heavy for her, or because it was jammed somewhere, possibly bolted. She climbed into the wardrobe, put her ear against the wood and held her breath so as to hear better. Nothing, not even breathing.

She took a gulp of air and the loud noise she made startled her. 'Mr Goldfaden!' she shouted, and hammered with her fists on the board. 'Mrs Goldfaden! Esther! Rachel! Yankel!' Nothing. Then she ran out into the garden and found the pipe hidden in the weeds that Yankel had told her about. She peered down it, but everything was dark. Again she shouted, 'Mr Goldfaden! Mrs Goldfaden! Esther! Rachel! Yankel!' and then she put her ear to the pipe. When she heard nothing, she went back into the bedroom.

She stood there for a long time staring into the cupboard, in which there were a few coats and other garments, left over, just like herself. Why shouldn't she take a coat? It had got colder and her summer jacket wasn't warm enough, and even the pullover didn't help. She tried the two coats on, but they were far too big. In the end, she decided on a jacket made of a dark-green felt-like material which came down to her knees. It made a good overcoat for her, but she had to fold the sleeves back quite a bit. She opened the little door to the compartments for underclothes and stuffed into her coat pockets two pairs of socks and then two pairs of woollen knickers, because she suddenly thought she heard the

136

voice of the lady doctor, telling Zofia the maid that changing your underwear regularly is important. Then she found something that set her heart racing: dark-blue trousers. She put them on, stuffing her dress in at the top. The trousers weren't even too big for her; they must have been Yankel's. They felt warm and comfortable.

As she left the bedroom in her clean woollen knickers and the new trousers, with the coat over her arm, she thought to herself, No, it isn't stealing, it's just taking. It wasn't her fault that it had got colder. She closed the bedroom door firmly.

In the hallway was her mattress. She lifted the blanket and there was her pullover, the one from Mrs Kowalski. As she pulled it on over her jacket she told herself that she would never leave the house without her pullover, nor the new coat. She fell down on to the mattress, covered herself with the coat and felt in her jacket pocket for Liesel, the only comfort she had left.

But Liesel wasn't there, nor was she in the other pocket. She must still be at Ciotka's. In an instant all her pleasure at the new clothes just disappeared, and this loss seemed unbearable, worse than anything she had experienced so far.

All she had in her pocket was the apple. She turned it over in her hand, smelled it, ran her finger over the smooth, cool skin and cried. She couldn't remember ever having cried so hard.

They were walking along a mountain track when it happened. The path wasn't particularly narrow, and the slope wasn't particularly steep, and so Hannah did not, at first, think that anything serious could have happened when she heard a shout behind her, and then the sound of agitated voices. She turned round. Mrs Waiss, Mrs Kohen and her husband were standing at the edge of the hill path, leaning over and waving their arms. Hannah ran back. Some distance below them lay Mrs Frischman, lying awkwardly across a rocky outcrop, clearly hurt. Her husband was sliding down the slope and had nearly reached her. He bent over her, spoke to her and then looked up and shouted, 'Doctor! Please can you come here?'

It wasn't as easy as all that. The slope wasn't particularly steep, but it was slippery, and as Hannah slid down it on her backside she kept having to pull down her skirt to keep her legs covered. She almost imagined that she could feel a disapproving look from Mrs Waiss when at one point her knees were actually uncovered. Then she bent over Mrs Frischman.

The woman had abrasions on her legs, arms and face, but that wasn't the reason she was groaning in pain. Her left arm was stretched out in an unnatural position, and even through her clothes Hannah thought she could see the distorted outline of her shoulder joint. She kneeled down by Mrs Frischman and felt the woman's left shoulder, making her shout out in pain. Hannah felt the top of her upper arm, which had been pushed backwards out of its socket. 'I'm sorry,' she said softly. 'This is going to hurt you even more, but I have to do it. You've put your shoulder out of joint.'

She was shaken – re-setting a dislocated shoulder under these conditions was no easy matter, especially as she had no way of telling whether the muscles and ligaments were torn at all, but she had to get it back into place. She called to Mr Waiss, the strongest of the men. While he was sliding down the slope Mr Frischman helped her to turn his wife on to her back and get her coat off. The woman clenched her teeth, but couldn't keep back a scream when Hannah pulled her coat over the damaged arm. Hannah kneeled down, undid the woman's blouse and pushed it aside. Luckily Mrs Frischmann was slim and not very muscular, so that the upper ball-joint could be seen clearly. She hadn't broken anything. Hannah told the two men to hold her still. Mr Frischman threw himself on to his wife's good arm, while Mr Waiss held her round the body.

Hannah put her foot into the woman's armpit, grasped the dislocated arm a little above the wrist and pulled on it with all her force. The woman screamed in agony, but Hannah pulled and pulled until she felt the joint give a slight turn and then move forward, until it snapped back into its socket with a clicking sound. 'Done it,' she said, and sat down on the ground, her legs trembling.

Mr Frischman, who had gone as white as if he had been the patient himself, wiped the tears from his wife's eyes. 'Thank you, doctor, thank you.'

Hannah got Mrs Waiss to throw her down two headscarves and used them to bandage the arm tightly to Mrs Frischman's body.

'Is it any better now?' she asked.

Mrs Frischman tried to smile, but could only manage a grimace. 'It's not as bad as it was,' she said. 'Thank you.'

'And now we have to get her back up,' said Hannah. The men pushed and supported the woman up the slope and Hannah crawled up behind them on all fours. It took quite a while before they were all up there again. Hannah was trembling from the effort. Minna smiled broadly at her, visibly proud that her mother had played such an important part in the drama.

After a very long pause they moved on. Mrs Frischman was clearly still in pain, but it was decreasing and she walked supported by her husband, so they made slow progress. But they couldn't simply stay where they were in the mountains. 'I'm afraid it will hurt for a few days,' said Hannah. Mrs Frischman nodded and said that she would cope. Hannah smiled at her. This wasn't her professional smile, the one she always had ready. It was a smile of real affection for this woman, who, in spite of the pain that she was obviously suffering, was showing so much courage.

Malka stared up at the ceiling of the hallway, which was crumbling in various places, and tried not to think of anything, but it didn't work. Besides, she was gradually getting hungry and thirsty, and the smell of the apple was getting to be unbearable. She pushed it into her jacket pocket where by rights Liesel ought to have been – Liesel, who was probably lying comfortably in Ciotka's bed, where Malka had slept. Or on the kitchen table. Malka simply couldn't remember where she had seen her last.

There was still some water in a bucket in the kitchen, so she got a mug and drank some. But wherever she looked she couldn't find anything to eat, just a small amount of flour. She tipped the flour into a bowl and mixed it with water to make a kind of lumpy porridge, and because she couldn't find any sugar she put some salt in it. It tasted vile, and she had to struggle to get it down, and with the struggle came the tears again. She didn't want to cry; she mustn't cry.

She put on her coat and left the house, then walked through the ghetto. She didn't know why, but she just kept moving as if she were bound to find something.

Her foot coverings were already wet when it started to get dark. The empty windows, with no lights burning in them, stared down threateningly at her from the fronts of the houses and frightened her, so she went back to the Goldfadens' house. She opened the bedroom door, knocked again on the board at the bottom of the wardrobe, but there was still no sound. She looked at the beds. The house was empty, so no one could stop her sleeping in a proper bed. But there was always the wardrobe, which got more and more worrying. Maybe they were all lying dead down there under the floorboards – Mr and Mrs Goldfaden, Esther, Rachel and Yankel. Perhaps they had all collapsed, as silent as rag dolls, down there in their hiding place.

As she left the bedroom, Malka saw that there was a key in the door. She took it out and locked the door from the kitchen side. Now she felt safer. She dragged her mattress into the kitchen. It was small enough to fit under the table. It was a cosy place, almost like a cave, and from there could keep an eye on the door. There was, once again, no electricity in the ghetto. Malka was scared of lighting the oil lamp, so she lay there in the dark on her mattress, wrapped up firmly in her blanket, as she had always done. The coat, neatly folded, lay beside her.

She felt alone, abandoned, unwanted.

She had always known the people around her, and she had known the names of practically everyone she had met in Lawoczne, and could point out the houses where they lived – not just of neighbours and friends, but even of people that she had had nothing much to do with. Since that day when she had had to go to Kalne suddenly because Doctor Mai, who had still been her mother at that time, said she had to, she was forever seeing new people who seemed to come from nowhere and disappear back into nowhere, a never-ending series of people. She no longer even remembered what many of them looked like – the Ukrainian, for example, who took them from Farmer Sawkowicz to Mrs Kowalski's. She remembered Mrs Kowalski very well, though. Wlado, too, who had carried her on his shoulder and had sung. But the faces of the Kopolowicis were already fading. She thought about Shlomo and Yossel, who hadn't taken her with them, and felt something like anger. But that was only because she was trying to stop herself from thinking about Teresa. Instead she thought about the Goldfadens, and this made her very sad because they were not there any more. She hadn't liked them particularly, but they were a link to Zygmunt – and Zygmunt was the connection to Teresa.

Malka tried to think about nothing, to wipe out the pictures. She was sure that she could manage to do that in the end – she would just have to make an effort and practise, practise, practise. But she couldn't do it. Even as she fell asleep she could still see faces which flew past her as if they were autumn leaves blown past her by the wind, one face after another.

Hunger woke her up in the morning. She crawled out from under the table. There was still some of the flour-gruel left over from the night before. Cautiously she put a spoonful into her mouth, but once again the revulsion rose up like a bitter lump, blocking her throat. She

142

poured in some more water, tipped the now liquid white stuff into a mug, held her nose and drank it down – just like she used to drink cod-liver oil when she had been ill, and the lady doctor had thought that she needed strengthening.

In the dawn light the ghetto looked less menacing than it had at twilight. She set off towards the pump to drink some fresh water and get rid of the horrible taste. When she turned into the main street she saw in front of her, just a short way away, two boys, Shlomo and Yossel. Excited and happy, she ran after them and grabbed Yossel by the arm, laughed and shouted, 'Hey, how did you two get here?'

The boy turned round. It wasn't Yossel and the other one wasn't Shlomo.

'What do you want?' asked the bigger boy. 'Clear off.' His voice was rough and he said the last words in the same tone of voice as Shlomo had.

Malka dropped her hand; all the pleasure drained from her face and body and suddenly she felt very weak. She leaned against the wall and looked at the pair of them as they walked on, then followed them from a safe distance until they went into a building and into an apartment. She waited in the hallway, hidden behind the stairs until they came out and went into the next apartment. She went up a flight of stairs and decided not to lose sight of them. When they came out this time one of them was carrying a loaf of bread. Malka leaned over the banisters.

The bigger boy saw her. 'What do you want?' he asked with his mouth full.

'I'm hungry,' said Malka.

The boy laughed. 'Then go and find yourself something

to eat. After there's been an operation it's not too hard to find food. And stop following us around like a dog – we don't want a girl with us.'

Then they both disappeared. But they were right. It wasn't hard, that day, to find something to eat. It took a while before Malka plucked up the courage just to go into a strange house and search a strange kitchen for something to eat, but when she did she found plenty. On lots of the tables the breakfast was still there from the morning of the operation. The milk had gone sour and the bread was hard, but anything was better than the floury gruel.

Malka spent the whole day going through the apartments and houses, eating what she could find. She looked around in the rooms, too, considered the beds and wondered which apartment she might like to move into, or which bed she would sleep in. Beside one bed was a little book of Bible stories, similar to the one she had read at Ciotka's. She put it in her pocket, even though she could hardly imagine a time when, as she had done before, she would be able to sit down and just read.

In a cupboard she found a pair of child's boots. They were too small for her. There was a knife in the kitchen drawer. Patiently and with much effort she sawed off the toe-caps and took the foot-cloths off her feet. Her wounds had healed up now – the scabs had come off the scars, but the new skin that had formed underneath still looked lighter, and it was tender. When she took off the socks Ciotka had given her she had to fight against the tears once more. She put the boots on. They were brown, brown as the earth, and her toes stuck out like little mushrooms. This made her laugh. Unfortunately the shoes were so narrow that they only fitted her if she wasn't wearing socks, so she put the socks and the foot-cloths into her coat pocket and went into the next apartment.

By evening she was stuffed so full that she felt sick. She went back to the Goldfadens' house, lay on the mattress and wondered what she could do with all the food she had seen. A mixture of porridge-oats and jam would surely taste good. In a kitchen in one of the houses on the main street, on the first floor, she had seen a jar still half-full of strawberry jam that she hadn't been able to eat.

A whole ghetto full of empty houses. And it was all for her; she could take what she wanted. In her mind she went from one kitchen to another, from one room to another. And although she was still not feeling too well, she laughed happily.

The happiness didn't last long, and the next day it was over. Malka was standing in the kitchen with the straw-berry jam when she heard a noise and quickly ran out of the apartment. Suddenly the ghetto was full again. People were coming from everywhere, some with luggage, some without – women, men, children, old people, they all poured into the houses. Dumbstruck, Malka watched as everything changed from one hour to the next. And then she was so frightened that she felt sick. What about the Goldfadens' house? And her mattress?

The house had been taken over. At least ten people had squeezed into the kitchen and the bedroom, and were trying to sort out their things. Malka stood at the kitchen door, looked at them and didn't dare say any-

145

thing. But she saw that her mattress had been taken out from under the table.

'We're full,' said a man when he eventually noticed her. 'Go and find somewhere else. You can see that we're more than full here.'

Malka turned and left. She was miserable and depressed. If only I had stayed in the house, she thought, then maybe they wouldn't have come in. If the Goldfadens had still been there, if there hadn't been an operation, if Ciotka had kept her with her, if the Germans hadn't told Zygmunt to get rid of her ... all those 'ifs'. And then she thought of the worst 'if' of all. When she had heard the noise earlier on, if only she'd thought of taking the jam with her. Half a jar of strawberry jam!

Malka sat by the pump and watched as more and more women and children came along with buckets to fetch water – different women and children, strangers to her. She hadn't really known the ones before, but at least she had recognized their faces.

Slowly it got dark, the streets emptied and no one had asked Malka to come with them. No one had said, 'Come on, child, we've still got a bit of room.' And no one had asked, 'Are you hungry?'

She *was* hungry. She was very hungry indeed. But the thing that was worrying her most was that it was nighttime and she had no idea where she could go. Then she remembered the coal cellar where she had hidden during the operation, the coal cellar in a house on the main street. Because there were no street lights she had to grope along the walls of the buildings on her knees in order to find out by touch where the cellar window was, and it took a long time before she found the small opening. She squeezed in backwards, felt with her feet for the chute, slid down and buried herself in the corner with the sacks. She was alone. She had never been so alone. Alone in a little coal-hole in the middle of a strange and dangerous world.

Liesel, she thought, if only I had Liesel with me. But she had lost Liesel. Malka pressed herself further into the corner. Perhaps Liesel had run away because she was missing Veronika. Perhaps even now she was walking along on her cloth legs with the coloured socks, down the road from Skole to Lawoczne. Don't get tired, Liesel, whispered Malka. Keep on walking, Liesel. Sometimes you'll find a stream, and there you can drink. Drinking is more important than eating, Liesel, that's what the lady doctor always said. Maybe you'll find some brambles; you can eat them. Don't forget to eat. I think there are still brambles, Liesel, but you won't find any more raspberries. Brambles make your mouth dark red, but they taste good. You have to be careful with mushrooms. You mustn't eat the really white ones with the ragged bit round the stem – they're poisonous. But you know that – you know as well as I do which mushrooms you can eat. Keep moving, Liesel, keep moving. You'll soon be in Lawoczne. Today or tomorrow or the day after, you'll find the house where Veronika lives. You'll be safe there, everything is clean there. That's where you've got your own bed and you can sleep warm and cosy. There's enough to eat there. They speak German there.

At last they reached Mukačevo. Their hiding place here was a small storage warehouse, no longer used, which belonged to a Jew. It wasn't far from the station, surrounded by old corrugated iron huts in which hardly anyone lived. They arrived early in the morning when it was still dark and the streets were completely empty. They were tired from the overnight walk, but not as exhausted as usual. After the days of recuperation with Hersh Rapaport and his wife they had coped with their exertions relatively well. Only Mrs Frischman was still pale and spoke little.

Hannah was relieved when she saw the town, because somewhere here Malka would be waiting for her. She took Minna's hand and said, 'Today we'll get Malka back.'

Mr Stern, the Jew who owned the warehouse, had bread and cans of hot coffee sent to them, and a bag with dark-red apples, which they fell upon hungrily, even though they tasted rather sour. In one corner there were three mattresses piled up, and next to them a heap of blankets. 'The women can have the mattresses,' said Mendel Frischman, and Reuben nodded. Mr Waiss and Mr Kohen kept quiet, though they clearly found it rather hard to play the role of gentlemen and to nod in agreement.

Hannah had watched this, and was surprised how the little scene had amused her. We haven't forgotten our roles in life after all, she thought, never mind what situation we might be in. She suggested that they sleep in shifts, first the women, then the men. Waiss and Kohen protested weakly, but then gave a relieved nod. Firm rules of behaviour are not a bad thing, thought Hannah, even if they do get on your nerves sometimes. Without civilization we'd be fighting over the mattresses by now and the strongest would win. Long live a decent upbringing! She thought the same thing as they went, one at a time before breakfast, to the water-tap and drain in the corner of the warehouse, and the others, without prior discussion, discreetly sat with their backs to the tap each time.

Hannah lay down between Minna and Mrs Waiss. Minna went to sleep at once, but Hannah lay awake, too agitated to sleep. Minna's elbows dug into her ribs and she turned over and found herself lying face to face with Rachel Waiss. The woman's face was pale; she had dark rings under her eyes. Her pupils were big, the eyelids swollen, red and inflamed – she had conjunctivitis. Hannah closed her eyes to avoid the other woman's searching look, but she didn't turn her face away. When she opened her eyes again Rachel Waiss was still looking at her. Then she smiled, and Hannah smiled back. The woman had never been a friend, but the dangers and exertions they had gone through together had brought them closer.

After she had slept for a few hours Hannah was woken up by Minna: 'Mama, get up, it's the men's turn now.'

Hannah got up. She wanted to go to Doctor Rosner at once, to see if Malka was already there. 'I'll come too,' said Minna, but Hannah looked at her daughter and turned down the offer. "You stay here and rest properly,' she said gently. She didn't want to say how awful Minna was looking. She had washed, it is true, but her clothes were dirty, her hair hung down in rat's tails over her eyes, her face was puffy and her lips chapped. Hannah was afraid that with Minna they would stand out too much.

Hannah walked along beside the track to the railway station, because she knew the way from there to Doctor Rosner's house. She'd visited him twice in the past few years, and he'd occasionally sent her medical supplies when they'd become scarce in Poland. There were lots of people about on the streets and things looked so normal, so everyday, as if there were no such things as German operations and deportations.

But once or twice Hannah saw a man or a woman whom she assumed to be refugees too. It wasn't just their shabby clothes – there were poor Hungarians in Mukačevo too – but their cringing attitude, their rapid movements and the way they seemed to be looking quickly all around themselves. Hannah forced herself to walk calmly and straight-backed, and concentrated on looking forwards, always forwards. A woman with a particular and immediate goal, heading there without fear or worries. A woman on her way to pick up her little daughter from acquaintances of hers, where she had been for a few hours on a visit.

Mrs Rosner, whom she remembered as a friendly woman and a generous hostess, opened the door and stepped back in alarm. 'It's me,' said Hannah softly. 'Doctor Mai, from Lawoczne.'

Mrs Rosner shook her head and tried to shut the door again at once. Of course, Hannah knew that she didn't look much better than her daughter Minna, but she hadn't expected a reaction like that. She was suddenly furious, furious with these people who were just going on living their everyday as if nothing had changed. She put her foot in the door and hurled herself against it with all her weight.

Mrs Rosner gave way, shocked. She gestured helplessly with her hand and led Hannah into the living room, where her husband was sitting at the table drinking coffee. There were pastries on a plate in front of him, large and shiny, with a dusting of sugar.

'Where is my daughter?' asked Hannah. 'Did Chaim Kopolowici bring my daughter to you?'

150

'Who's Chaim Kopolowici? What daughter?' asked Doctor Rosner.

Hannah saw very clearly not only astonishment in his face, but also repugnance and fear. But she couldn't take any notice of that, nor did she want to. She explained quickly how she had left Malka behind. She spoke rapidly, rushing the words out, and she had to stop several times because she was so disappointed and couldn't hold back the tears.

The Rosners shook their heads. No, they had heard nothing of any Chaim Kopolowici, and nothing about her daughter Malka. No, they would never have taken in a child anyway in times like these; they were only glad that their own children were grown-up. Doctor Rosner assured his lady colleague that she should not imagine for a moment that things were all right in Hungary; the Arrow Cross Party was becoming increasingly powerful, especially here in Mukačevo, and it was important to be careful and to keep one's head down. No, they couldn't do anything for her, much as they regretted it. Doctor Rosner then fetched from his surgery a little bottle of tranquillizers, pressed it into Hannah's hand and said, 'Try not to get too worked up, my dear colleague, it doesn't do any good.' And that was it. Then she was out in the street again.

Now all she had was the address of Kopolowici's sister. She asked how to get to the Jewish quarter, and by now she no longer cared what she looked like or what people thought of her. But Kopolowici's sister knew nothing about Malka either, and hadn't had a letter from her brother for weeks. The last time she had seen him had been at Passover, much earlier in the year, when she,

151

her husband and children had gone to Pilipiec for the holidays.

With her remaining strength Hannah dragged herself back to the warehouse. Then she sat upon the ground and wept.

DECEMBER, 1943

Malka was sitting by the pump when a woman went past her who looked like Teresa. It wasn't Teresa, of course it wasn't – what would Teresa be doing in the ghetto anyway? But she looked like Teresa. She was wearing a blue hat with blonde hair spilling out underneath. In one hand she was carrying a bag and she was leading a child, a little girl, by the other. The woman walked past Malka without looking at her; the little girl said something, and the woman laughed.

Malka got up and followed the pair of them. They went along the main street, then turned into the street with the little wooden tower, then into the first lane on the right. The woman was wearing a long, full-skirted dress, which swayed as she walked. The girl at her side had a blue dress and long brown stockings on. Whenever she said something to her mother she turned her head so that Malka saw her profile with the fine, small nose. But she could not make out what the little girl said, not even what language she was speaking, because the wind blew the words away before they reached Malka's ears.

They went into a narrow, two-storey house with a small front garden, and their outlines were silhouetted for a moment very clearly against the dark hallway; then the door closed behind them.

Malka stood and stared at the door for a long time without moving and without thinking. As if she might be able to make the door open again just by looking at it. Nothing happened. Malka crossed the street and sat down on the ground opposite it. Her eyes were fixed on the windows of the house on the other side of the street, and behind one of them must be the woman she had seen. There were four windows, one each side of the front door and two more upstairs. The little front garden was overgrown with weeds and at the side grew a slight, leafless tree.

Malka had not thought of Teresa all day, but now the memory was there, so clear that it hurt. Teresa was standing in the kitchen peeling potatoes, cleaning carrots and chopping leeks and onions for the soup. The soup smelled wonderful. Antek was playing on the floor with the cloth ball that Malka had made for him, and Zygmunt, Marek and Julek sat at the table. 'Wouldn't it be nice if Malka were here as well now?' Zygmunt was saying to Teresa as she put a bowl of the steaming soup down in front of him on the table. He started to eat and said between mouthfuls, 'But you know the Germans.' Julek wrinkled up his little nose, which was so turned up that you could see his nostrils, and announced, 'When I'm grown-up I'll chase the Germans out and then Malka can come back.' 'It's a pity that it will be such a long time till you're grown-up,' said Teresa. And Zygmunt sent Marek out to bring the goats in from the field into their shed, where Teresa would milk them. And she would sing while she was milking them.

Malka saw a shadow pass behind one of the windows, the one on the right of the doorway. The shadow didn't stop to look out of the window to see Malka. Maybe next time, she thought, and started to undo her plaits. Her hair was a bit matted, but it was pretty. She knew that because the lady doctor, in whose house she had once lived, had told her so often enough. The prettiest hair in the family, she had said, not platinum, not flaxen and not reddish, but proper gold.

Malka lowered her head and the hair fell like a curtain in front of her face. She thought about the day when the lady doctor had taken her along to the German military administration to try and get a relocation permit for her grandfather, so that he could move in with them. Before they turned down the street where the German office was, the lady doctor had suddenly stopped and undone Malka's plaits. She had told her to shake her head a couple of times and then had run her fingers gently through her hair. 'I want them to see how pretty you are,' she had said. And sure enough the German officer had made out a relocation permit for her grandfather, but then he hadn't come after all because he wanted to stay with her Aunt Golda.

Malka lifted her head and shook out her hair, then looked across the road. The house became blurred before her eyes, the windows turned into dark holes and the garden became distorted. The weeds grew up into a forest and the door opened and Teresa came out, stepping lightly with her skirt swaying, came over to Malka, picked her up and said in that happy voice that Malka had almost forgotten, 'Come on in – I've made some soup and I know how much you like it.'

Malka wiped away the tears with the back of her hand. The house was clear again, and now it looked forbidding. Teresa, or the woman who looked like Teresa, was nowhere to be seen and the windows and doors stayed firmly shut. People walked past without taking any notice of her. A small beetle scrabbled on her leg. She picked it up, looked at it and watched its tiny legs twitching, and put it down again on the pavement.

Twilight came, and then it got dark. A light came on in the right-hand window of the house across the street. The woman who looked like Teresa was clearly visible for a moment, then she closed the curtain. A little bit later, lights appeared in the upstairs windows, and in one of them a white-haired woman came and drew the curtains. They were drawn in the other by a man whose hair colour she couldn't make out. Somewhere a baby was crying. Malka stayed there, sitting on the ground in the dark street until all the lights went out in the house opposite.

That night she ate the apple Ciotka had given her. She had kept it for so long as her most treasured possession. Now she had nothing.

They stayed for three days in Mukačevo, because the man who was going to take the group on had not yet turned up. Stern had had extra mattresses and blankets sent, so that they could all sleep at the same time. Hannah didn't care; she moved about as if in a nightmare – she couldn't sleep and she couldn't eat. Part of it, of course, was to do with the filth. She couldn't understand how her companions came to terms with the unhygienic conditions so easily. Even Minna ate anything she was given without pulling a face, because hunger now drove her to it. Here in the warehouse, she again often sat with Reuben in a corner. Hannah sometimes asked herself what they talked about – she herself had never talked much with men, not even with Aleksander – but then she forgot this train of thought again. In fact it suited her, because Minna was friendlier and more helpful now than she had been for the past few months. Sometimes she even laughed, and looked, at least for a moment, as happy as she had been during the time Zofia was with them. At least Hannah didn't have to worry about Minna at the moment.

In the morning, after their meagre breakfast, Hannah went to Doctor Rosner, even though both the man and his wife had begged her fervently *not* to come there again, not to endanger them, and to have some consideration for their advancing years. If absolutely necessary, they said, she could ring them. Hannah took no notice and felt little sympathy for these people who were sitting well-fed and content in their own home with no concern for the problems of others, just for their own skins. She did not give way, and only left the house when both had assured her over and over again that they had heard nothing of Malka. Then she went to Kopolowici's sister, who also begged her not to come again. The sister swore on her life that she would bring the child to Stern's warehouse if her brother were to turn up.

Hannah didn't know what to think. She didn't dare return to the warehouse for fear of Minna's questioning looks, or the would-be comforting comments of her travelling companions. Instead she walked for hours through the town, not even trying to be careful, driven by her thoughts and by her conscience.

She should not have left Malka behind; surely somehow they could have managed to get there themselves without the group, and after all she had made it from Lawoczne to Pilipiec. Perhaps she had just misread the situation, as so often before. And time and again she

157

asked herself whether she had done it for fear of the difficulties, for fear of the problems, the police or the danger. Or whether she had maybe left the child behind just to make things easier for herself. And another thought was beginning to gnaw at her – the thought of Issy, Malka's father. What was she to say going to say to him when he asked about his little daughter? At least I've saved one of them for you while you were happily picking oranges and milking the cows out there in Palestine. Where were you when we needed you? But it didn't help, and time and again she saw her father's words in front of her, in his spiky handwriting: *When someone is in trouble, you can't abandon them.*

She felt that she had done everything wrong. If Issy were here now he would help her. If she hadn't stayed in Poland because of her job, then presumably she, too, would have spent the last five years in Palestine. It couldn't be worse than here, even though all that talk about a Jewish state and the Land of the Patriarchs rather got on her nerves. My father, she thought, comes from Kraków, my grandfather from Skawina, and where my great-grandfather was born I no longer have any idea, except that it was somewhere in Poland. But however you looked at it, if she had gone off with Issy to Eretz-Yisrael as he had wanted her to, then Malka would still be with them, and none of this would have happened. Issy had had a travel document from the British Mandate authorities, and his wife and children could have gone with him. But then she hadn't believed that Hitler would invade Poland. Or she hadn't wanted to believe it, because she was scared of the idea of living with Issy as man and wife. And now it was too late.

Hannah wandered through the streets. She stood for

hours at the station waiting for a train to come, and when one arrived she ran along the platform looking at the people getting off. Sometimes she saw in the distance a blonde child and ran forward full of hopes, but she was disappointed every time. Malka didn't come.

The third night, Hannah slept like the dead after she had decided to travel by train back to Pilipiec the next day and fetch Malka, no matter how dangerous it was.

But the next morning, when it was still dark, the guide came along very early indeed and made them get up so that they could be on their way. Sleepily they all got out of their beds and started to get their things together – except Hannah.

'I'm not coming,' she said. 'I'm going to Pilipiec. I have to fetch Malka.'

'And what about Minna?' asked Shmuel Waiss. 'Doctor, be sensible.'

The others talked to her as well. She could write to Kopolowici from Budapest, and once she had arranged to get herself some false papers she could even take the train back and fetch Malka.

Hannah felt herself being torn both ways. She looked at Minna, who hung her head and wept. Hannah decided she had to go on with the group. Whatever she did, it would be wrong. You can't abandon a person when they are in trouble. But what were you supposed to do when there were *two* people in trouble – one here and one there?

The days passed. In the mornings, at the crack of dawn, when the cross-pieces of the wooden frames in the windows in the house opposite were just about visible, Malka would leave her cellar, and she only came back when it was dark. She didn't want to be seen because she was frightened that someone might try and take her hiding place away from her. There was no other way in. Of course, there was a door connecting her coal-hole to the other part of the cellar, but it was locked.

At first Malka had thought about trying to break it open by kicking it or by throwing herself at it until the lock gave, but then she decided that she wouldn't even try. She needed the door as protection against the threat of the rest of the house, against all the people who lived there and had access to the cellar and who could drive her out – people who didn't know about her, and who mustn't find out. The cellar was her home, her fortress against the horrors of the night.

In the mornings, straight after getting up, she went to the pump and washed her hands and face in the basin. For the first few days she had tried to get the coal dust out of her coat and trousers, but she had given that up long since – it didn't matter what she looked like because there was no one there to look at her; she was alone. Washing was different. Washing was hygienic, that's what the lady doctor had always said. When she felt herself to be more or less clean, Malka set off through the ghetto. By now her boots had stretched and they fitted even when she was wearing socks, which was good, because her feet stayed warmer.

She had also discovered by now that she wasn't the only person living alone; there were lots of others. She realized this from the fact that she always saw the same set of faces, people who stood around, like her, either by the pump or begging in front of the shops. They had no family. They had no table where a woman would put a

160

pot of food. Just like her they almost certainly didn't even have a pot in which to cook food.

She got to know every street, every lane, every court-yard, every earth-closet and every passageway. That was important, because when Germans came into the ghetto, which luckily wasn't too often, she could listen out for the direction that the sound of their boots, their voices or their cars was coming from, and then escape into the nearest courtyard that had a way through to a neigh-bouring one, and from there into a parallel street. The Germans couldn't be in all the streets at the same time. Often Malka would run up the stairs in an apartment block until she got to the very top, and crouch down in a dark corner until the sounds told her that the Germans had gone again.

She had even discovered a shed where a group of boys lived, though she never found out how many of them there were, because the number seemed constantly to be changing. All she knew was that the boys she had thought were Shlomo and Yossel belonged to this group. She had heard them talking to other boys, and found out their real names. The bigger boy was called Micki, the smaller one David. She was always pleased when she saw these two because then she felt less alone. At least, that was how she felt at the beginning, but as time went on it wasn't so important to her because she had become used to being alone. All the same she went past the shed once, twice or three times a day, keeping a decent distance, and kept an eye open for Micki and David. When she saw them, that was satisfaction enough for her.

No, the loneliness wasn't so bad; the hunger was worse. She could think of nothing else. Hunger filled her mind every minute of every hour, and when she woke up in the morning she felt that she had been hungry in her sleep and had even dreamed about being hungry. Hunger became the very centre of her thoughts, however much she did her best not to think of food. Hunger made her chew her fingernails and suck her fingers. At night on her coal sacks she even chewed at her toenails.

Since that heavenly day after the operation, in the empty ghetto, she had been living off what other people gave her. If she saw a woman come out of the bakery – where she particularly liked to stand – or out of some other shop, she would stand in their way and say, 'I'm hungry.' Often, she would just get pushed aside – in fact, that was what happened usually, but from time to time someone would give her a piece of bread. Whenever she got something to eat she chewed it slowly and thoroughly before she swallowed it, because she thought that the bread would get more liquid the longer she chewed it and she would have to crap less.

Crapping was the worst. Crapping meant that the body was emptied and that should only be allowed to happen when there was something to fill it up again. She didn't have much idea of how her insides worked. Of course, she knew that she had a stomach and guts, but she didn't know what they looked like; she just knew with absolute certainty that they had to be full. And she felt it too, because after she had crapped, her hunger was especially great. She imagined that her body only kept its shape because it was somehow stuffed. If it got empty she would collapse like a flour sack that someone had cut a hole into. Malka didn't want to lose anything, nothing at all, and she wanted to keep everything inside her body that could fill her up.

The days went past but Malka didn't count them. She

162

divided her days into 'food days' and 'no-food days'. The food days had names, and were like rays of light in the grey of the flowing days of hunger, which she just called 'other days'. One day, a day she particularly liked to remember, was called 'loaf-of-bread day'. A woman had given her a whole loaf of bread when she had stood in front of her and said, 'I'm hungry.' When the woman asked, 'Where is your mother?' Malka had started to cry because she didn't want to hear that word, and because the hunger hurt so much and because despair just flooded over her.

Without a word the woman had pressed the loaf of bread she had just bought into Malka's hand and gone back into the bakery. Malka had hidden the bread under her coat and had run away before the woman could change her mind.

Another day – it must have been two or three days after she had come back from Ciotka – she had named 'turnip day'. She had gone into the western part of the ghetto, where amongst the houses there were a few gardens – well watched-over – in which potatoes and vegetables were growing. That day a man had been digging potatoes in one of the gardens, and another man was digging turnips. Two women had been watching them, one of the women with a baby in her arms. Malka was quite sure that the Jews harvesting these potatoes and vegetables were not the ones who had planted them in the spring, because the German operation had come in the middle.

Malka had stood at the fence and watched until the man digging the turnips had come over to her with an angry face, pressed a turnip into her hand and told her to make herself scarce. The turnip had been bitter-tasting, but she had had something to chew on for a long time. And even now, when she shut her eyes she could still see the scene, so clearly and so vividly that she could smell the dank earth and the bitterness of the dried-up greenery. The man digging the potatoes pushed his spade into the ground so far that when he turned it up, the earth and the whole withered plant came up with it. Then, when he twisted the spade over, the earth fell off just by the hole and the potatoes rolled out, round and gold-coloured. The man bent down, felt in the loosened earth and picked out every individual potato and put them all into a sack. Then he shook out the plant, from the bottom of which hung one or two tiny potatoes, and he took these as well. The sack had been half full when the other man had told Malka to clear off.

There was also an 'egg day', although Malka was a little bit uneasy when she remembered that one. A woman had been sitting by the pump on a stool with a basket of eggs in front of her. Malka watched her for a long time, then she slipped unnoticed behind someone who was buying three eggs. When the customer fished out a handful of coins to pay for the eggs, Malka had ducked down, reached between the customer's legs, grabbed an egg from the basket and run away.

She hadn't looked round and didn't know whether anyone had chased her; she had just run on and on, through courtyards and lanes until, by an involved detour, she reached the Goldfadens' house. There she sat on the ground and took the egg, which luckily had not broken, out of her coat pocket. She had tried to make a hole in it with a sharp stone, but it didn't work. Only when she had tapped the egg carefully until it cracked could she break away a piece of the shell and drink the egg, sucking it out the way Zofia used to do.

Now Malka felt her legs trembling, and her stomach hurt because of the hunger. But that was her own fault; she had been thinking about food again. And by now it was dark. This was one of the 'other days'. Before she set off home she went to the pump and got a drink. On the way, she found an earth-closet and pissed. Luckily she didn't have to crap.

They went the last stretch of the way to Budapest in a truck, hidden under sacks that smelled of hay. Once upon a time Hannah had loved that smell, but now it was too much associated with flight, with exhaustion and collapsing as if one were dead. She longed for other smells, cleanliness, soap, disinfectant. The smell of hay made her feel sick.

'It smells like it used to in Lawoczne,' Minna whispered to her. 'Remember how it smelled when the farmers had just cut the hay?'

Hannah squeezed Minna's shoulder to show her that she knew what she meant. But she didn't want to think about Lawoczne. She didn't want to think at all. The fact that she was unable to move in the truck was hard for her, and she felt as if she had been deserted like a small child. She had pins-and-needles in her feet and hands, and had to make strenuous efforts to stop herself screaming. Any amount of effort, any exertion would have been preferable to this, just lying there helpless. Not moving meant death. She started to tremble, it was like a seizure that began somewhere inside her and spread out over her whole body.

'What's the matter?' whispered Minna, alarmed.

'Mama, what's the matter with you?' When Hannah didn't answer, Minna put her arms round her mother and hugged her tightly.

Hannah let her; she couldn't do anything to stop her anyway. That's me, she thought. Always moving, always pressing on from one day to the next, without a real goal, as if I were possessed. I've always been like that. Driven but aimless. That's what's behind all this, my aimlessness and that relentless urge forward. That's how I got through my studies, that's how I fell in love, married, had children. That's how I did my job, and that's how I sacrificed Malka.

Minna held her tightly and stroked her until she calmed down and the trembling stopped.

When the truck stopped and they got out it was night. They were taken into a house, up the stairs – lots of stairs – to the attic. There they found a kind of dormitory with camp-beds and mattresses and people everywhere. Many of them were asleep. Others bombarded the newcomers with questions about where they had come from, whether they had heard anything of this or that, whether it was still possible to get across the border. Hannah didn't answer. She just flopped down next to Minna on a mattress, helpless, incapable of thought, more like a sack full of old rags than a human being. She hadn't only lost her child; she had lost herself.

It had been snowing. The snow had only lasted a few days, then it had disappeared again, although it hadn't got any warmer. Quite the reverse. The cold was biting and wicked. Malka was freezing. She lay in her hiding place on a sack, with the other sack wrapped round her legs. She tried to imagine that she was in Lawoczne, lying in her own bed. But it was hard to imagine a soft mattress and warm bedclothes when you were lying on a hard floor and freezing.

She pulled her legs up and wrapped her arms round them to give herself a little more warmth, or maybe to preserve what warmth she had, but it didn't help. Even her feet were cold, although she had pulled on all three pairs of socks that she owned, and the rough skin on her hands and arms was itching. She tucked her hands into the trousers to warm them on her naked skin. Her thighs felt bony and strange, as if they didn't belong to her – strange hands touching strange legs – but it was still pleasant to rub her legs. It's a pity you can't bend right forward, she thought, because her bottom would be a lot softer and maybe warmer. She pushed her hands behind her and then pulled them out again. Her bottom was icy cold.

She curled up even tighter, pulled her jacket over her head and tried to warm her body with her breath. But although her breath felt warm on her hand, it was cold by the time it got to her chest. She was happy to have the coat and the trousers – of course she was happy about that – but it would have been better if she had had a coat with fur lining like the one hanging in the cupboard in Lawoczne. A lovely warm coat – leather, with coloured patterns on the outside and fur on the inside.

She had a very precise memory of the day the lady doctor had bought it for her, at the start of last winter. Malka had put it on and danced about the house, then she had run out through the little garden down to the stream. In the field on the other side of the stream Tanja was walking along, pushing a pram in which her eternally runny-nosed little brother was sitting. Malka stepped on

167

to the wide plank balanced across the stream that served as a bridge. Later on she couldn't say why she had done that, since Tanja was no longer her friend and hadn't been for a long time. Nor could she say why she had suddenly stopped in the middle of the plank and started to bounce up and down. All she remembered was how proud she had been of her new coat. She hadn't even minded very much when Tanja started shouting 'Jew-girl, Jew-girl,' because Tanja only had a kind of shawl made out of an old grey horse-blanket.

Malka bounced and bounced and laughed and laughed and then she stumbled and fell into the stream, which was deep and fast-flowing after a long, rainy autumn. She tried to scream, but the icy cold wouldn't let her and not a sound came out of her throat. She was carried along by the current, gulped for air, flailed around with her arms, heard Tanja screaming, and then the water was thundering in her ears, loudly, more and more loudly. She was spun around, her head met some kind of obstruction, she felt a blow but no pain, and then she was hurled onwards.

When she came to, she was in bed, with the covers up to her neck. Under the bedclothes she was naked, and when she moved her legs she felt the rough surface of warming-bricks and the scratch of their sharp edges. Later on she found out that the neighbour, the kosher butcher, had pulled her out of the water, alerted by Tanja's screams. When the lady doctor and Minna had asked her, Malka pretended not to remember anything, but when she shut her eyes she could see herself standing in the middle of the plank-bridge, pleased and proud – and then the fall into the water, the fear. A sense of shame had stopped her from talking about it, a feeling that she had done something wrong and been punished for it. But now, here in the cellar, she simply thought longingly of the coat with the soft fur, and the memory of the warming-bricks in her bed brought tears to her eyes.

She didn't want to think about Lawoczne – better to think about the next German operation. Last time she had been too stupid to think about getting hold of some warm blankets for herself. Next time would be different, because by now she'd found her way around and knew what was what. She wouldn't be able to get a mattress through the window, but an eiderdown to sleep on and one to put over herself would be wonderful. She could just stuff them through the window. She mustn't forget. Or maybe two or three blankets as a mattress? After the last operation there had been lots of blankets lying around, but then all she had been able to think about was food. She hadn't known at the time what cold was really like.

The next morning Malka woke up stiff from the cold. She sat up painfully. Her legs and arms were numb with the cold and hurt when she moved them. Nevertheless, she stretched out and moved her limbs until she felt the blood flowing again. She had to force herself to climb out of her hiding place, force herself to go to the pump and drink the cold water and then run around until she got a bit warmer and the pains in her arms and legs got a bit less. Luckily her boots were now so worn that they still fitted her even if she put on two pairs of socks, one over the other. Malka walked between the pump and the garden where the man had been digging the potatoes, back and forth, back and forth. It was easier not to think of food when she was walking. She knew too well that thinking about food made the hollow feeling in her stomach so much worse. But she remembered precisely how the porridge and goat's milk had tasted at Teresa's. And chicken soup at the Kopolowicis'. And the food at the wedding party and the bread and sausage with Ciotka. If she concentrated she could even feel the actual taste in her mouth.

She bent down and picked a few blades of grass that were growing in a crack in the pavement, and put them into her mouth. The taste of the grass drove away the memory of all the other things she had eaten, so long ago. She chewed and chewed until the tough stalks had turned into a bitter wet mass, and then she swallowed it.

Around midday, when it got warmer, she sat by the garden fence. Amongst the weeds there was a plant growing that looked like a wild carrot, and you could eat wild carrot roots – Tanja had once shown her. Malka pulled the plant up, carefully wiped the roots and put them into her mouth. At first all they tasted of was earth, but then slowly the carrot taste came through, sweet and full of memories. Teresa had had carrots in her garden. She would have harvested them all by now, and would have made wonderful dishes with them, adding potatoes and a few onions and a little bacon. Perhaps even now Antek was opening his mouth, and Teresa was putting in a full spoonful and saying, 'One spoonful for Marek, one spoonful for Julek, and one spoonful for Malka,' and Antek would have beamed when he heard Malka's name.

Malka shook herself, grabbed at the weeds and pulled them up, chewed at leaves and roots and swallowed it all until she felt sick and had to go to the pump to wash away the sick feeling with cold water.

It wasn't until she felt better that she smelled them. Near the pump was a woman roasting chestnuts over a little coal-brazier to sell them. Malka was drawn by the smell, captured, pinned down. Suddenly, there was nothing else in the whole world, and all her desires and longings were concentrated on those fragrant chestnuts.

She crouched down on the ground in front of the woman and put her hand out. The woman shook her head, but Malka didn't give up. She breathed in with her mouth wide open as if she could get nourishment from the smell alone. It entered into her being, flowed with the blood into her legs and down to her fingertips. She couldn't think of anything else, couldn't look at the woman; she could only smell. Her outstretched hand began to shake and the square all around her began to blur.

Then she felt something hot on the palm of her hand and she opened her eyes wide. Three chestnuts – the woman had given her three chestnuts. A present. Malka closed her hand over this treasure and stood up to go and find somewhere to eat them without fear of being disturbed. Saliva gathered in her mouth, she swallowed and then swallowed again. The chestnuts were so hot that she had to change hands. The woman smiled and Malka smiled back.

That was the 'chestnut day'.

They were in a house that belonged to the Jewish community, and which provided a base for several Jewish organizations. The refugees were housed in the attic, but it was made clear to them right away that they wouldn't be able to stay there long, since more refugees were expected. However, people would do their best to

171

provide false papers for them. Hannah didn't want to stay anyway, as the hygiene arrangements were hardly better than during their escape, the food was terrible and the lack of space oppressive. But before she could make any plans, she had to get Malka back. She went from one floor to another, from one office to another, telling them about Malka and begging the people to get her daughter back. Until one of them said, 'You're not the only mother to have lost her child, so please stop going on about it. We have plenty of other problems.' And when she heard that she went back to her grubby mattress and lay down.

Slowly, Hannah regained her self-control. Only sometimes did she think, somewhat awkwardly, of the journey in the truck. If Minna looked at her, she avoided her eyes. But that didn't happen much anyway, and Minna was miserable and depressed because the group was breaking up and she would be separated from Reuben. The Frischman and Kohen families were the first to move on, heading for Istanbul, where Mr Frischman had business contacts. Perhaps they would start again there, he said.

Mr and Mrs Waiss had relatives in Hungary, in Szeged, who were due to come in the next few days to collect them. Reuben said that he wanted to stay, but Mrs Waiss insisted that he went with them. 'I promised your mother I would look after you like my own son,' she said. 'Do you want me to betray her?'

Hannah saw the way Reuben looked across at Minna, and saw her daughter look down. Children, she thought, did they really think they could just stay together under circumstances like these? But she felt too empty, too drained to comfort her daughter. When the time actually came to say goodbye she could say nothing, although she, too, was sad and downcast. Even though they had had hardly anything to do with each other earlier on in Lawoczne, it was still hard to accept that she would never see these people again. Minna cried. Reuben cried as well.

One morning when Malka went to the pump she saw a dead child lying in the street, the lower part of the body in the gutter and the upper part on the pavement. She saw what looked like an abandoned bundle of rags from a distance, but somehow she knew at once what it was. Of course she had seen dead people in the ghetto before; suddenly they would be lying somewhere in the street and Malka would either make a detour or walk past looking the other way. But this time it was different, this time she could see from the size that it was a child. She didn't want to see the dead child, but still she went up to the bundle as if drawn by an invisible cord. She didn't know what it was that drove her there, whether it was curiosity or fear or just the feeling that she had to face the worst. It was better if you knew for certain, so that it didn't come as a huge shock to you if some time it caught you unprepared.

And then she was standing in front of the boy. She knew him – that is, she had seen him often, because he belonged to the group with Micki and David, but mostly he went around the ghetto on his own, in a coat that was far too big and boots that were far too big as well, so that he moved along with a kind of shuffling progress. He was lying there in an unnaturally twisted position, his broken legs on the roadway, his arms on the pavement, outstretched as if they were pleading for something, his face towards the sky. His eyes were open. Malka noticed now for the first time that they were hazel-coloured, with long lashes. His mouth was open too, as if he were screaming, but no sound came from his mouth.

Malka stood there and stared at the boy. Any dead people she had seen in her earlier life had always been old. And nicely laid out, with flowers, and their hands folded over their black clothes. Like Zofia's grandmother, to whose funeral Zofia had taken her and Minna.

She saw that picture in front of her, a picture which had been frightening for her at the time, but now seemed peaceful and calm. The old lady lay in a coffin, surrounded by flowers and with a cross in her folded hands. Her jaw had been tied up with a white cloth and her face, with its sunken cheeks, looked almost as if she were trying to smile, as if she were pleased about being dead. And after all, she had done her own dying, and this boy had not.

Malka realized that she kept looking at the checked scarf the boy had round his neck. The scarf looked so warm that she thought the boy couldn't have frozen to death – not with that scarf – so it must have been something else. But she didn't care what he had died of; his face had become just a pale blob above the scarf, and his arms no longer seemed to be spread out because they were pleading, but seemed to say: take the scarf if you like, I don't need it any more.

But still she hesitated. She didn't know how you touched a dead person. She had touched dead rabbits and dead birds, but they had fur or feathers over their skin. The boy had tied the scarf so firmly round his neck that she would have to touch him to loosen the knot. She looked again into his hazel eyes and thought, you could have undone the scarf before you died – you know what it's like here. Then suddenly she understood why the boy's coat and boots had been so big – it was because he had taken them from a dead person, a grown-up dead person, an old dead person. Because dead people still have everything, coats and boots and scarves, but they don't need them any more, so you can take them. There you are, she said to the boy, you knew that. So why didn't you loosen the scarf so that I could just take it?

She had hesitated for too long, because suddenly she wasn't alone any more. People were standing around her looking at the boy. A woman said, 'He can't have been more than ten. These are really bad times.' A man said angrily, 'What do you mean, bad times? It's not the fault of the times – it's those damned Germans.' And he bent over, unknotted the scarf and pulled it away from under the boy's head. The head moved and fell to one side, and its open mouth touched the filth of the street. Malka walked away, disappointed. Again she had been too slow.

Later, sitting by the garden fence again, she squashed a snail with a stone. Slowly, and without feeling anything. The shell broke with a crack and a rustling noise, the snail rolled up, and only stopped moving when Malka had squashed it completely.

Hannah was always on the go. She sought out every possible aid agency and was sent from one to another, but nobody could tell her how to get Malka back. She telephoned Doctor Rosner every day, having decided to get on his nerves so much that he would make contact with Kopolowici.

On the third day, late in the evening, she found herself with someone called Nathan Hecht, who was, so people had told her, very influential, with connections to the government. Nathan Hecht ushered her into his office. She sat down on a leather sofa. She had lifted the back of her skirt so that it didn't get crushed, and now the leather felt unpleasantly cool on the strip of bare skin at the top of her legs. The stockings that the organization had given her were too short for her.

Nathan Hecht listened to her story, then said that he knew plenty of people who traded on a 'per head' basis, that being the term they used in Hungary when they meant smugglers who specialized in getting people across the border. 'Please, Mr Hecht, please help get my one little head back to me,' she begged. 'I'll work and pay you back all the money.'

'The money isn't so important to me,' said Nathan Hecht. 'It would be a pleasure for me to help such a beautiful woman.'

Hannah hung her head. The words sounded so unbelievable, so strange. She knew perfectly well how thin and run-down she looked. But still, it was nice to hear something like that.

Very late in the evening, when she got back to the place where she was staying, Minna was crying. She had been worried. 'I thought I might never see you again,' she said.

Hannah put her arms round her and said, 'We're going to get Malka back, it's going to be all right.'

But it wasn't all right. Nathan Hecht was, she was told, 'not available' when she went back to see whether he had made any progress. On the third or fourth time she tried to see him, the housekeeper handed her some money – one hundred Hungarian pengö – and said that the gentleman did not wish her to bother him again.

Hannah felt more ashamed than she had ever been in her life, but she needed the money, so she took it.

The next day she went with Minna to Erzsebet Street, where she had been told that she would find the Palestine Office. The people there promised to keep their ears open to find out if anything could be done about the child, but that these days it was very difficult to find a child, because so many had gone missing. And they asked what she was planning for her other daughter, and suggested they try to find her a place on the Youth-Aliyah, the rescue programme for getting children out of Europe to Palestine, to Eretz-Yisrael.

'No,' said Hannah. 'My daughter is staying with me.' She took Minna's hand and dragged her out of the office after her.

Minna followed dumbly. But when they got out into the street she suddenly stood still and said with a new, hard edge to her voice, 'But I want to!'

'What do you want?' said Hannah. 'It doesn't matter what you want – you're staying with me until we get Malka back. Do you really think I want to lose another daughter?'

Minna looked straight at her. 'You never change,' she said. 'Everything always has to be the way you think it ought to be. It doesn't matter to you what I want.'

Hannah raised her hand.

'Go on, hit me!' said Minna with suppressed anger in her voice. 'Hit me, then.' Her face was white and her eyes dark with fury. Then she said, 'I want to go to Palestine. I want to go to my father. I want to get away from here. And if you don't let me go, I shall die. Then you won't just have Malka on your conscience.'

Hannah dropped her arm. It hung helplessly at her

177

side. Then she nodded, turned round and went back into the office. Minna followed her.

'I want to go to Eretz-Yisrael,' said Minna to the man at the desk. 'Put my name on that list. Besides, my father is there.'

'That will help a lot,' said the man. 'What is his name and where does he live?'

Minna's name was put on the list.

Both of them were silent on the way back. At some point Minna said, quietly and without any note of triumph in her voice, 'Reuben wants to go to Palestine as well. He doesn't want to stay with his aunt and uncle. I'll see Reuben again there.'

Hannah didn't answer, and suddenly she felt very old and quite exhausted. She merely thought: right, so he *was* just a poor relation of those two.

Then came the day when the Jewish Committee gave her a set of false papers, according to which she was Catholic, a refugee from Poland. She and Minna were to leave Budapest to go to a place called Korad. There was a camp for Polish refugees there, where she was to take up a position as a doctor.

The day before she left she heard from Doctor Rosner, who had been in touch with Kopolowici's sister, that Malka had been taken back to Poland. His voice sounded indistinct and a long way off, but Hannah understood every word. 'Kopolowici couldn't find out any more than that, just that the child is in Poland.'

JANUARY, 1944

Time was like a great grey cloud into which Malka was sinking, without her feet ever touching the bottom. Everything seemed to be interminably long to her. Days and nights just stretched out and were hardly different from one another because the hunger never went away. It was a feeling that she never became hardened to, never became used to. Hunger and cold determined her days; hunger and cold determined her nights.

And then she developed a fever. It began so slowly that she hardly noticed. At the start it was just a feeling of warmth – almost pleasant, if you ignored the feeling of tenseness in the skin around the face. But every day the fever got a bit stronger, and now she couldn't ignore it. I mustn't get ill, she thought. You can only get ill when you live in a proper house with a proper bed, with somebody like the lady doctor around to give you medicine and cold compresses.

Malka didn't stay lying down, not only because it was too cold in her cellar, but also because then it would be true that she was ill. As long as she was on her feet, everything was all right, more or less. She was also afraid of being alone, afraid of the fear that she must not allow herself to have. She had to walk, to put one foot in front of the other, and above all to drink, to keep on drinking.

I'm not ill, thought Malka on the way to the pump. I can still walk – that's a good sign.

After a few hours she really did feel better. Her skin still felt taut and hot, and her stomach hurt, but she went her usual way, as she did every day, with her head bent down, staring at the ground. Her field of vision had changed, and now she really only took in small details. Only rarely did she raise her head and look at the fronts of the houses, or the sky, or sometimes people. It was as if she didn't want to see anything. On the other hand, her hearing had become much sharper – she had acquired big ears, perceptive and movable as a hare's. They picked up any noise. Especially the sound of boots, or German voices. Those sounded like the crack of the coachman's whip, something she had always found so funny in Lawoczne. But then she hadn't known anything, certainly not real things. In those days she had sometimes sprawled on her back in the grass looking at the sky and thinking up stories about the clouds.

Now she didn't bother about the sky; only the ground interested her. Her eyes were good, and she could see things that were invisible. Like thick roots, buried deep in the earth, roots that you could eat. Or potato peelings lying hidden under a pile of paper and rubbish, which someone, for reasons she could not imagine, had actually thrown away.

A few days earlier she had even seen a coin under the accumulated mud in a gutter, invisible to everyone. But her eyes were good, and she knew that she just had to dig into the dirt a bit – and then there it was in front of her, a silver coin. It was a foreign coin; she hadn't recognized it. She picked it up reverently and carried it off to the bakery.

The baker had looked at the coin for a long time, then he had taken a loaf of bread, cut it in two and given her half. That had been a ray of sunlight in the grey of the ever-passing, hunger-determined days. It was the 'day of the bread-coin'.

For two days Malka had been sitting from morning till night by the pump, not far from a group of men who were gathered around a coal-brazier, because it had got colder again after a few days of milder weather. Malka had chosen her place carefully, just far enough away so the men wouldn't chase her off, but near enough to get at least some of the warmth. She was hungry. She felt as if she had been hollowed out, as if she consisted just of skin with nothing at all inside it. On top of that she had a funny sort of stomach-ache, down in the bottom part, a pressure and a pulling and a turning-over and a griping. She hadn't crapped for days.

The warmth of the brazier reached her face and took the edge off the cold wind, which had suddenly come up. She stretched out her hand and moved her stiff fingers. One of the men sitting by the fire kept looking across at her, but she avoided his glance. Just don't chase me away, she thought; this is a good place, I want to stay here. She crept into herself and made herself invisible. She had learned how to do that. You had to shut your eyes and just creep into yourself, into your own inside, then nobody could see you. She assumed that from outside she would look like a stone or a rag doll, even though she was so empty and hollow inside. Every time there was a strong gust of wind she was afraid that she might be blown away into the air, and at the same time she wished that it would happen.

She saw herself flying through the air, over the ghetto and over the Aryan district of Skole. But however much she tried she couldn't pick out Ciotka's house from all the many houses, nor, strangely, could she even see the church that had saved her. The wind carried her in the direction of Lawoczne. She knew that, even if she didn't recognize the roads and villages and woods beneath her; it just had to be taking her to Lawozcne.

There was the forest and the hut at the forest's edge. She could see Teresa standing in front of the house looking up at the sky. Teresa shaded her eyes with her hand and then suddenly let it drop. 'Marek!' she called. 'Julek! Come and see! Isn't that Malka flying up there?' Marek and Julek came running along and stared up at the sky with their mouths open as Malka whisked past them like a cloud and waved. 'Where's Antek?' she shouted down. 'I'd like to see Antek.' But Teresa, Marek and Julek didn't hear her. They just waved and waved and soon they vanished behind the trees.

Then she flew over Lawoczne. She saw the house that she used to live in, the little garden, the stream, the hill with Kalne behind it. The hills beneath her got higher, the wind whistled in her ears and she became dizzy. But then she could see Mrs Kowalski's little farmyard; she could pick out the house, the cattle-shed and the barn. And behind it the field with the two cows and the calf. The calf had got a lot bigger.

'Let me down,' Malka begged the wind. 'Please let me get down here.' If she couldn't go to Teresa she wanted to go to Mrs Kowalski. But the wind hissed and whistled: *to Hungary, to Hungary.*

At that moment Malka felt a hand on her shoulder and opened her eyes. The man who had been looking at her bent over her and held out a packet wrapped in newspaper. Malka's nose had become just as sensitive as her eyes, and through the newspaper she could smell bread and onions and a boiled egg. I must say 'thank you', she thought as she tore off the paper. But the man had gone back to sit with the others and was talking to the man next to him. He had a wide face and a large nose, big eyes and a big mouth.

I must take note of that face, thought Malka as she started to chew. I must never forget it.

Strangely, the stomach-ache didn't go away, even after she had eaten the food.

The Polish refugee camp was as bad, though no worse than Hannah had expected. A few hundred people were living on the edge of the town in barrack-like buildings. The sanitary arrangements left something to be desired, but the food was adequate, even if a bit low in protein for children and old people. Polish and Hungarian aid organizations looked after the refugees; above all, they had medical supplies, more than had been available in Poland in the last few years. Hannah had a room to use as a surgery and a nurse to help her.

The administrator of the refugee camp had asked her about her experience when he interviewed her on arrival, and also whether she, as a woman, would be able to cope with looking after a camp with so many people. She had concealed her annoyance at this arrogant question, had looked at him coldly and said, 'For years I worked as a regional medical officer and I can do everything from midwifery to major surgery. In an emergency I can pull teeth, help deliver a calf or castrate a bull.'

He had laughed in a slightly strained manner.

'Castration probably won't be called for here, but you might need your experience with teeth.'

Hannah threw herself into the work. She spent the mornings in the medical post, a kind of emergency hospital where the most serious cases were brought and looked after by volunteers, then in the afternoons she held a surgery or visited patients where they were living. There were all the usual diseases, dysentery, colds, infections, wounds. What annoyed her most was when strong, healthy men would try to get her to give them a sicknote, so that they could get off work. And every time she had to treat a child of Malka's age, it gave her a jolt. Apart from that, she enjoyed her work. For the first few days she was still very worried about giving herself away with an unguarded word, but people treated her politely, even respectfully, and she slipped more and more easily into her new identity as a Polish Catholic.

She had been allocated a small room with a single bed, in which she and Minna both lived and slept. To be crammed in like that with her elder daughter was not something she found very pleasant, although she did not admit this to herself. She noticed only that she was putting off her house calls until late in the evening, so as not to have to go back to the room where Minna was lying on the bed reading novels that she had borrowed from the Polish library. She read like someone possessed, perhaps so that she didn't have to speak – as if it were an addiction, reading one book after the other indiscriminately. Hannah knew that she was suffering from the separation from Reuben, and though she said nothing, she resented the fact that she wasn't suffering because of Malka.

During the day Minna worked in the kitchen where

they got the food ready for the sick and the old. It was only with some reluctance that she had taken the job, but she was aware that a young Polish girl ought to make herself useful, and the alternatives – looking after small children or the sick – seemed very much worse to her, so working in the kitchen was preferable. She got up every morning and went off to work, but she wasn't prepared to talk about it. If Hannah asked her how her day had been, she shrugged her shoulders and picked up a book. Even when Hannah warned her to be careful, to say little and not to give herself away, she just shrugged and buried herself in a book again.

It was a strange, tense kind of normality in which they were living – a stolen normality based on lies and deceit. During the day, when she was working, Hannah could keep her mind off things, but hardly had she been back in the room with Minna for a moment when the tension returned.

Both of them avoided talking about Malka. Nor did they talk about Reuben.

The next German operation came. Just like the last time, cars with loudspeakers drove round the ghetto, and just like last time Malka smelled the fear. She had had bad dreams, perhaps because she was feverish, but at any rate she was awake early and was already sitting near the pump when she heard the first cars and the first words of German. She knew that she would have to get away. Hiding would be no good – the Goldfadens had had such a good hiding place and despite that, they weren't there any more – so she got up and set off. But the world was covered in thick fog and she couldn't make out a thing. Just occasionally, a face appeared in front of her, or a window, or a lamp-post, then disappeared again into the mist.

She groped aimlessly along the side of the houses as if she were blind, just trying to get away from the German voices, which got quieter and quieter and then faded completely. Malka walked and walked. At some point the fog lifted, and she noticed that somehow she had got to the church where she had met Ciotka. Then she was standing by the railway station in Skole, in the Aryan district. She couldn't see any Jews around, nor Germans, just Poles and Ukrainians.

Blurred memories of train journeys came back to her, train journeys to Kraków, or to her relatives in Skawina. Travelling by train meant lots of strangers – nobody knew anybody else, nobody stood out. She stood there for a long time and stared at the legs as they hurried past her into the station, then she stepped forward and let herself be carried along by the crowd. The back that she was following, a back in a thick, warm, grey overcoat, went towards a platform, and Malka followed.

There seemed to be a lot of people waiting for a train. Malka had to concentrate to see them, because everything kept getting blurred. She spotted a family with four children. Without giving it much thought, she went over and stood near them. Not too near, so that the people themselves didn't notice anything, but again not too far off, so that it still looked as if she belonged to them. Near children she always felt more secure, almost invisible. Nobody notices a child, and a child will always make it somehow, she thought to herself. She wondered where she had heard that sentence before, but she couldn't remember at all.

A train thundered into the station. Clouds of steam

came hissing out and Malka stepped back in fright because she felt as if the engine were aiming straight at her. But then she heard the squeal of the brakes, the banging noise became slower and more rhythmical, and then with another hiss of steam the train stopped.

People poured on to it. Malka made sure that she didn't lose sight of the family with the children, and pushed herself in behind the father, who was helping his wife and children get on board, up the steps and through the door, with his arms stretched out protectively. There were two long benches along the wall of the compartment, and they sat down quickly next to the father, who put one of the children, a little boy, on to his lap.

Malka shut her eyes and could just hear that the compartment was getting full. From the right she was pushed nearer to the father with the child on his lap. She felt dizzy, she was hot, she couldn't think. And she didn't want to think. Especially not of what was going on in the ghetto now. Here on the train there was a slight smell of coal dust, almost like her cellar.

Eventually the engine made a few complaining noises and the train started moving, slowly at first, but then faster and faster. Malka heard the steam hissing and felt herself shaken from side to side, The shaking didn't stop – it just got a bit more regular and a bit quieter – and the rattling didn't stop either. There were voices mixed in with the rattling – words and sentences that she couldn't understand because her head was so fuzzy. It all merged together into a kind of music, rhythmic, with a melody of which she could only pick out the high and low notes.

The train stopped, started again, stopped, went on. Then the ticket inspector came along. She had been prepared for him – she knew that you had to show a ticket, and she had thought out in advance what to do. When he got close to the family with the children, she got up and went past him towards the toilet. She needed to piss anyway. When she came back the inspector had gone again.

The woman who had been sitting next to her moved up a bit and made space for Malka. She sat down, leaned back against the wooden wall, shut her eyes and gave herself up to the noise, which was made up of lots of different noises that couldn't be distinguished from one another and which all merged together into a sort of rushing sound. The time passed for her in a twilight state between waking and sleeping, and Malka only came to herself when she heard the shrill whistling of the engine.

Then the train stopped again. This time everyone got out, including the family. Malka got up and followed them. They were on an unknown station, which looked strangely gloomy. People were moving away from the platform, others were arriving. She stayed where she was and waited for children. A woman with three children appeared. She had a suitcase and a bag, and the two bigger children, two girls with plaits and with bundles on their backs, were looking after their little brother. Malka moved nearer to them and waited till they got on. This time she felt safer, because the trick with the inspector had worked so well. Nobody notices a child; a child will always make it somehow.

The train was travelling for a long time. The woman with the children opened her bag and put her hand in. Paper rustled. When she brought her hand out again she was holding a sandwich that she handed to the bigger of the two girls. Her hand disappeared into the bag again, paper rustled once more. Malka couldn't take her eyes off the bag and the smell of the bread was becoming unbearable. She hadn't been hungry before then – in the last few days she hadn't been feeling the hunger so much – but now, when the hand reappeared with a sandwich for the second girl, it took Malka's breath away. A third sandwich came out of the bag, the little boy took it and bit into it at once.

Malka felt everything going dark. She was hungry; now she was really hungry. The woman looked at her. Malka looked back and put into the look all her longing for some bread, please; but she didn't say a thing and couldn't even manage to hold her hand out as she had so often done before. The woman put her hand back into the bag. The rustling of paper became very loud indeed and Malka almost drowned in its noise. Then the hand came back and held out a piece of bread for Malka too. Malka didn't dare to move. The woman nodded and smiled, and Malka took hold of the bread. She had to force herself to eat slowly, because she really wanted just to gobble it down. But then she would only crap it out again without getting the full value. Chew slowly, almost let the bread dissolve in your mouth so that you can suck out the last fragment of nourishment.

When the train stopped, the woman and the children got out. At the door the woman turned round and smiled at Malka, and Malka smiled back, grateful for the bread that filled her stomach. She would have liked to go with them, but didn't dare. She felt safer in the train.

It stopped again. People got off, others got on. Malka's head become more and more fuzzy, filled with fog, as if the clouds of steam puffed out by the engine, which she sometimes saw drift past the window, had gathered inside her head, blocking her ears and dimming her eyes. She felt that she really wanted to collapse, but knew that she mustn't, not now. Only after the German operation, she thought, when I'm back in my cellar.

And then she dreamed of all the things she would do after the operation. Look for blankets. Woollen blankets, eiderdowns, pillows. She would push it all through the window. In the evening she would tidy it up – she wouldn't need any light – and then lie down in her new bed. Then at last she'd be able to collapse and sleep, just sink into it, not think of anything, not keep a look-out. Sleep.

When everyone got off the train Malka could barely walk because her stomach hurt so much. She had to hold on to the handrail as she went down the steps. She was back at the station in Skole, but it was still daylight, so she couldn't go back to the ghetto yet. She would have to stay away at least one night to be sure that the operation was over.

She leaned against a lamp-post, then held on to it so that she didn't fall down. Then she simply couldn't just stand there and wait any longer. Without looking around to see if anyone was watching her, she crawled back into the train, which was still standing in the station, and lay down under one of the benches. She stretched out and lay pressed up against the wall without moving, and waited. Down here the smell of coal dust was stronger than up in the compartment.

Just lying down did her good, and slowly she began to feel better again. She was just wondering whether she should get up and sit on the bench, because she knew now how to behave unobtrusively in a crowd, when people started to get on – lots of people – and sit down on the bench. All Malka could see were shoes, calves in woollen stockings, trouser legs, a pair of men's shoes with a hole in the left heel of one of them. Right in front of her were a child's feet, in black shoes and brown socks. The child must still be small, because the feet swung in the air between the bench and the floor. The train set off. Down here the rattling felt different, much stronger but at the same time gentler. She shut her eyes and gave herself up to the rocking, and to the familiar smell.

Now and then, scraps of conversation would reach her ears. 'I'm going to see my aunt in hospital,' said a man. 'She's in for surgery.'

The voice of a woman directly above Malka – so it must be the one with the brown woollen stockings, the mother of the child swinging its legs – said, 'Hospitals, yes. I was in one as well last year, having my appendix out, but it was horrible . . .'

And another woman, whose voice came from the right-hand side, joined in and said, 'My father had a stroke and the doctor just let him die. I tell you – it was all that Jewish doctor's fault.'

A man, presumably the one with the hole in his shoe, gave a derisive grunt and said, 'At least these damned Germans have done one thing – they've got rid of our Jews.'

Malka didn't want to hear any more. She crept into herself again, into the hollow in her inside, and made herself invisible. She didn't want to hear any more or see any more, and just felt the rattle of the train on the rails. From time to time she heard a shrill, complaining whistle, as if the train itself were howling at the heavens.

Eventually she noticed that the train had stopped. She opened her eyes and there wasn't a single leg in sight, no feet and no shoes. She was alone. She felt sick and dizzy and her stomach hurt. But she wasn't really hungry – after all, she had eaten the bread the woman had given her – so why did her stomach hurt so much?

Outside, it was nearly dark, and the lights were on in the station building. She heard voices, German voices, and opened her eyes in fright. Over there, in the lights by the station, boots were gleaming beneath German uniforms.

Desperately she looked around and spotted a large rubbish container, made of wood, and big enough to hide her. With her last resources of strength she pulled herself up and fell into it. She felt paper, but underneath the paper there must be something else – a rotting stench reached her nose. She pulled sheets of newspaper over herself and sank down.

Suddenly she felt that she had to crap. But she couldn't get up; she couldn't go and find a lavatory – the shining boots were out there, and she could still make out voices speaking German. She would have to try and hold it in, absolutely, she couldn't get out, the voices, so she shoved her hand under her bottom and tried to hold it shut, bent double with pain, and then started to tremble, and then it just burst out of her. She crapped and crapped and felt as if her life was just flowing out of her so that nothing of her would be left. She felt it on her hand and on her skin, soft and warm, and sank deeper and deeper into it and then there was nothing.

She heard voices in a dream. She was carried, driven, carried. Other voices came to her ear, from a long way away, a very long way away, and then vanished again. She felt someone undress and wash her, and the cold water on her skin made her shudder. Someone's teeth were chattering, and when she noticed that it was her own teeth she felt the urge to crap again, an urge she couldn't resist. But I'm not there any more, she thought in astonishment, I've crapped myself away. And then she sank into darkness.

Malka was lying in bed under a cover and was so weak that she couldn't move. She kept her eyes shut, slept, dozed, drank what was held to her lips, and then, later on, ate what was put into her mouth, allowed herself to be lifted on to a pot, and pissed and crapped and wondered whether anyone could experience all that twice and whether she was with the Kopolowicis at the mill again without having crossed the border back into Hungary. Then she noticed that there were no hens clucking outside, and that the voices were speaking Polish rather than Yiddish.

She opened her eyes and saw a woman's face in front of her, a broad face with brown eyes and a flat nose, a face framed with dark hair. A nice face, but it dissolved at once into the darkness and she wondered when she had fallen into the black cotton wool again, but she couldn't remember. She couldn't remember anything; she was deaf and blind and only in her dreams could she see.

She dreamed about Teresa and saw in front of her the face that she loved so much, and watched in amazement the way the face changed, how the blue eyes got darker, the creases appeared around the eyes and how Teresa's small and slightly turned-up nose got bigger and more hooked, and how her smooth skin developed pores, and how the cheerful, laughing mouth became slightly twisted, with a few hairs coming from a little wart on the chin. It was Ciotka. It made her laugh. She laughed in her dream, and she woke up.

'Are you back with us again?' asked the woman who had been bending over her. 'Well, at last you can tell us who you are, can't you?'

'Malka,' said Malka. 'My name is Malka Mai.'

'Malka,' repeated the woman. 'That's a nice name – it means a queen. And where are you from, little queen?'

Malka didn't know what to say – she didn't know where she had come from – but luckily she didn't have to answer because everything went dark again. All she heard was the voice saying, 'Sleep well, Malka, sleep and you'll get better.' She had heard those words somewhere else, too, though she didn't know where and when that had been.

Malka woke up again when someone in the room screamed – a loud complaining scream, like nothing she had ever heard before. It was dark and the scream got louder. It cut through the blackness, hit Malka and pierced her flesh. Then there were footsteps, voices, there was light in the darkness all around, some furniture was moved, it got dark again and the voices and the footsteps disappeared. But Malka imagined that she could still hear the dreadful scream. It pursued her in her dreams, and in a dream she knew who it was who had screamed – it was the scream that the boy with the coat that was too big and the boots that were too big had given, and that she had only now heard – a scream that had been with her without her knowing, from the moment she had seen him on the pavement. Now the boy lay there again with his arms stretched out and pleading, his mouth wide open, pointed towards the sky – and it was out of his mouth that the scream came.

She woke up again whenever she was lifted out of bed and taken to the toilet, but it was a long time before she

194

could open her eyes and look around. She was lying in a large room with lots of beds. The light was dim in her corner because her bed was behind a jutting-out wall, but behind it there must have been a window, because a ray of sunshine lit up another bed which had a girl sitting up in it – a girl in a white nightdress, but with a bald, bony head, who was staring at her with enormous eyes. Malka quickly shut her eyes again and drew back.

The next time she woke up she saw the girl in the white nightdress, the one with the enormous eyes, sitting on the bed of a boy. The two were talking very loudly. Suddenly the boy started to shout, tore back the bed-covers from his body and roared, 'I'm never going to be able to walk again, damn it, never! Get that into your head, can't you! Three Germans, three machine-guns and a pile of dead bodies with me in the middle. And that was it.'

'After the war you'll get a wheelchair,' said the girl. 'After the war—'

'Shut up!' shouted the boy. 'After the war, after the war . . . There won't be any "after the war" for me.'

Malka pulled the covers over her head and blocked her ears. She didn't want to hear anything, she didn't want to see anything, she wanted to sleep.

Whenever she had a day free Hannah went to Budapest. She was fetching medical supplies – that was the official reason for her visits – and she also went to the Palestine Office to see whether there was a date yet for Minna to leave. Then she went round from one organization to another, got to know all the members of the various aid agencies – the religious ones and the socialist ones – and asked everyone to help her get her child back.

195

When she heard that some more refugees from Lawoczne had arrived, she went back to the house where she and Minna had stayed when they first got to Budapest. In the attic room they found a married couple with teenaged children. Hannah knew them, but hadn't ever had much to do with them. Malka had been back in Lawoczne, said the wife; she had been seen, and there were rumours that Zygmunt Salewski, from the Polish police, had taken her in, though she didn't know if it were true or not. Hannah thanked her for the information. She knew the Salewskis; they were good people. Now at least she had a starting point for her search.

From the Jewish community she got the address of a Mrs Ronay, of the Red Cross. She was reputed to be a very influential lady, and if anyone could, then she would be the one who could get Malka to Budapest. Hannah found the house, an enormous villa, and was taken by a maid into a splendid sitting room. Hannah went to the window and looked out on to the street along which she had just walked. She felt uncomfortable in these surroundings, although by now she was looking more or less respectable again; at least she was no longer dirty, her hands were clean, with short fingernails, and she was dressed normally.

Mrs Ronay came in. Hannah stood up involuntarily. This was undoubtedly a real lady coming towards her, dressed in a simple but elegant dress. When Hannah introduced herself as Doctor Mai, Mrs Ronay asked her to sit down. She rang a bell and ordered tea and cake for her guest. Only then did she ask Hannah what she could do for her.

Hannah began to tell the story, but when she explained how she had left Malka behind in Pilipiec with the Kopolowicis the lady's face changed, and it became suspicious and hostile. 'How could you do such a thing?' she exclaimed. 'How could you leave your own child there alone?'

Hannah tried to defend herself, but noticed that the woman was no longer listening. Suddenly she had lots of other things to do. Before she dismissed Hannah, she gave her some underclothes for herself and Minna. Underwear was very hard to come by in Budapest, everyone knew that. She gave her the huge sum of two hundred pengö as well. 'Apart from that, I can't help you,' she said. 'In times like this who can possibly track down a lost child?' Hannah thought that she could hear disapproval and condemnation in the woman's voice, and that she could see disapproval and condemnation in her face.

In the train back to Korad she thought, That arrogant lot, so full of themselves! She doesn't know what it's like to be in danger of her life. She doesn't know what it's like to be responsible for another daughter, that well-fed lady with her maidservants and a husband to keep her free of any worries.

That evening she got back home completely defeated. 'Nothing works,' she said. 'Nobody wants to help me.'

Minna didn't look up from her book as she said, 'Why don't you try your old boyfriend? Peschl is bound to be back in Lawoczne. Write to him, or better still, ring him. He owes you something, doesn't he?'

Hannah would dearly have loved to tear the book out of Minna's hand and slap her, but she didn't. Nor did she want to think whether it was shame that stopped her, or fear that she and Minna might have a loud argument and draw unnecessary attention to themselves. They mustn't do anything out of the ordinary and make people doubt their identity as Polish Catholics. She turned round without a word and left the room.

It was silly for a woman to wander around alone at night, but she needed to move. It had always been like that – whenever she was unsettled she had to move about or do something, even if it was only shifting things from one place to another; just as long as she wasn't sitting still. Even at school it had been a problem for her, then when she was studying, and later still when she was working in the hospital. 'Just stop fidgeting around all the time, can't you,' her consultant had said – the one who couldn't stand her anyway, either because she was a woman or because she was Jewish, or both.

She wandered around the camp without noticing where she was going, and in her thoughts she was back in Lawoczne with Heinz Peschl, who had been such a wonderful violinist. Back then, in the first flush of enthusiasm, he had promised to look after her and her daughters. He had said he would get hold of false papers and take all three of them to Germany. Hannah had laughed and refused. She loved her job – why should she give it all up? She hadn't seen the danger; she hadn't wanted to see it and it had come so unexpectedly.

If the houses of the Jews had been invaded by blood-thirsty, murderous hordes she would have understood the danger; the fear of the pogroms was in her blood and she had grown up with stories about them. Pogroms meant violence and death. But a German in a neat suit or a neatly pressed uniform, who just signed a piece of paper? She had believed that it was all just irritating bureaucracy, and had thought that you could just keep your head down and let it pass over you. Maybe it would have been different if they had lived in a large town, but you didn't hear much about the world in Lawoczne.

She shook her head, as if some invisible person were providing the counter argument. No, even in a large town it wouldn't have been any different – frivolity and naivety were part of her character. She only had to look at the wealthy Jewish citizens of Budapest. They felt safe; they weren't trying to escape, even though they knew from Jewish refugees what the German army was doing. More and more stories of Jews having to dig their own mass graves before they were shot, tales of whole trains of cattle-wagons, all full of Jews, going off to some unknown destination and coming back empty. And in the middle of it all was a child with blonde plaits – her Malka.

Maybe she really *should* try to call Peschl. But she knew that he wouldn't help her. At the time she had lost her job as district medical officer she had asked him for help, but he had just shrugged his shoulders and said that it was the law and you couldn't change it. He had made excuses and his visits became less frequent and in the end he had stopped coming altogether. She had been sorry about that, but hadn't run after him because she was too proud. Heinz Peschl was a good-looking, well-educated man who had attracted her right from the start even though he was a German. Or because he was a German? That thought shook her, and made the blood rush to her face.

No, she wouldn't call him, and not because her pride wouldn't let her do so. Her pride wasn't worth anything now; it was a superfluous and indeed a dangerous quality to have in her situation, a pointless luxury. No, she wouldn't call Heinz Peschl because she couldn't expect him to give her any help. Heinz Peschl was a good-looking coward and nothing more. And his cowardice was more likely to hurt Malka. An over-persistent mother getting on his nerves might lead him to make a child disappear, just to get rid of the problem.

When Hannah got back to the room, Minna was in bed with her face turned to the wall and her eyes shut. But Hannah knew that she wasn't really asleep. She undressed, lay down on the outside half of the bed and turned the light off.

'Minna,' she said into the darkness. 'Minna, I don't know what to do.'

Minna hadn't been asleep, and Hannah heard her swallow. It was quiet for a while, and then Minna said, 'You left Malka there, you'll have to go and fetch her back.'

Suddenly it was all clear. 'Yes,' said Hannah. 'I'll have to go and fetch her.'

Both were silent. Hannah didn't know why she had said that. Maybe the words had just slipped out in response to Minna's reproach. Because the idea of going back into the lion's den was so crazy that she would never have thought of it herself. But that was irrelevant now. The decision had been made, and a good thing, too. At last she had a goal. She would go and fetch her child.

Malka burrowed deeper into her warm, dark cave and pressed herself against the wall to get away from the hands that were trying to pull her out into the cold, into the harsh light. 'No,' she shouted, 'no, no,' – but the hands grabbed hold of her mercilessly and pulled her out. 'Malka, wake up, Doctor Burg is waiting for you,' said a woman.

Malka opened her eyes. It was the woman with the

broad face. She was standing by the bed and had Malka's things over her arm – her dress, her jacket, her trousers. 'Where is my coat?' she asked anxiously. 'Where are my shoes?'

'They're all there,' said the woman in a calming voice. 'Your shoes are here by your bed and your coat is still drying.'

The woman pulled back the covers and Malka now saw for the first time that she was wearing a thick, sky-blue flannel nightdress, like the one Ciotka had worn, only smaller. 'Where am I?' she asked.

'In hospital. You were very ill – you had typhoid fever,' answered the woman. 'I'm Nurse Rosa.'

She helped Malka to dress. The clothes had been washed and the smell of soap filled Malka's nose. Her socks had been washed, too, and they felt surprisingly soft. When she put her shoes on she suddenly remembered the train and the shoes she had been able to see from her hiding place under the bench, and the unknown station. 'What town am I in?' she asked.

'In Stryj,' answered Nurse Rosa in surprise. 'Where else?'

'In the ghetto?'

'Where else?' said Nurse Rosa again. 'What silly questions you ask! Now come on, I've got other things to do.'

Malka followed her, past the head with the enormous eyes, past other sets of eyes. The door was open to the next room and she could see cots, and a little child crying. Nurse Rosa knocked on the door of another room and ushered Malka in. It looked like the lady doctor's surgery at Lawoczne, but it was a man who sat her down on the examination couch. While he felt her stomach he asked her name. 'Malka Mai,' she said.

201

He listened to her chest and checked her ears. Then she had to open her mouth, stick out her tongue and say 'aaah', and then breathe deeply, in and out.

Then he sat down at his desk. 'Good,' he said. 'You're better again and you can go home. Where do your parents live?'

'My father lives in the land of Israel,' said Malka quickly.

He looked at her. 'That's a long way away. And where is your mother?'

Malka looked down. 'In Hungary.'

'And what's her name?'

Malka stared at the wooden floorboards, which had once been painted dark red, but were now worn through in many places so that you could see the bare brown wood underneath.

'Well?' asked the doctor impatiently. 'I haven't got all day.'

'Doctor Mai,' whispered Malka.

For a moment there was silence, and she heard him drumming his fingers on the desktop. 'Doctor Hannah Mai from Lawoczne?' he asked eventually.

She nodded.

'I know your mother,' he said. 'We did one or two things together a while ago. And how old are you?'

Malka didn't answer.

'Surely you must know how old you are?' he said.

Malka raised her eyes and looked at him. 'I used to be seven once,' she said. 'But that was a long time ago.' Then she stared down at the floor again.

Everything was quiet for a long time, and his fingers had stopped drumming. In the end he said, 'Very well, we'll keep you here with us.'

Malka didn't react. She didn't care. She didn't look up when Nurse Rosa came to fetch her and take her back to the ward. She took her shoes off, lay down in the bed in her clothes and turned to face the wall.

Nurse Rosa dragged Malka down the stairs, though she had to keep turning round because Malka was clinging on to the banisters. Malka didn't want to go down to Shmulik, the janitor, and she wanted to keep her hair. In her ears rang the voice of the lady doctor who had said, 'The prettiest hair in the family, not platinum, not flaxen and not reddish, a colour like proper gold.' With all her force she pressed against the steps. Not until Nurse Rosa turned round and slapped her face once, and then a second time, did she give up. With drooping shoulders she allowed herself to be led through the vestibule, where there were camp-beds set up, then the passageway, with mattresses on the floor, and down the basement steps into Shmulik's workshop.

'Shmulik, here's another one,' said Nurse Rosa. 'Everything off.' And then she disappeared.

The old man nodded and put a box containing scissors and a razor on the table. 'It's a shame about the nice hair,' he said. 'Come on, child.' He pulled Malka towards him, clasped her between his knees and picked up his scissors. 'What a pretty colour,' he said. 'Just like gold.' His breath smelled bad.

He held on to her right-hand plait so hard that her head was pulled down towards her shoulder. She heard the creaking noise as the scissors opened, and felt the metal on her neck, and then the scissors were at work, sawing and chopping through her plait. It was pulling and tugging and Malka felt as if her head was being wrenched from her body. Suddenly she felt a jolt and her head was free again. Shmulik laid the severed right plait on the table and took hold of the left one. Malka's head was pulled the other way – she couldn't prevent it – and then the cutting noise again, the tugging at her head and the sudden relief. It was over.

No longer with any will of her own, Malka just gave herself up to the scissors and watched the clumps of blonde hair fall on to the old man's trouser legs and on to the floor, and then she felt the scratch of the razor. 'You've got some sores on the back of your neck,' said old Shmulik, 'so you'd better tell Nurse Rosa about them. You couldn't see them under your hair.'

He took a little mirror with a green frame out of his pocket and said, 'Do you want to see yourself?'

Malka didn't answer. Her head was light and it felt alien, as if it didn't belong to her any more. Slowly she lifted her hand and ran it over her head. It was smooth, and the small patches that were still there felt scratchy, not soft, like a sheep is when it's just been shorn. Who's ever going to give me anything now I look like this? she thought. It's a trick – they're doing this just so I can't run away. I'll have to stay here because no one will ever give me anything now. The road back was barred to her. People only gave bread to pretty children.

Suddenly she started to cry; she just couldn't go on. What had just happened to her was worse than all the rest put together, because now she was definitely no longer the little girl she used to be. No longer was she Malka Mai, the daughter of Doctor Hannah Mai; she was some other girl who happened to be called Malka Mai. Nobody would recognize her, and Teresa would say, 'Look at that, Marek. Look, Julek, this ugly girl reckons she's our Malka!' Antek would beam when he heard her name, but when he saw her he would start to cry and Teresa would take a broom and drive her out of the house.

Despair flooded over her. She was aware that old Shmulik had taken her on to his lap, and was stroking her shorn head. When she struggled, he only held her closer. She kicked at him, hit against his chest; she wanted to die. The boy with the coat that was far too big and the boots that were far too big must have felt as empty and as false as this, and now she understood why he had spread his arms out. It wasn't pleading, it was just helplessness; he simply hadn't known how to go on. I'm like him, she thought, and she saw herself lying there in the dirt. She spread her arms out, but Shmulik held her tight and she didn't fall into the dirt.

And then eventually she ran out of tears. Shmulik pulled out a handkerchief; she wiped her face and blew her nose loudly. 'Right,' said Shmulik, 'things go on. Don't be too sad, your hair will grow again.'

She nodded, although she didn't believe him because she couldn't imagine it, and because it didn't matter anyway. She would have to come to terms with it; it had happened.

'Lice always get the upper hand with long hair,' said Shmulik. 'And believe me, you can't have a war without lice. The lice are always there and they win every war.'

Malka smiled, because she saw an army of lice marching against a German soldier. David against Goliath.

He picked up the two plaits he had cut off and looked at them. 'I had a granddaughter once,' he said, 'and she had hair exactly like yours, exactly – it was just like gold. Will you give me your plaits?'

Malka nodded. The plaits didn't belong to her any more; she didn't care what happened to them. She didn't ask what had happened to his granddaughter – she didn't want to know, because she suddenly remembered the white-haired woman in the Hungarian prison, the Polish woman from Kraków, and what she had said about her mother and her children. She had forgotten the woman's name, but her voice had sounded just as empty and lost as Shmulik's.

Shmulik got up and pulled a small leather suitcase from under a low bed, which Malka noticed now for the first time. Malka watched as he unlocked it with a key. There was a prayer shawl in it, which she recognized because her grandfather had had one, and a couple of books. He put the plaits into the case, locked it and pushed it back under the bed.

But by then Malka was already outside. She didn't turn left to the stairs that would take her back up, because she didn't want anyone to see her, so she walked off to the right and opened a door at the end of the corridor, hoping she would find something like a coal cellar. But it wasn't a coal cellar.

She was standing in a fairly large room, lit only by two small casement windows. The first thing Malka noticed was a strange smell, and then, once her eyes got accustomed to the half-light, she saw that the room was nearly empty, with only a couple of tables in it. They weren't really tables either, just blocks of wood with tiles on the top. And on them were longish boxes made of rough, untreated wood. She recognized at once that they were coffins, even though they looked different from the coffins she had seen before because they were not a solemn black and they had no decoration. Two were empty. There was the corpse of an old woman in the third.

A shudder ran down Malka's spine. Suddenly old Shmulik was standing there beside her; he must have followed her without her noticing. She jumped when she heard his voice.

'Do you know what I do when the Germans mount one of their operations?' said Shmulik, still whispering. 'I take out the base board of the coffin, lie down in it instead, cover myself with a white cloth and pull the body on top. The Germans are frightened of corpses – they're afraid they might catch some contagious disease, so they always put the lid back on quickly.'

'What happens if there aren't any corpses?' asked Malka, whispering as well, in spite of herself. She glanced at the old woman, who was lying there cold and stiff with her eyes shut.

'There are always corpses,' said Shmulik. 'It's always worked so far.'

'Did the Germans shoot her?' asked Malka and pointed at the dead woman. 'Were the Germans here?'

'No, she was lucky – she just died because she was old,' answered Shmulik. 'Or did you think maybe the Germans had put her into a coffin?'

He took her hand. 'And now I want to show you something.' He opened a wooden door at the other side of the room, and they went out through a short but wide passage and through another door, and suddenly they were standing on a little paved area with steps leading up to the garden.

'When this house used to be an old people's home,' said Shmulik, now in a normal voice, 'the gravediggers used to fetch the bodies from here. Probably they didn't want the other old people to see, because otherwise it might have upset them.'

He held her hand more firmly and went up the steps with her. 'If you have to, you can get out this way and hide somewhere.' He pointed to a couple of trees. 'If it was summer you could climb up, but that won't work in winter, because everyone would be able to see you.' They went on a few paces to a tall lattice fence behind which loomed a block of flats with boarded-up windows. You could only see the roofs of other houses. 'There,' he said, and pointed. 'Between those bushes is a hole in the fence – can you see it?'

Malka nodded.

'If you crawl through you come out in the Aryan district. With your looks you won't stand out – it might work.'

Malka ran her hand over her prickly head, and Shmulik said comfortingly, 'Lots of children have had their heads shaved because of the lice – you're not the only one. Don't think about it any more.'

They went back.

When she came into the ward, the boy, who was called Mottel, said, 'Look at that, our little queen's been shorn. Hey, Malka, you're no better than us now – you can deign to talk to us.'

Malka hung her head. She didn't like Mottel; she was afraid of him, even though he couldn't do anything to her. His legs dangled uselessly when the nurses lifted him out of bed and put him on to the commode. She walked past him with her head down. Henya, the girl with the shaven head and the enormous eyes, was sitting up in bed mending a child's blouse. She sat in bed all day mending clothes that Nurse Zippi brought her, and only occasionally looked across to Mottel's bed. She smiled at Malka. Malka didn't smile back.

FEBRUARY, 1944

In Budapest, Hannah had been given a contact for a group of smugglers from Bereksis – people who made their living on the 'per head' basis, smuggling other people. She had given them all the money she had, and they had promised that a woman would take her by train to Bereksis, and from there they would smuggle her across the border. Everything was in place. Hannah had told the camp administrator that she needed two or three weeks' leave because her mother was dying and she had to go and see her. He had given it to her, but only reluctantly. Before she set off in the morning Hannah talked the whole thing over again with Minna. Minna would stay for another two weeks in Korad. If Hannah hadn't returned with Malka, she should go to Budapest to the Jewish Committee and wait there until she could leave with the Youth-Aliyah. Then she should go to Palestine to her father, who would look after her. Hannah would follow with Malka as soon as possible.

On the train to Budapest Hannah felt more anxious than she had ever been before. Minna had been cool and distant; she had displayed no emotion and no fear, even though this parting might well have been a parting for ever. Hannah was completely aware of the danger. 'You're crazy, going back into the lion's den,' Mrs Kohn, an acquaintance of hers from Budapest had said. 'You should just come to terms with the situation. You've got another daughter and you're responsible for her.'

That's true, thought Hannah. Of course that's true. Minna wasn't grown up yet – who would look after her if her mother didn't come back, and how would the Poles in the camp behave? Was Minna sharp enough not to give herself away, and to plan her visits to the Jewish Committee so that nobody noticed? She thought about Minna and worried about her until she realized that she was doing so out of fear – fear of what she herself was about to do. Minna was old enough and clever enough, and she would manage. She herself ought to concentrate on her own plans and she mustn't let herself be put off by her fears. She was heading for Poland.

But that same evening she was back in Korad telling Minna what had happened. She had had to spend a long time looking around Josefvarosy Station in Budapest until she found the woman who was supposed to be taking her to Bereksis, because the Hungarian woman was wearing a blonde wig and wasn't wearing the glasses she had had on when they had made all the plans. She had nodded to her, and Hannah had followed the woman on to the platform. The she had lost her in the crowds and had rushed from one compartment to another in panic before she found her and sat down next to her.

'Well, what happened?' asked Minna.

'Then the ticket inspector came along,' said Hannah. 'I asked the woman for my ticket and she said she had already given it to me.' Hannah put her hands over her face as she went on, 'She was so short-sighted without her glasses that she had given the ticket to some other woman she thought was me. Just when the inspector was getting near to us she told me in Yiddish to get out quickly or we'd both be arrested. I got out and came back. What else could I do?'

'Didn't you go straight to the group and ask for your money back?' asked Minna.

'Of course,' said Hannah, 'but they wouldn't listen. The business was done, and that was it.'

'Something that stupid could only happen to you,' said Minna nastily. 'How much money did you give them, then?'

'Almost everything we've got,' confessed Hannah. 'I'll have to go out on the scrounge again.'

Minna said nothing. Her expression was blank and dismissive as she went back to her book.

Malka lay in her bed, staring into the darkness. She always woke up very early, before anyone else in the room. In that strange state between waking and sleeping she waited for Nurse Rosa to bring breakfast – tea and bread and jam. Malka had got used to the hospital because with her shaven head she had no choice. After her hair had been cut off she spent a few days just lying in bed under the covers, until she had set out to go and find herself a proper hiding place in the hospital. She had looked around very carefully – every corridor, every room, all the little ante-rooms and even the attic. The only room that was really suitable as a hiding place was the room in the cellar with the dead bodies, and Shmulik had that one already. So she had got used to her bed by the wall, and at least she wasn't as freezing as she had been in the coal cellar, though she was often homesick for it. Especially when the others made stupid comments.

She didn't want to talk to them, and what could she say, anyway?

Things had got better after she got to know Rafael. She had seen him by chance when she had looked into the room with the cots. He was in one of the beds by the window, standing up and holding on to the cot bars, and he had beamed at her as she walked slowly towards him. 'Antek,' she had said. 'Antek, what are you doing here?'

'That's not Antek,' Nurse Zippi, who was sitting in a chair giving a baby a bottle, had said. 'That's Rafael. But it's easy to make a mistake – all mongoloid children look a bit alike.'

Malka had stood by the little child's bed, stretched her hand out and touched him hesitantly. He had taken hold of her hand and chewed on her fingers.

'Do you want to feed him?' Nurse Zippi had asked. 'His porridge is over there on the table.'

Malka had fed him, and then she had grabbed the slice of bread that Nurse Zippi had given her, an extra piece of bread, and had run away.

Rafael couldn't speak, just like Antek, but he beamed at her, just as Antek had beamed at her. Whenever he saw her his eyes narrowed down to little slits, his mouth opened and he stuck his tongue out, started to jump up and down and held his arms out to her. Malka wiped his face, kissed him and whispered into his ear all the words that Teresa had always said to Antek. 'You're special, Rafi, something very special, aren't you? You're our sweetest little boy and we love you.' Rafael beamed, babbled and put his damp hands on her face.

Malka had sewn him a cloth ball made from old bandages, because of course Nurse Zippi didn't have a sewing basket like Teresa. The nurse had given her two walnuts for doing that, real walnuts, that she had cracked open with some stones in a narrow alleyway between two houses, and then eaten. Malka's mouth still watered when she thought of those nuts.

Slowly the dawn light crept over Malka's bed. And then the door opened. Nurse Rosa pushed in the trolley with a tray of bread and jam, a big pot of tea and some mugs. Malka reached for her trousers which were at the bottom of the bed, under the cover, and then her pullover and got dressed.

Hardly had Nurse Rosa poured out the first mug of tea when Malka was standing at her side. The tea was only lukewarm. Malka had finished it in a couple of gulps. She took a bit longer with the bread. She was still chewing when she went into the next room to see Rafael. She changed his nappy, then took him on to her lap and fed him, and if Nurse Zippi wasn't looking she popped a spoonful of his porridge into her own mouth. She thought about Antek and the polished wooden blocks. If she could get old Shmulik to make some building blocks like that for Rafael, maybe Nurse Zippi would be so pleased that she would give her some more nuts.

When Rafael had finished she wiped his face, kissed him and went back to her own room to fetch her coat, which she always kept hidden under the bed. Then she went downstairs to see old Shmulik.

This hospital was quite different from the one to which the lady doctor had once taken her to see an old aunt. That had been in Kraków, the day before war had broken out. In that hospital the rooms had been white, with white beds and bedside tables with flowers on them, and the old aunt had been lying there in a clean nightdress. Here there were camp-beds and mattresses with people

214

lying on them in their clothes, with their belongings in bundles next to them. Malka went past them, down the steps to the basement.

'Ah, there you are,' said Shmulik. He was rolling up freshly washed bandages. Malka watched him for a while, and then asked if he couldn't maybe make a couple of wooden building blocks for Rafael. When he nodded she added, 'They've got to be really smooth, though, so he doesn't hurt himself.'

Shmulik smiled and ran his hand over her shorn head, on which the hair was starting to grow again. 'I'll see if I can find something today,' he said. 'Come back tomorrow.'

She nodded and left the hospital.

She always went the same way, just as she had in Skole, and, just as she used to do in Skole, she stood in front of shops and held out her hand to people coming out and said, 'I'm hungry.'

It was true; she was hungry. Since she had been living at the hospital she got food more regularly than she had before, but it was too little to drive away the hunger. She often thought that hunger had become so much a part of herself that it wouldn't matter how much she ate, she would never be able to get rid of it.

At midday, when they dished out a thick soup, she joined the queue on the ground floor, with the grown-ups. The portions the grown-ups got were slightly bigger. Anyone not confined to bed took a plate from a pile and stood in the queue until it was their turn, and the nurse poured a ladleful of food on to the plate.

After the midday meal she went upstairs and fed Raphael if he hadn't eaten already, and then she went back around the ghetto. By now she knew her way about very well and had her regular spots; for example, just in front of the bakery, which she had found very quickly indeed just by following her nose. Often she interrupted her walks to run quickly up just to see Rafael, to stroke his head and, if there was no nurse in the room, to plant a quick kiss on his wet cheeks.

In the evenings, she got back to the hospital early and crept into her bed so as not to miss out when they distributed the nightly bowl of soup, and when she went to sleep she always lay with her back to the others. She had learned to hear nothing, to see nothing, and to retreat into herself.

That day it was cold and grey. The clouds hung deep over the ghetto and seemed to merge with the roofs of the houses. Malka had done two rounds of the ghetto and was standing in front of the bakery, begging, when she suddenly heard loudspeakers, shots, German voices: 'Out! Out! Get in line! Faster!' Shots rang out again, dogs barked.

She looked round in horror. The people were moving quickly, disappearing silently into their houses. Suddenly the street was empty.

Malka ran back to the hospital, down into the cellar, through the passageway and the room with the coffins, through the wooden door, up the steps and across the garden to the fence. All the outlines were blurred as she groped through the bushes for the hole, found it, and crawled out on the Aryan side.

The house with the boarded-up windows was occupied, though you couldn't tell that from the ghetto. Malka found that out as she ran through the narrow alley between the house and a half-ruined wall, and now saw the house from the other side – the Aryan side. From the front it had normal windows with curtains, and in one of the windows of the ground floor sat a fat old woman with her elbows on the window sill, looking out. A cat was arching its back next to her. When the woman saw Malka staring at her she brandished a fist threateningly at her. Malka ran off as fast as she could. Behind her she could still hear the voices of the Germans and the occasional shot. Panic-stricken she ran and ran, always straight ahead, until she was so far from the ghetto that she couldn't hear anything except the normal noises of a normal street. Ciotka, she thought; if only I were in Skole, I could go to Ciotka.

She ran and ran. Here, too, the sky was low and pale grey over the houses, sucking up the smoke which rose from the chimneys. Malka did not stop until she reached a market place. There weren't many stalls, because it was winter and the farmers had nothing to sell except potatoes, cabbages and turnips. At one stall there were apples. Malka automatically put her hand out when the stallholder, sitting heavily wrapped up behind her apples, looked at her.

The woman picked up a couple of apples, turned them round, inspected them and then held one out to Malka – an apple that was starting to go bad on one side. Malka took the apple in amazement, thanked the woman and rushed on. She didn't eat the apple, just put it in her coat pocket and thought about Ciotka, who had also given her an apple once. As a farewell gift.

She came to a kind of eating place, which smelled wonderfully of soup, vegetable soup with meat in it. There was a throng of people in front of this place with bowls in their hands. When Malka noticed that there were children there, too, she simply joined in, just so she wouldn't lose the smell. Strangely, she wasn't at all worried. Several of the children also had shaven heads, just like herself. Shmulik had been right – lice clearly went for Christian heads as well.

Malka allowed herself to be pushed along. It was pleasantly warm amongst the people. She was surprised that no one was pushing or shoving, and that the people simply stood in line quietly and sometimes took a pace forward. Like a huge snail made out of people, thought Malka, as she was pushed on a bit further forwards. It started to snow; thick flakes fell on the heads of the people waiting, but nobody left the queue, and nor did Malka.

Then she couldn't feel the snow any more; she had been pushed through the door and was standing in front of a counter where a couple of women were ladling soup out of huge containers into the bowls that were being held out. A woman held out her hand to get Malka's bowl, but Malka shook her head, raised her hands and gestured helplessly. Without a word the woman turned round, took an old tin down from a shelf, filled it with soup and held it out to Malka.

Malka took the tin, which was hot against her chilly fingers, but not so hot that it would burn her. With both hands clasped round the tin she carried her prize carefully past the people still waiting. A few snowflakes fell on to the tin and melted before they reached the soup. Only when she had left the people a long way behind did she squat down in a doorway and drink the soup, carefully, so as not to hurt her lips on the jagged edge of the tin. There was no meat in it – her nose had deceived her on that – just cabbage and turnip and potatoes, but it tasted wonderful and warmed her from inside.

Because it was snowing harder now and starting to get dark, Malka went into a church. It wasn't warm, but at least it was dry. The church was empty, apart from one woman kneeling at the front. Only a couple of lights illuminated the place, though there were candles burning in front of a couple of the holy images. On either side of the pews, amongst pictures of the saints, was the dark row of confessionals. Malka stared at them. She crossed herself quickly and sat down.

She closed her eyes and thought, but couldn't find anything wrong with her plan. She was safe in a church; nobody came to confession at night and the priests who normally heard the confessions were certainly tucked up with hot-water bottles in their soft beds. She would stick to her idea. She would sleep in a confessional. It was cold here, that was true, but no colder than it had been in her coal cellar in Skole. She would manage.

She stood up carefully. The woman in the front pews was praying and didn't turn round; presumably she hadn't noticed Malka coming into the church at all.

It was dark in the confessional. Malka sat down in the corner, pulled in her knees and laid her head on her arms. She was glad she had practised not thinking. Her head emptied, and she waited. When her legs got stiff she stood up, moving carefully, until the blood flowed in her legs again, then she lay down on the ground and curled up. Luckily, it was a wooden floor and not as cold as she had feared it would be.

Later on she heard someone with heavy, echoing foot-steps walk through the church; the door was closed and a key turned in a lock. When she was sure that she had heard nothing for a long time she pulled down the curtain of the confessional and wrapped herself in it. Before she fell asleep she ate the apple. The rotten part tasted horrible, but she ate it anyway, and the core as well. The pips had a strange, bitter taste that she already knew. She even chewed the tiny stem for so long that it became pulp and then she could swallow it.

Hannah was half frozen when she knocked on the door of the forester's house. The forester didn't recognize her and she couldn't make a sound, just stared at him and raised her hands. The forester's wife came running out and caught Hannah as she collapsed. Hannah was aware of them taking her into the kitchen. The woman took off her cold and damp outdoor things, washed them in warm water and rubbed them dry with a towel. She gave her some warm things of her own to put on, and made her walk up and down in the kitchen and tell them where she had come from.

Hannah, completely distraught and with no control over what she was saying, told them about the successful flight to Hungary, about Malka's illness and that she had had to leave her child with strangers. She had tried once to get back to Poland to fetch the child, but someone had messed it up for her or she had messed it up herself, but that didn't matter. Mrs Kohn from Budapest – may she live and thrive for a hundred years – had helped her when she realized that Hannah would not be put off from going back into Hitler's jaws and so here she was in Poland at last and she had to get to Lawoczne to fetch her child – nothing else mattered.

The forester's wife, who hadn't understood much more from this rambling than the fact that Hannah had come back to Poland from Hungary, asked in astonishment, 'You came through the snow?' And Hannah started off on her story again, incapable of making herself understood.

Not until some hours later, when she had eaten, drunk and walked around again, could she speak normally. She sat with the forester and his wife at the table. 'It was dreadful,' she said. 'The mountains in winter are hell. My guide had to pull me along on a rope or I wouldn't have made it – I'd just have collapsed in the snow.'

'The snows were very late this year,' said the forester, and poured her a glass of vodka. She drank the glass off at a gulp and told her story again. When she saw the approving, almost admiring looks on their faces she said very quickly, to take full advantage of the moment, 'I have to get to Lawoczne, somehow. Without my child my life means nothing any more. Without my child I might as well give myself up to the Germans.' She started to cry, the way she had cried as a child, loud and unrestrained. What a relief it was to be able to cry like that, even if she didn't know whether she was crying for Malka, or out of self-pity because of all she had had to go through.

'Come on,' said the forester's wife in a calming voice, as if talking to a child. 'First you have to get some sleep. Here, sleep by the stove. This time you needn't go out to the barn. Nobody is going to come up here in this weather, certainly not German soldiers. They don't take any unnecessary risks. Sleep, and tomorrow morning we'll see what else can be done.'

Hannah climbed on to the place by the stove and lay down on one of the two blankets the woman gave her, covering herself up with the other. The stove was warm,

221

and as she stretched out she realized clearly for the first time what she had gone through since she had left the train in Bereksis. Every single muscle in her body hurt. But for all that she was weeping with relief.

The sun was already pretty high when Malka at last realized that she was lost. It must have snowed while she was in the church, snowed for quite a long time, because a thick, white layer covered the streets, the roofs, the trees. Everything looked different, strange, and the houses could hardly be distinguished from one another, as if the world had put on a white veil just to hide itself from her.

Malka wandered from one street to the next. If she could only find the market where the peasant-woman had given her the apple yesterday she would know what direction to take. In desperation she began to run, but it was all unfamiliar – every house, every lane, every square. Slowly the damp crept along from the toes of her socks, which stuck out of her cut-off shoes, until her feet were wet through. She skidded on the snow and stepped into puddles with a thin layer of ice, which cracked under her feet.

Once she passed the railway station, but that didn't help – she couldn't remember how she had got from the station to the hospital. Over and over again she looked at people in the street and wondered whom she could ask for help, but an inner voice warned her against asking the way to the ghetto. She walked and walked, and realized that she must have been going round in a circle, because she recognized squares and houses that she had already seen that morning after she had left the church.

In the end she stopped a girl not much older than

herself who was coming towards her, a thick woollen scarf around her neck and a knitted cap on her head. She was carrying a basket with its contents covered up by newspaper.

'Please can you tell me where the ghetto is?' asked Malka.

The girl put the basket down; the paper slipped aside, showing some potatoes. 'Oh, there's nothing much going on there today,' she said with a friendly laugh. 'You should have seen it yesterday when they rounded up the Jews and took them away – that was worth watching, with all the dogs.'

Malka stared at the girl dumbly, incapable of saying a word.

The laughter drained from the girl's face; she became uncertain and visibly uncomfortable. 'There,' she said, turned round and pointed down a side street. 'Down there and straight ahead.' Then she grabbed her basket and hurried off, practically running, down the street.

Malka turned down the side street and soon after got to the market place. The peasant-woman from yesterday was standing there again, and her apples were shining a more vivid red against the white background. Malka stopped. The woman recognized her, laughed in a friendly manner, held out another apple to her and said, 'You can't come every day, though, or you'll ruin me, do you hear? This is the last one.'

Malka nodded and tucked the apple into her coat pocket. She'd give it to Rafael, who liked eating – they rarely got apples in the hospital. She could picture his face, beaming as he bit into it, and she could see him dribbling from the side of his mouth. Perhaps he would even clap his hands. He'd just learned how to do that.

223

Malka found the houses by the ghetto fence, went along the side of the big block and stopped in front of the hole. There were no sounds, no shots, no German voices, no dogs barking. As if it were night-time, with everybody asleep. But it was daytime.

Malka crawled through the hole and ran right across the garden, which also looked strange under its white cover. Her feet left deep imprints in the snow. She went hesitantly down the steps and opened the door. Then she started to run, through the passageway, through the room with the coffins, through the hall.

The door of Shmulik's workroom was open. He was sitting on the low bed, his hands on his lap, and he looked at her without a word. Malka nodded and went past him.

Upstairs, on the ground floor there wasn't anybody lying on the mattresses and the camp-beds were empty too, but a woman was sitting in a corner at the back. She had pulled her scarf over her face and was rocking backwards and forwards as if praying.

Malka went up the stairs. Suddenly she felt so weak that she had to hold on to the banisters. It was as if her arms and legs already knew what her eyes hadn't yet seen. The ward was empty. Mottel's bed was empty, Henya's bed was empty. All the beds were empty. Completely devoid of all feeling, as if she were quite dead inside, she went to the next room, the one with the cots. She took from Rafael's bed the ball she had sewn and pressed it to her face. It was still damp from him sucking it.

Malka couldn't cry. Even when Nurse Zippi came and put her arms round her, her eyes stayed fixed and dry, and only Nurse Zippi was crying. 'They took everybody,' she kept saying. 'They only left us to look after the next lot of children that will come here. And then they'll take them as well.'

She took Malka into the nurses' room and sat her down on a chair. Malka held the ball in her hand and didn't say a word. Not a word for the whole day. Nor the next.

Hannah had to wait for three days until Wojtek, the forester, could make arrangements – three days in which his wife did everything to help Hannah get her strength back.

Wojtek built a false base on to his sleigh, just high enough to give Hannah a place to hide in if she lay flat. Horse blankets were draped over the top so that they hung down at the side and covered the gap between the two bases. Then he loaded it up with baskets of freshly shot venison. There were also a few hares, frozen and stiff.

'I've got customers in Lawoczne for the meat,' he said, 'even as far as Skole. Everybody is hungry nowadays, and people are grateful to get anything.'

The next day Hannah said her goodbyes to the forester's wife, Jadwiga, and crawled down beneath the two bases of the sleigh. Wojtek had already harnessed the horse. Hannah heard the whip crack, and they were off.

She lay there hardly able to move. To distract herself she tried to imagine how the sleigh was gliding through the snow. It was dark all around her. From time to time she felt a jolt as the sleigh hit some obstacle, maybe a stone, but otherwise all that she could hear was the crunching of the snow, the muffled sound of the horse's hooves and the squeal of the brakes. Hannah was excited, because soon she would see Malka again, if it were true that she was with Teresa and Zygmunt Salewski. She would have been in good hands with the Salewskis. They were both decent people who loved their children dearly, even poor little Antek.

The journey took a long time and gradually Hannah started to feel panic rising inside her. She was lying there between the two wooden floors as if she were in a coffin. She couldn't move, her face was pushed to one side, her neck hurt and she was beginning to get cramp in her thigh. Just as she was about to kick out in panic at the wooden cover she heard the forester crack his whip and shout out a greeting to someone. At once she calmed herself, the muscles in her thigh stopped twitching and only her neck hurt.

They must have reached a town, maybe it was even Lawoczne. She pricked up her ears. Often she heard voices, and occasionally a dog barking, and then she heard the noise of a car engine or a motorbike, the sound of children playing, and once the noise of a hammer from a smithy. Then it was quiet again. Hannah had explained to the forester exactly how to get to Zygmunt's house, and had even drawn him a map of the route that – since Antek's last dangerous illness – she would have been able to follow in her sleep. He had studied the piece of paper thoroughly for a long time before throwing it in the fire.

At last the sleigh stopped. Wojtek opened the cover, put his hands into the space and pulled Hannah up. She grabbed at his hands like someone being rescued from drowning.

She fell over in the snow, got back on to her feet and moved her head about until the painful muscles in her neck loosened up again.

The sleigh stood in front of the house at the edge of the forest. Teresa tore open the door, rushed to Hannah and embraced her. 'Doctor,' she said, and started to cry.

'Where is Malka?' asked Hannah and looked all round her.

Teresa led Hannah and the forester into the house, into the warm kitchen. Marek sat at the table and was carefully removing the skin from boiled potatoes with his fingertips. Julek and Antek were sitting on the floor by the warm stove, their legs wide. They were rolling a coloured ball made out of cloth backwards and forwards to each other.

'What about the children?' said the forester. 'Shouldn't we send them out?'

'No,' said Teresa, 'that isn't necessary. Marek and Julek love Malka, and they know that they mustn't talk about her. Even Julek knows that. And Antek...' She smiled, bent down and stroked the boy's head. 'Antek can't talk, so he won't give anybody away.'

She poured tea for her guests from a pot which was on the stove, and told them how and why Zygmunt had taken Malka to the ghetto in Skole, to a family he knew. Hannah was so disappointed that all she wanted to do was cry, just cry.

The forester looked at her. 'Come on then, doctor,' he said. 'We'll just have to go to Skole.'

Hannah was about to get up when Teresa put her hand on her arm. 'Malka's not there any more. When we heard that they had taken the Jews out of the ghetto, Zygmunt went along to see, but the Goldfadens, the people who had taken Malka in, weren't there any more. Zygmunt asked a friend of his to check the transportation lists, and Malka wasn't there, and there wasn't a fourth child under the name of Goldfaden.' She smiled at Hannah. 'Zygmunt has a lot of friends. We've found out that Malka is in Stryj, in the Jewish hospital. Nobody knows how she got there, but we hope that things are more or less all right there.'

The forester's face clouded. 'Stryj is too far away,' he said. 'My horse won't manage that.'

Teresa nodded and said encouragingly, 'We'll have to wait for Zygmunt. He'll know what to do. He'll do everything so that you can get your Malka back, doctor.'

They drank some tea and waited. Out of habit Hannah gave the three boys a medical check-up, as far as she could without a stethoscope. This was a pleasure, and for a little while she had the feeling that everything was back to what it had been before, that after this she would just go back to her house in Lawoczne. Minna, or maybe Zofia, would have cooked supper, and Malka would be out playing somewhere or reading. The boys were healthy, and Antek squealed loudly when she tickled him.

At last Zygmunt arrived. He soon grasped the situation. 'You can't stay here, doctor,' he said. 'We're under suspicion. People have been coming here to check up on us ever since the business with Malka. I was supposed to turn her over to the Germans, but I took her to Skole and told Commandant Schneider that she had run away. I'm sure he didn't believe me.'

He put his arm round Teresa. 'Couldn't we take the doctor to your mother?' He turned to Hannah. 'My mother-in-law lives with Teresa's sister Bronja and her husband, Frantek and their children, right in the middle of the forest, about two hours from here. Frantek is a charcoal-burner. He and Bronja won't arouse any suspicion – I don't think the Germans even know they exist.'

So the forester drove Hannah and Zygmunt into the woods. By sleigh the journey was less than two hours, and Hannah didn't have to crawl into the secret compartment because nobody would be about in the forest that late, in the twilight, and with all the snow. She sat on top, between the two men.

The plan was developed that same evening. Babka Agneta, Teresa's and Bronja's mother, would go to Stryj to fetch Malka.

The men were really enthusiastic, but had to persuade the old lady, who had never travelled alone by train before. Hannah watched the scene as if it were nothing to do with her. The men's voices got louder, their faces redder. The objections of the old lady got weaker, and eventually she nodded in agreement. Hannah pulled the shawl that Bronja had put over her shoulders, tighter round herself. Again, there was nothing she could do but wait.

Malka was struck dumb. It was as if the pain had driven her voice too deeply inside her, as if she would never speak to anyone ever again now that she could no longer speak to Rafael. Time and again she stroked the apple in her coat pocket, the apple she had been going to give to Rafael. She didn't want to eat it, ever. It was going to stay in her pocket for ever, to remind her of Rafael. The beds in the hospital filled up again; different people came in, different children. Malka didn't look at them – she didn't want to see any faces. She wouldn't even look at Nurse Zippi or Nurse Rosa. The two of them kept trying to talk to her, and Doctor Burg tried as well, but nobody could get through to her, not even old Shmulik. It was as if Malka were under a glass bell;

she moved, she ate and drank what they gave her, she went to the lavatory, she slept. But that was all.

After a few days she started her wanderings through the ghetto again. There were fewer newcomers this time than there had been people taken away. The ghetto was strangely empty, whereas before it had been too crowded. Every so often Malka recognized a face from before, and saw that these people were just as startled as she was – as if they felt guilty for still being there when the others were not. Malka felt guilty as well. She should have taken Rafael with her to the Aryan side. She had only thought about herself.

The only feeling that hadn't been anaesthetized, and which stayed lively and vigorous and ever-present, was her hunger. But Malka had learned to love hunger, because it was only hunger that kept her in contact with life. She ate a slice of bread in the mornings at the hospital, then she walked through the ghetto without begging. Only when she got back to the hospital late in the afternoon did she eat her bowl of watery soup, and then she lay down in bed with her face to the wall.

One day, when Malka came back to the hospital late in the afternoon, Nurse Zippi came up to her. 'Malka,' she shouted, 'there you are! We've been looking for you everywhere.'

She pulled Malka, resisting, up the stairs and pushed her into Doctor Burg's office. The doctor came over to her, held her by the shoulders and turned her to face a chair where an old peasant-woman was sitting, dressed in black with a white headscarf. 'Malka,' he said. 'What do you think of this? This lady has come to fetch you. Malka, do you hear? Your mother is waiting for you.'

Malka looked at the woman, she looked at Doctor

230

Burg, then she tore herself away from her and ran out. She didn't stop until she had crawled through the hole and was on the Aryan side of the fence, and then she stopped and waited until she got her breath back. She stood in the narrow gap between the house and the fence, freezing cold and with nothing at all in her head, and she waited. Once she heard Nurse Zippi call her name, a long way off, from the hospital, and then it was quiet again.

Malka waited until it was properly dark, then she crawled back. That night she didn't sleep at the hospital. She went into a house in the middle of the ghetto, up the stairs to the attic, ate the apple that Rafael was really supposed to eat, and went to sleep pressed against a chimney, which at least gave a bit of warmth.

She didn't return to the hospital until the next evening, driven there by hunger and just in time to get her evening bowl of soup. The unknown woman was no longer there.

They were all sitting around the big table with the oil lamp hanging over it – Hannah, Bronja, her husband Frantek, and Zygmunt, who had been happy to make the long journey just to see Malka. But Malka wasn't there. Babka Agneta had come back alone.

She was sitting with her legs apart in her basket chair, her hands resting helplessly on her lap. They were old hands, worn and covered in brown age-spots. 'She didn't want to come,' she said in a despairing voice. 'She just jumped up and ran away.' She wiped her eyes with the corner of her apron before she went on. 'We went everywhere, we looked all over the ghetto for her, the nurses and me, but we couldn't find her anywhere. Then I had to come back to catch the train.'

When nobody said anything, Babka Agneta whispered into the silence, 'What else was I supposed to do?'

Hannah felt numb. Suddenly all the phrases came into her head that she had thought on the way to Mukačevo. She's all right. She's in bed. She's asleep. She's warm. She's got enough to eat. Pointless phrases – as if her thoughts had just taken on lives of their own.

With an effort she pulled herself together. 'How did she look?' she asked. 'Is she all right?'

Babka Agneta raised her hands and then dropped

them again. 'All right? How can a child in that situation be all right, there without her mother? She's very thin and her head has been shaved and her eyes are very big. No, she's not all right. I know what children look like when they are all right.'

'Her head has been shaved?' exclaimed Hannah in horror. 'They've cut off her lovely hair?'

Babka Agneta nodded. 'Because of lice, I should think.'

Hannah put her head down on her arms and wept. Bronja laid a hand on her shoulder, but Hannah was not to be comforted. She was crying for Malka's hair, and she knew that she was crying in disappointment because Malka hadn't come. She was crying because she felt so helpless and robbed of all hope.

Gradually, she realized what it was she had been suppressing all this time. Even if everything turned out all right, even if she got Malka back, she wouldn't be the same child Hannah had left in Pilipiec. Not just because she had lost her blonde plaits. Maybe she was physically ill, maybe she would never get better – but even if she escaped without any physical harm she would never be the same child as she had been before. What had happened would leave scars on her soul, for ever and ever. What Malka had been through would cancel out her childhood as a beautiful and protected little daughter; it would lie there on her heart and on her soul. That could never be made better. And it was her mother's fault.

Hannah had stopped crying, but she didn't dare raise her head for fear that people might be able to read what she was thinking from her face. She would have to lock her guilt away inside herself. And suddenly another thought came into her head, one that shook her even

233

more. Perhaps this was the price she had to pay for her own stuggle against her family, for her desire for status and for a position which her birth had not intended for her. She saw her father in front of her, this time the man with the naked face that she only knew from a photograph. He looked at her sternly and said, 'If you had listened to me none of this would have happened. But you always wanted things your way. Now look where it's got you.'

'Doctor,' said Bronja, 'pull yourself together. You have to be strong.'

Hannah raised her head. Her nose was running but she didn't care. 'I'm not going back without my child,' she said with force. 'I'll go to Stryj myself and fetch Malka.'

'Impossible,' said Zygmunt. 'That's far too dangerous. We'll have to think of something else.'

Hannah was incapable of thought. She felt as abandoned as she had felt as a child when her father had punished her. At the time she had often not understood what she was supposed to have done wrong, but this time she knew exactly.

'Maybe she simply didn't believe that Babka Agneta was telling the truth,' said Frantek. 'Maybe she thought it was a trap?'

Babka Agneta shrugged, and Bronja said, 'Babka, you've got to go there again, please. I'd go myself only I can't leave the children.'

'What if Teresa went?' asked Babka Agneta. 'She knows the child, after all.'

Zygmunt shook his head. 'Teresa mustn't take the risk, not with Antek. It's impossible.'

There was another depressed silence. Then Zygmunt said, 'Babka Agneta must go again and take something with her as proof that Malka's mother is here. Perhaps a necklace or something.' He turned to Hannah. 'Doctor, have you got a chain, or some piece of jewellery that Malka would recognize?'

Hannah shook her head. 'I had to sell everything I had long ago, and I didn't have much anyway,' she said in a downcast voice.

Another silence. The quietness hung so heavily over the room that Hannah felt as if she were suffocating. It was so quiet that you could hear the spluttering of the oil lamp. Suddenly Zygmunt brought his hand down on the table. 'I've got it!' he shouted. 'I know what you must take with you, Babka Agneta. Antek's ball. Malka sewed it for him when she was with us, and she's bound to recognize that.'

Everyone laughed with relief and they all started talking at once, as pleased as if Malka were already there with them.

'I'll take Babka Agneta to the train on my sleigh,' said Frantek. 'We'll go first thing tomorrow, and on the way we'll come by and pick up the ball.'

'No, not tomorrow,' put in Bronja. 'Babka Agneta needs a couple of days to have a rest. Next week.'

The two men nodded; their pleasure couldn't be dampened. 'And when we've fed Malka up a bit,' said Frantek, 'I'll take her and the doctor to the forester's house. Perhaps the weather will be better by then, but if not I'll use the sleigh. The trick with the false bottom isn't a bad idea.'

Zygmunt nodded to his brother-in-law. 'I've got some planks you can have and I'll give you a hand.'

Bronja stood up and took her mother's hands. 'You

need to get some sleep,' she said gently. 'A journey like that was a strain. Come on, I'll help you to bed.'

Zygmunt and Frantek were already planning the journey across the border and discussing which routes would be passable with the sleigh, and they already had Hannah and Malka on the train at Mukačevo.

Hannah felt how contagious their delight was and that worried her, because it was tempting fate and maybe God would punish them for it. 'Stop it,' she said. 'Let's not talk about it any more. Let's get Malka here first.'

Frantek got up and poured out three glasses of vodka.

Nurse Zippi took Malka by the arm and dragged her into Doctor Burg's room, then stood with her legs wide and her arms spread out in front of the door so that Malka couldn't run away. The old peasant-woman was sitting there again, her hands on her broad, dark skirt with the black apron, just like last time. Malka stepped back into Nurse Zippi, who grabbed her shoulder and pushed her forwards again.

'Just listen, will you,' implored Doctor Burg.

Malka put her hands over her ears. Why wouldn't they leave her alone? They ought to leave her alone, that was all she wanted. She stared past the woman at the window and looked at the sky. It was going to snow again, there was the right sort of heavy sky for it. Suddenly she wished it would snow and snow and never stop so everything would be covered with a white blanket – the hospital and all the people in it, and the ghetto and all the people in it, and all of Poland and all of Hungary and all the people in them, and all of the whole world.

From the corner of her eye she saw the old woman

put her hand under her black apron and bring something out. 'Look at this, Malka,' she said.

Malka heard her voice for the first time. Through her blocked ears it sounded far off and dull. Reluctantly, still resisting, she looked at the woman.

On her outstretched hand was a ball, Antek's ball. Malka knew it at once. One side was red checks, the other was blue with yellow flowers – she had chosen the scraps of material herself from Teresa's sewing basket. Malka looked from the ball to the woman, from the woman to the ball and then back to the woman. Tears ran down her face. When the woman smiled, her eyes almost disappeared into all the wrinkles.

Malka hesitantly took her hands away from her ears, held them in the air for a while and then dropped them to her side.

'I'm Teresa's mother,' said the woman, her voice now clear. 'I'm Antek's *babka*, his grandmother. I've come to fetch you because your mother is waiting for you.'

Malka didn't understand. The lady doctor was in Hungary, wasn't she, but the old woman was Teresa's mother and Antek's *babka*. She had Antek's ball . . . Tears were still running down Malka's cheeks although she wasn't really crying, and she couldn't make a noise. Nurse Zippi wiped the tears away with a handkerchief but she hardly felt it. She couldn't look at anyone except the old woman.

And then she nodded.

Doctor Burg and Nurse Zippi laughed with relief.

When they left the ghetto through a side street, it really was snowing. The old woman took Malka's hand. Malka allowed herself to be led along. After she had nodded, she had simply let things happen to her

237

regardless. She had allowed herself to be hugged by Nurse Zippi and Nurse Rosa, she had nodded when old Shmulik, with tears in his eyes, had said, 'See you again one day,' even though she knew she would never see him again. He was just one of the faces which had blown past her like autumn leaves since that day in Lawoczne.

The old woman asked her something, but when Malka didn't answer, she was silent, too.

In the train they sat next to each other on the bench. Malka looked straight ahead, gazed at her chewed-down fingernails and ragged fingertips and retreated into herself. But a woman's voice drew her out of her emptiness.

'The child looks pretty bad,' said a woman sitting on the bench opposite. She took some bread out of her bag and offered it to Malka. Malka took it automatically; you mustn't turn bread down, even if you were in such turmoil that you didn't feel hunger. She started to eat it at once, and after the first mouthful her hunger was back. She chewed it slowly and thoroughly, almost letting the bread dissolve in her mouth so that she could suck out the very last scrap of nourishment.

'Thank you,' said the old woman next to her. 'Yes, the child has been ill for a long time. She was in hospital, and you know what hospitals are like.'

The woman opposite her nodded. 'You'll have to do a lot of feeding up, the way the little one looks. What was wrong with her?' In her voice was a mixture of sympathy and curiosity.

'Fever,' said the old woman, who perhaps really was Antek's *babka*. 'A terribly high fever.'

Malka chewed and looked out of the window. She didn't listen as the two women started to talk about illnesses. The woman opposite had had a child die of a bad fever several years earlier, and you never knew what was going to happen with fever.

Outside the window a white landscape was rolling past – mountains, trees, fields, the occasional house. Malka tried not to think. She had to keep her head empty; thoughts were dangerous, hopes even more so. She let herself be lulled by the shaking of the train and the rattle of the wheels. But when the engine let out shrill whistling noises, it made her jump. At last the train stopped and Malka thought with surprise that this time there hadn't even been a ticket inspector. The old woman stood up and pulled Malka up, although she would rather have gone on sitting there. For ever.

Malka recognized the station at once; she didn't need to see the sign hanging over the crudely repaired building which the Russians had destroyed as they withdrew. Snow had fallen through the holes in the roof on to the ground and melted into brownish sludge. They were in Lawoczne.

Malka tried to tear her hand away, to run back to her own house, to her bed. She wanted to pull the covers over her head and never wake up again. But the old woman held her hand firmly and pulled her onwards.

There was a horse-drawn sleigh waiting for them outside the station. A man got down from it and said, 'I'm Frantek, Teresa's sister's husband.' When he saw Malka's frightened look he added quickly, 'Antek's uncle.'

He helped the old woman, whom he called Babka Agneta, on to the sleigh, then he picked up Malka by the waist and lifted her up. The old woman took a folded blanket from the floor, shook it out and wrapped it round Malka. The man cracked a whip and the sleigh set off, not through Lawoczne, not through the streets she knew,

239

but in a wide detour around the houses. She had lost the chance of fleeing to her old house. Again she had been too slow.

The fields were under a white cover and the trees at the edge of the road were bent under the weight of the snow. Malka no longer knew where they were; she didn't recognize where they were going, not with all this snow covering the roads. Then they reached a forest. It was silent as the grave; all she could hear was the horse's hooves and the scraping of the sleigh runners in the snow. Malka crept back into herself. She was overcome with fear. She longed to be back in the ghetto where she knew her way about, never mind whether it was in Skole or in Stryj or anywhere else – it just needed to be a ghetto. She hadn't been careful enough; she should have known better. The old woman didn't seem nearly as friendly up here in the forest, and it suddenly came to Malka that she had been tricked. The back of the man driving the sleigh seemed to get bigger and bigger.

The journey through the forest was endless. The branches were black against the snow; everything else was white, even the sky – there were just the black branches and the black tree trunks which looked from a distance like soldiers in uniform with raised rifles. When the sleigh went past a thicket, Malka tore off the blanket and jumped off the moving sleigh.

She heard the woman shout out, heard how the man reined in the horse and she ran as fast as she could into the bushes.

Hannah was lying on the shelf of the stove. She had been there for hours, since Frantek had harnessed the horse and set off with the sleigh to the station. She didn't want

240

to talk to Bronja and certainly did not want to see the children, two sweet little girls, twins, not quite two years old. She lay there on the stove ledge and tried not to hear Bronja laughing with the little ones and calling them pet names. She couldn't laugh, and she couldn't be nice to other little children, not today.

She had slept very badly the night before, and even the three or four glasses of vodka she had drunk with Frantek hadn't helped. She had dreamed about her mother and in the morning, when she had woken up, her mother's face was clearly there in front of her, clearer than it had been for a very long time. Now, lying above the stove she thought about the first time her mother had visited her after Malka had been born. She had given birth in the hospital, because she had thought there would be complications. Even Minna's birth, which had been nine years earlier, had not been easy.

She recalled that she had been lying in bed exhausted and alone, because Issy hadn't been there – she had been alone when Minna was born, too. In addition she was feeling a little disappointed that she had had another girl. Not that she herself had desperately wanted a son, but she *had* wanted a grandson for her father, who had so badly wanted a male heir in the family who could say kaddish, the prayer for the dead, for him when he died. Her mother had come in and looked at the newborn baby.

Hannah could picture her exactly, the way she had leaned over the bed and stroked the baby with her finger. 'The red marks are from the forceps,' Hannah said apologetically. 'They'll soon go away.'

'What a lovely little girl,' said her mother, taking the baby out and sitting with her on the edge of Hannah's bed, so completely absorbed in looking at her that Hannah thought jealously for a moment: she's behaving as if it were her child, as if *she'd* just given birth. She's more pleased than I am.

Her mother looked up. 'I would be so happy if you'd call her Malka.' And when Hannah said nothing, she added, 'Please.'

Hannah didn't know what to say. Malka had been her elder sister, who had died as a child. Hannah had no memory of her, but this dead Malka had been with her like a ghost throughout her childhood – this pretty, good-natured, ever-obedient child who had been a pure joy to her parents as long as she had lived.

When Minna had been born her mother had asked her even then to name the child Malka, but at that time she had refused and said that she was afraid of the name because her sister had died so young. The name would be a bad omen for a newborn child. She was just about to bring that argument out again, when her mother started to cry. 'Please, Hannah, I don't want the memory of my own child to fade away. Call the little one Malka – she will live, I can feel it. I promise you that she will survive.'

Her tears had fallen onto the little face, and the newborn baby had moved her mouth and had waved her tiny hand about.

'Very well,' Hannah had said. 'She'll be called Malka.'

The visible delight on her mother's face had, at least for a short time, brought them closer together than they had ever been. It had made Hannah happy as well, and she had felt less lonely.

Down below a chair fell over with a bang, and one of the little girls started to cry.

*

Malka ran through the thicket. Taking no notice of the twigs scratching her face and hands, she sank into the snow, pulled her shoes out with difficulty, stumbled over a branch, fell, got up, ran on. Why don't they leave me alone, she thought, I only want to be left alone . . .

Behind her she heard twigs snapping, heavy boots running through the snow. She gasped and could barely get her breath, but she didn't give up. She ran as fast as she could, but the boots still got closer and closer. And then the man had caught up with her. He threw his arms round her and pressed her hard to himself. His face looked angry and hurt, and she turned her face away. Nobody could help her now, she was in the hands of the old woman who had pretended to be so friendly and this man who was carrying her back and swearing as he did so.

He climbed on to the sleigh with her, wrapped her in the blanket again and pressed her on to the old woman's lap. 'Don't you dare do that again,' he said, 'or I'll tie you down.'

Malka lowered her eyes. The man climbed back on to the box and cracked the whip. The cracking sounded just like the Germans shooting. The old woman held Malka so tightly that she couldn't move, and her arms were pressed against her body as if they were in a vice. On her neck and head she felt the warm breath of the woman, who murmured words that were presumably supposed to be comforting. But Malka would not be comforted and just resigned herself to her fate because there was nothing left for her to do. After a time the old woman's grip relaxed a little, but not enough to allow Malka to get free. She wouldn't have tried it again anyway – it was pointless.

With the onset of twilight, the whiteness of the snow turned slowly to blue. By the time they got to a house in the middle of the forest it was dark. The man lifted Malka down from the sleigh but didn't let her go, and carried her, still wrapped in the blanket, into the house. He stood there and waited until the old woman had climbed down and had opened the door for them.

Only when they were in a kitchen with a huge central stove did the man let Malka out of the blanket. She stood there stiffly and didn't move. At a big table sat a woman with a little girl on her lap, looking at her, while another little girl was playing with building blocks on the floor. The woman pointed with her free hand towards the stove. Malka lowered her head and her shoulders fell forward.

'Up there,' said the old woman. 'Up there on the stove seat.'

Malka felt the man who had driven her there pick her up around the waist and lift her on to the stove. She just let it happen.

'Malka,' said a voice that she remembered from before. 'Malka, love.'

And there she sat, the lady doctor, whom she had last seen in Hungary, at the mill, when she was ill in bed.

Malka slipped down backwards off the stove seat, grabbed the old woman who had brought her here by the arm and said, 'Where is Teresa? I want Teresa.'

The old woman laid her hand on Malka's head, a cold and heavy hand. She was breathing hard. The woman sitting at the table gave a startled gasp. Her face could hardly be seen. The oil lamp flickered, shadows crept across the floor. It was very, very quiet. When Malka heard the woman up on the stove-seat start to cry, she looked up in bewilderment.

AFTERWORD

In 1996, four years before I wrote this book, I met Malka Mai in Israel and she told me her story – or at least, what she still knew of it. In 1943, she was living with her mother and her elder sister in Lawoczne, a town in the Carpathian Mountains. The area belongs to the Ukraine nowadays, but then it belonged to Poland and Poland had been occupied by the Germans. Not far from Lawoczne was a border that doesn't exist any more, the border between Poland and the part of the Ukraine that had been occupied by Hungary.

Malka is a real person, then, but for all that, the story told in this book is fictional to a large extent. I had to work out a story for myself, because Malka Mai can only remember certain key points. She was too young then, and her mind has suppressed much of what happened in those days, times that were very hard for her. The actual Malka Mai, who was brought by her mother from Poland a second time and taken to Hungary, to Budapest, went to Palestine in 1944 with the Youth-Aliyah. The Youth-Aliyah had been set up by various Jewish agencies to help rescue Jewish children and young people from Nazi-occupied Europe. Malka and her sister Minna came to Palestine that way, and lived first of all with their father on a kibbutz. Her mother emigrated to Israel only after the foundation of the new state in 1948. The family didn't live together again; Minna was already grown up, Malka had settled down on the kibbutz.

Today Malka Mai lives in a suburb of Tel-Aviv. She has three children and two grandchildren.

Other books published by Young Picador

Julie Bertagna

As the waters rise, the old world is lost. But a new world waits to be found . . .

Mara's island home is drowning, slowly but surely, beneath storm-tossed waves. As the mighty icecaps melt, the Earth is giving up its land to the ocean – and a community, a way of life, are going to die.

But Mara has seen something extraordinary. Far out among the dizzying electronic information stacks of the Weave, there are hints of a New World – of cities built out of the sea and reaching high into the sky. Cities where desperate refugees can surely find safety.

In a terrifying gamble for survival, Mara and the islanders of Wing take to their boats in the ultimate exodus. Somehow they must find a new home in a world they no longer understand – a world where anything and everything is possible.

But Mara's epic quest becomes something even greater. An extraordinary journey into humanity's capacity for good and evil. And a heart-wrenching story of love and loss – and the triumph of the will to survive.

Thrilling, inspiring and deeply challenging – Mara's unforgettable story will stay with you long after the final page.

JULIA BELL

massive

'I'm fat,' I *hear myself saying.* I *look in the mirror. My face has gone hot and red;* I *feel like I'm going to explode. 'I'm fat.' It sizzles under my skin, thick yellow layers of it, puffing me up, pushing me out, making me massive.*

Weight has always been a big issue in Carmen's life. Not surprising when her mum is obsessed with the idea that thin equals beauty, thin equals success — thin equals the way to get what you want. And somehow her daughter is *going* to be thin.

But with a long list of failed diets behind her and a mountain of empty wrappers under the bed, Carmen knows the comfort of forbidden food.

Then everything goes pear-shaped. Swept off to Birmingham by her mother, Carmen finds her old life disappearing — her home, her friends and her family. Now at last she's landed right at the heart of her mum's dieting obsession.

With everything to gain and absolutely nothing to lose, Carmen starts to ask: if she were thin, very thin, could it all be different?

A shocking, moving, bittersweet novel about all kinds of nourishment — and the lack of it.

BROCK COLE

The Facts Speak for Themselves

'The subject is female, age thirteen. She appears to be in good physical health. She is small for her age. Her periods are scanty and irregular. Sexually active . . . molested by her mother's employer . . . evidently very distraught . . .'

The social worker's report on Linda records the brutal facts. It attempts to explain Linda's involvement in the murder of one man and the suicide of another. But can the facts really speak for themselves?

Linda doesn't think so and demands to write about her life in her own words. Everyone has their own version of the truth – this is Linda's.

It is a ruthlessly honest and unforgettably moving account that challenges readers to make their own judgement on Linda's shocking story.

'Tremendously touching and sad. Brock Cole has found the perfect tone for this very raw and very real novel' *New York Times Book Review*